SECRET SCARS

Lucy shrank from letting Richard see her legs, scarred as they were by an accident long ago. But he was her husband now, and she could hide them from him no more. She froze as she felt his eyes on them. Then his lips found one of those white scars on the inside of her thigh. She gasped, wanting to tell him to stop but enjoying the sensation too much to force the words from her.

He raised his head and smiled at her. "These are the marks of life," he said. "No one who truly lives is free of them. Perhaps someday I will let you explore mine."

That kiss, those words, freed her. The fear that had held her disappeared. Her heart was on fire, her lips opened under his, her arms pulled him close.

Tomorrow might bring fresh doubts about this man whose own child accused him of the darkest deeds.... This man who let her know so little of himself while forcing her to lay her own soul bare. But right now the dawn of dread seemed far away, and the night was lit with love....

An Amiable Arrangement

An
Amiable
Arrangement

∽

by

Barbara Allister

Ⓞ
A SIGNET BOOK

SIGNET
Published by the Penguin Group
Penguin Books USA Inc., 375 Hudson Street,
New York, New York 10014, U.S.A.
Penguin Books Ltd, 27 Wrights Lane,
London W8 5TZ, England
Penguin Books Australia Ltd, Ringwood,
Victoria, Australia
Penguin Books Canada Ltd, 10 Alcorn Avenue,
Toronto, Ontario, Canada M4V 3B2
Penguin Books (N.Z.) Ltd, 182–190 Wairau Road,
Auckland 10, New Zealand

Penguin Books Ltd, Registered Offices:
Harmondsworth, Middlesex, England

First published by Signet, an imprint of Dutton Signet,
a division of Penguin Books USA Inc.

First Printing, July, 1994
10 9 8 7 6 5 4 3 2 1

For my niece Ryan Elizabeth Teer

Chapter One

"You can still change your mind," Edward Meredith reminded his sister. He stood in the vestibule of their parish church, looking down at her. Although the day was warm, the church was cool, and he had felt her shiver in spite of the dark blue spencer she wore over her ivory sprigged muslin. He tilted her face up so that he could see her face more clearly under the blue bonnet she wore. "Father would not even ask any questions."

"But Richard might. I thought he was a friend of yours," Lucy said quietly, aware that at times even the slightest whisper echoed throughout the stone structure. And she knew she did not want her father to hear this discussion. "And if the *ton* discovered I had cried off from yet another wedding, I would be the talk of London." She glared at him, her head tilted slightly and one eyebrow raised, wishing she had not insisted on preserving the formality of the occasion. If they were with the others at the front of the church, Edward would not have had an opportunity to question her decision once again.

"Two engagements in eight years is not excessive. And Richard insisted that we not announce your engagement. Therefore, he could not complain that you had held him up to ridicule. He may be my friend, but you are my sister. Our friendship should not be a factor in this discussion." His sister stifled a laugh because he sounded so like her father. Her brother glared at her and continued. "If Richard were in a more sensible frame of mind even he could see—"

"Enough. We have been through this before. I gave

Richard my word. Let us begin. The others are waiting."
Lucy looked up at her brother, her blue eyes serious in
her lovely face. "I am not going to change my mind,"
she said firmly. Then she prudently held her tongue and
simply tugged at his sleeve. Sighing, her brother led her
into the church. As her attention was on the man at her
side instead of the worn stones on which she was walking, Lucy stumbled and would have fallen except for her
brother's arm. "Are you all right?" he asked anxiously.
One of the men waiting at the front of the church stood
up as if to hurry to their aid and then stopped as they
started forward again.

"I am fine," Lucy said quietly. She carefully smoothed
the pain from her face, hiding it from him as she had
learned to do during the last eight years. Each step was
an effort at first. Then as usual walking grew easier.

Edward Meredith slowed his steps, knowing without
having to be told that his sister needed to move more
slowly. He glanced at her again, wishing he could
change what had happened to her eight years earlier. Always adored by her family, she had been the Incomparable of her Season, sought after by every eligible man of
the *ton* and many of the ineligible ones as well. She had
accepted their compliments naturally. Fortunately, her
sense of humor kept her from becoming too puffed up
even when her laughing blue eyes and rich brown curls
had inspired many of the young men of her acquaintance
to create poems praising her eyes, her lips, even the tips
of her fingers.

By the end of that Season, she had had offers from
several eligible men. When she accepted the Earl of
Haversham's offer, everyone in the family agreed that
theirs would be an ideal match.

As soon as the Season ended, the family and their
guests had returned home to prepare for the wedding.
Then in the space of one morning, everything had
changed. An intrepid rider to hounds, Lucy had jumped
a fence and had come to grief on the other side. Someone had piled stones to repair the fence behind the wall.

Her mare had landed on them and fallen. With her leg firmly anchored in her sidesaddle, Lucy had not been able to roll free before the mare had fallen on top of her.

Fortunately, someone had seen her fall and was with her almost immediately. It was too late for her mare, and Lucy's injuries were such that for a time they despaired for her life.

At first she had been oblivious to the seriousness of her injuries. However, when she had recovered enough to start asking questions of her doctor, questions she refused to allow him to avoid, the answers were as devastating as she had feared. Although she refused to let the doctor see how badly his answers had affected her, she had broken into a storm of weeping when the door closed behind him, leaving her alone with her maid. After her initial shock had worn off and she had had time to think, she had realized what she must do.

Lucy had called her betrothed to her side. Edward had been an unobserved witness to that meeting. Seeing his sister's door open, he had slipped in, not realizing the earl was already there. To his horror, he was a witness when Lucy told her betrothed that the doctor did not believe she would ever be able to have children and that she was releasing him from their engagement. The alacrity with which the young earl accepted her decision had made Edward want to pummel him, but Lucy had maintained her pleasant, serene expression and said good-bye to the man without letting him know how badly his desertion was hurting her. When the door had closed and she had thought she was alone, she had covered her face and sobbed. Edward had hurried to her side, but as soon as she saw him, she hid her pain, saying merely, "George and I have decided we do not suit."

The earl's action had changed her life. She had withdrawn from society, refusing to return to London even when her injuries had healed. Her father had raged and complained, but she had not changed her mind. Nor did she accept any of the suits that were laid before her. And she had had opportunities to marry in spite of the fact

she always explained her condition. There were always
men who needed a wife but not more children. To her father's despair, she had turned them all down, all except
Richard Blount.

Lucy Meredith looked at the altar where the minister,
a man she had known all her life, waited, his serious face
framed by white hair. She smiled at him, and he allowed
the faintest of smiles to flicker across his face. In spite of
his reservations, he had agreed to perform the ceremony,
unorthodox though it was. He glanced at the front pew
where Lucy's father sat, his legs so crippled he could no
longer walk unaided. One look at Mr. Meredith's face
told the minister that the older man was no happier today
than he had been when the banns had first been announced. The minister glanced back at Lucy, her face
lovely and calm and her brown hair shining, and sighed.
He wondered if he was doing the right thing. He had
been present when Lucy had told her father and brother
what she intended to do. Nothing anyone had to say
could convince her to change her mind. She and Richard
had made this decision, an arrangement they both found
amiable, and she planned to abide by it.

Although the church would normally have been full of
well-wishers, only a few people invited personally by
Lucy were present. Most people in their small commu-
nity did not know what to make of the unorthodox wedding. No one in the area had been married by proxy
before. The inhabitants were aghast that the bridegroom
had not appeared at the ceremony. The minister himself
had had to research the proper ceremony for never before had he performed such a service.

Lucy stood before him, serene on the surface although
she was seething on the inside. Why had she agreed to
Richard's proposal? The wisdom of what she was doing
escaped her. She looked up at the minister, trying to
draw answers from the peace that always seemed a part
of the man. She turned her head slightly and saw her father in his place, a frown on his face. Nearby was Ara-

bella. The glimpse of her closest friend steadied Lucy. She took a deep breath and willed the minister to begin.

Long before anyone wanted it to, the ceremony was over, and they were signing the register, her brother signing as proxy for his sister's husband. "Edward Thomas Meredith, proxy for Richard David Blount," the words stood out boldly on the page. Although the banns had been read, Richard had wanted to take no chances. He had also arranged a license, which he had signed. Lucy now added her name to that as well. Then she smiled tremulously at her father and brother. "Let us leave this cold damp building. My bones are beginning to ache," her father said gruffly, hiding his emotion and his worry about his daughter's future.

Although everyone present tried to make the wedding breakfast that followed a happy occasion, no one was completely successful. "You will return for Edward's and my wedding?" Arabella asked, her face anxious.

"I would not dare be absent. Even if Richard cannot come with me, I will be here," Lucy promised even as she realized that her new husband might have a different opinion. Well, he would simply have to change his mind, she thought. "Have you decided on a date for the wedding?"

"We thought soon after Christmas," Arabella said with a smile, looking around the room until she caught Edward's eye. "I would rather not wait so long, but my family insists." Lucy saw the look the two of them exchanged glances and she smiled inwardly. Her brother had waited so long for his happiness.

Edward strolled over to join them, putting his arm around Arabella and pulling her close to his side. She sighed and let her head rest on his shoulder in spite of the fact that her mother would be sure to give her a scold for permitting such a caress in public. "Have you convinced her to stay for the wedding?" he asked.

"I have promised to return for it," his sister explained.

"But Arabella needs your help, don't you, sweet?"

"Arabella has her mother, and I have already given

her a tour of the house—as if she needed one. She knows more about the place than I do. And our house-keeper knows she must take her orders from her. She will do well, Edward," Lucy assured him. "I must take up the reins in my own household."

"Must you leave tomorrow?" her friend asked.

"I have promised Richard I will do so." Lucy glanced up at her brother, who recognized the firm set of her mouth and chin and prudently held his tongue.

"You will be so far away," Arabella said wistfully as she had so many times before.

"Nonsense. Richard has an estate just two hours from here."

"But he is not living there now," her friend complained.

Although he had earlier proposed the same arguments his betrothed had just voiced, Edward recognized the limits of the discussion. His sister was married. Seeing the white lines around Lucy's mouth, he realized his sister had endured as many complaints as she could handle and changed the subject. "Will you and Richard be in town for the Little Season?" he asked. Arabella's face brightened.

"That is one subject we have never discussed," Lucy admitted, taking a deep breath and smiling up at her older brother.

"I am surprised. From the size of the letters he sends, I would assume you had discussed everything," her brother teased her. "I hope your letters have been as long and expensive as his."

Lucy simply laughed. Then she caught sight of her father in his bath chair and moved to his side. He studied her face and then held out his hand. "It is too late to turn back now," he said quietly. "I hope you know what you are doing." He held her hand tightly as if he did not want to let go.

"Richard is a good man, Papa. You have always spoken highly of him. I will be happy with him," she assured him, hiding her own doubts under a mask of calm.

"I hope you are right." He paused and looked up at her, a serious expression on his face. "You know that this will always be your home if you need one, Lucy."

"I know, Papa." She kissed his cheek, her heart touched and her eyes stinging with tears. Then she turned the conversation to other subjects.

His words came back to her as she jostled around in the coach on her way to her new home. Dear stubborn Papa, she thought. Had he been willing to allow her some independence she would not be a married lady now.

All she had wanted was a home of her own. The first time she had mentioned her desire he had laughed. The laughter stopped as soon as he had realized she was serious. "No daughter of mine will live such a scandalous existence," he had declared. None of her arguments or continued pleadings had been able to sway him. Each time the discussion had come up again he had grown more adamant until he had finally altered his will, forbidding any of the money Lucy should inherit from him being used to set up a home of her own. Until she married, she would live in the family home.

Having finally recognized the futility of her plan, Lucy had put it behind her, resigning herself to managing the household. But when Edward had asked Arabella's father if he might court his daughter, Lucy had known she must do something. Arabella deserved to be the mistress in her own household, not to have to defer to her brother's sister. It would be hard enough on her brother and his wife to share a home with his father, who was already beginning to look forward to his grandchildren; Arabella did not need another woman sharing her home too.

Lucy knew how long her brother had waited for Arabella. He had fallen in love with her before her first Season but refused to offer for her until she had time to know her own mind. Then, before the Season had well begun, Lucy and Edward's mother had taken a chill and died. By the time Edward was free to return to town, if not to parties and balls, Arabella's fancy had been caught by a handsome young man in a glorious uniform with a title equal to her father's. Edward had retired in haste, letting no one but Lucy know his despair. By the Season's end, Arabella's father had announced her engagement to the handsome soldier. But before they could marry, he was sent to the Peninsula.

Arabella had waited patiently for him, worrying because she did not hear from him very often. Finally she received word that he was selling his colors and would be returning shortly. That return never happened. Contracting one of the fevers that plagued the battlefields, her betrothed had died in the arms of a Spanish señorita. Arabella had been devastated, turning to her friend Lucy for comfort, bringing Edward into close contact with her again.

At first, Edward was afraid to hope. Then as her time of mourning was finished and Arabella still did not return to her life in town, he began to dream. With his sister's encouragement, Edward had set out to woo Arabella, this time letting her see how much she meant to him. Finally, his suit had been accepted, but her parents had demanded that she spend one more Season in town and that the marriage be announced only at the end of that Season. As much as they liked Edward, her parents wanted to ensure that her decision had not been based on propensity alone. Lucy had raged at the implied insult to her brother, but Edward had only laughed and agreed. "I do not like it," he had told his sister privately. "But I understand her parents' viewpoint. I know they had hopes of her capturing a title."

Her parents' conditions had only strengthened the bond between Arabella and Edward. Watching their love grow stronger, Lucy was determined that she would not be a burden to that upcoming marriage. But until Richard's letter to Edward had arrived, she had not known how to accomplish her goal.

She would never have known about the letter had she not burst into Edward's study that morning, her mind on the party she was planning. He had a strange look on his face. "What is wrong?" she asked quietly.

He held out the letter. "Read this."

She glanced over the document and then dropped into the chair in front of Edward's desk to read it more carefully. When she finished, she looked up, an amused expression on her face. "He wants you to help him find a wife? Does he not know how long you waited to take one of your own?"

"You read the letter. When I wrote him of my engagement, he decided that should make me an authority on the young ladies of the *ton*," her brother said ruefully.

"You did not read his letter very carefully, Brother mine. He does not want a young lady. He wants an older one who perhaps did not take during her Seasons and who will be happy to marry and become a mother to his children," she reminded him.

"Either way I will be no help to him. I did not pay any attention to the Marriage Mart when I was in town. I was too busy with Arabella." He ran his hand through his thick hair and sighed. "When I saw him in town shortly after his wife's tragic death, I told him to call on me if there was anything I could do. I had no idea he would ask this." Edward's face showed his confusion. Richard was a close friend, and he knew his old friend must be desperate to write such a letter. "I suppose I could ask Arabella if she knows anyone," he said hesitantly.

Lucy had been rereading parts of the letter. Inside, an idea was churning. She smiled at her brother. "Let me talk to Arabella," she said. "Perhaps between the two of us we can suggest someone, perhaps someone who came out shortly after I did. If you promised him your help, we should at least try. Richard sounds almost desperate, not at all like the carefree young man who used to visit you here in the summer." Her voice was casual. However, if her brother had taken the time to look at her carefully, he would have realized that she was up to something.

Edward merely shrugged his shoulders. "That was

some time ago. None of us are the same. And Richard
has had to bear more trouble than most; all I can guess is
that his problems have influenced this decision of his.
Are you sure you wish to be involved in this mad
scheme? Otherwise I will write and tell him that I cannot
help."

"Richard was always kind to me. If I can help
him . . ." she explained.

"Well, I will write and tell him you have agreed to
lend him your assistance," he said indulgently. Only
over the matter of her setting up her own home had Edward or her father ever opposed her. She knew what he
was thinking: if this would give her something to do,
fruitless though it might be, Edward was willing to
agree.

The renewed jostling of the coach brought Lucy out of
her reverie. She glanced down at the letters she held on
her lap as though they were a talisman. "Shall I tell them
to slow down, Miss Lucy?" her maid asked, not liking
the strain she could see on her mistress's face.

"Nonsense. We will never arrive if you do that,
Betty."

Betty held her tongue, but when they stopped to
change horses a few miles further on, she insisted that
Lucy walk into the inn and rest in the private parlor that
had been engaged for her. After a few moments away
from the uneven ride, she was pleased to see color creeping up into her mistress's face. But a short rest was the
most she could convince her to take. Knowing that she
had done what she could, Betty climbed back into the
coach with her mistress, hoping that the coachman
would not press on much further that day. Lucy smiled at
her maid, wishing she could explain that not the journey
but what she would find at the end of it was causing the
tension.

The letters she once more held on her lap were her
only contact with Richard Blount in almost eight years.
He had danced with her during her Season, a welcome
respite from the men who had tried to dazzle her with

their charms. As a married man and a close friend of her brother's, he was safe. And he made Lucy laugh. When he had returned to his home to be with his wife when their first child was born, she had missed him. Together she and Edward had perused countless baby gifts to find the perfect one for Richard's first son. During the next two or three years when his second son and daughter had been born, Edward had taken care of the notes and the gifts.

Although Richard and Edward had corresponded for years, Richard had been part of the world that Lucy had turned her back on. She had listened when Edward had told her tidbits of what Richard was doing, enjoying the descriptions of Greece, Moscow, or wherever he happened to be. She knew from clues that her brother gave that Richard had served as an unofficial government courier even though neither he nor Edward ever referred openly to that fact. Sometimes Lucy wondered if Edward enjoyed Richard's letters so much because he wished that he too were free to engage in such an occupation. But Edward had been forced to take up the reins of estate management when their father had become incapacitated. Lucy glanced once more at the letters in her lap, her hand smoothing the ribbons that held them. As matter of fact as Richard had tried to make them, there was a hint of uneasiness there. She wondered if she had done the right thing. Then she sighed. If she had not, she would have to make the best of it. In these last few years she had learned that lesson very well. And she would be a mother. Not until she had read Richard's descriptions of his children had she known how much she had longed to have a family of her own. Hope filled her once more, and she settled back, her hands clasped around the letters.

Like Lucy, Richard Blount was considering what he had done. The morning of the wedding he had left his children with their governess and tutor and ridden out to one of the cliffs that overlooked the sea. The morning was clear and bright, and he made a striking figure as he sat there on his black horse, his light brown hair catching the sun until it was more golden than brown.

At the time Lucy had told him that she had arranged for their wedding, he closed his eyes, trying to visualize her. Even though she had given him a description of what she looked like, all he could remember that morning was a happy sprite who had laughed and chased Edward and him about the estate, wanting to share every moment with the much older boys.

Edward had often been frustrated by her persistent tagging along, but Richard had merely laughed and encouraged her. At the time he had wished that instead of being an only child who was often shuttled off to his Welsh grandfather that he too had a sister who obviously loved him so much.

In spite of his memories, Richard knew she had changed. Lucy had been very open with him in her letters. But he could not erase that earlier laughing picture and replace it with a more somber one. Surely, her original personality had not been erased.

Solemnly, he repeated his vows as if he were standing beside Lucy at the front of that church. In spite of the unpleasant relationship he had had with Julia, his first wife, he planned to make this new one succeed. He had a more realistic view of marriage this time, he reminded himself. His reasons were simple: his children needed a mother, and he needed a wife.

Besides dealing with the horror of his wife's tragic death, this last year had been difficult. Perhaps he had been wrong to run away, to uproot his family and move them here to this isolated estate out of danger. But they could not stay there where the burned-out ruins of the house would have been a constant reminder of the horror. And his hunting box near Edward's home had seemed entirely unsuitable for his children and not particularly safe. He loved this area of England, its green hills, the hidden inlets, and even the trackless moor.

The sea was one advantage of the place as far as the children were concerned. In the past year, they had become quite good sailors, learning to take orders and man the small boat he loved to take out. Idly he wondered if Lucy would enjoy the sea. There was an easy path to the dock; that should not cause problems. He shrugged his shoulders. Even if she hated it, they would manage.

The thought of her injuries bothered Richard. He had written to Edward, offering his sympathy when the news of her accident had first become the topic of conversation. What would she be like? Lucy had told him that she walked with a limp occasionally and that, more importantly, the doctor had said she would never be able to bear children.

Although he had heard the gossip about why her engagement had ended, he had not known the full extent of her injuries. That knowledge had made him evaluate her offer carefully. What if she had become bitter and hard? Richard thought of his three active offspring and wondered if the knowledge that Lucy could never have any children of her own would affect her relationship with them.

Her letters, though more sober than he would have expected, had contained no trace of anger in them, only a quiet determination. As he stood on the hillside that morning, he reminded himself that the decision had already been made. Even if there were problems, they would have to work together to solve them. And from his last marriage he knew that every married couple has problems. Resolutely, he forced the memories of the last terrible months of his previous marriage from his mind.

Richard lost track of time, staring out into the distance, his gray eyes reflecting the blue of the water on this remarkably clear day. "Da?" The shout brought him back to this instant, bringing vivid happy memories of the time he had spent in Wales as a boy. "Da? Are we going sailing today?" his oldest son asked, spurring his pony.

His father glanced around, making sure his son had not slipped away from the groom who was supposed to accompany any of the children whenever they rode. He let out a sigh of relief when he saw the man, deliberately holding his horse back so that David could reach his father first. Nothing had threatened them here, but he intended to maintain a careful watch.

"What are you doing here?" Richard asked sternly. In the year since the tragedy, he had supervised his children carefully, for the first time truly learning to enjoy them not as his children but as interesting people. Their acceptance of his role in their lives had not been easily won. They had known little about him. And since he had told the children about his upcoming marriage, David had needed more of his attention; they all had. After he had assured his youngest son and daughter that he did not plan to leave them for months at a time as he had once done, they had accepted the idea. Only David seemed to be having problems with the idea of his remarriage.

"I finished my lessons," David said even before his father could ask him a question. Richard gave him a questioning look. David hung his head sheepishly. "I finished my mathematics," he said quickly. "Mr. Avery said that we would do geography and Latin after luncheon."

"And he gave you permission to leave until then?" his father asked sternly. Knowing the tutor, Richard doubted his son's story.

"Not exactly." David looked up at his father, his eyes pleading.

"What did he say?" Although he knew he should send the boy back immediately, he did not have the heart to punish him. And if he was honest with himself, he did not want to be alone.

"He told me to read some history. But I had already read it. You and I read it together. Truly, Da," his son explained.

"And he gave you permission to leave?"

Once more the boy hung his head. "He was working with Robert when I left."

"And he does not know where you are?" his father asked sharply. The events of the time before the fire had made him insist that someone know where his children were at all times. That and that alone had enabled him to rescue them from the blaze that destroyed their home.

"I sent a stable boy to tell him I was going riding," David explained quickly. When his father got that hard line around his mouth, he did not want to be the one his father was displeased with.

"Good." Richard smiled at his son. "But I do not think it would be fair to go out in the boat without your brother and sister, would it?" He glanced once more at the sturdy little boy beside him and felt his heart catch. If anything were to happen to him or to his brother and sister, Richard did not know how he would bear it. The death of his wife, estranged though they had been at the time, had been devastating.

As the memory of that fiery night over a year before began to sweep through his mind as though it were painted on canvas, he resolutely put it behind him. "Perhaps we can persuade Mr. Avery and Mrs. Stanhope to release Robert and Caroline," he suggested. "Then we can go sailing."

Thoughts of both his wedding and the tragedy were pushed from his mind as they sailed down the river and into the Channel, the soft breeze that was merely cool on land, turning cold quickly on the water.

"Let us sail to France, Da," Caroline suggested, her face rosy under the scarf tied about her head.

"We are at war with France. Isn't that right, Da?" her older brother said scornfully. "Why would we want to go there?"

"Mrs. Stanhope says every educated person once had to speak French. Do you speak French, Da?"

His second son, more talkative than the other two, asked, "Why would he want to speak like the enemy?" Both turned to face him. "Well?"

"I speak French," Richard explained, remembering that last secret trip as a courier when only his knowledge of the language had saved his life. "My tutor insisted. We will not be at war forever," he continued, noting their disapproval. "Then we all will go to France. You may need to learn French too."

"And see Napoleon?" Robert asked, his gray eyes wide.

"Napoleon will be gone then," his brother said firmly. "Isn't that right, Da?"

"I want to go to Wales," David said, his face very serious. "To see where you were born."

"Me too," Robert added.

"Will the lady who is to be our new mama go with us?" Caroline asked. For the first time Richard noticed that her teeth were chattering.

"I hope so. Now let us see what you remember about returning a boat to shore," he said quickly, wrapping his jacket around his daughter. Then he changed course. The change in direction altered their conversation, making them forget the subject for the moment.

Unlike his children, the thought of his new wife was never far from Richard's thoughts. As he lay in bed that night, he wondered if Lucy had any idea of the demands that his family and he might make on her. He had been as honest as he could in his letters. Although he had told her he expected her to be his wife in all senses of the word, he had tried to word his expectations so that they would not offend her.

Thinking of the last year, here on the coast of Devon, Richard acknowledged that his isolation had made his decision to remarry a necessity. He refused to leave the children alone for more than a few hours. He supposed that he could have imported a mistress, but he would not subject his children to that type of atmosphere. And the few women in the area had no appeal for him even though some of them had cast out lures. If he had felt less responsible for his children's safety, and had been able to get away for a day or so . . . He laughed ruefully. That was as much an impossibility as his bringing a mistress in had been.

Then he smiled. He had solved his problem. In a few days Lucy would be here to take up her roles as wife and mother. He looked around the room and wondered if she would want to change any of its furnishings.

Chapter Two

The journey had given Lucy too much time to think. What if Richard decided that she had as little to offer as George, her former fiancé, had thought? What if they did not suit? She pulled back the curtain over the window once more so that she could look at the passing countryside.

They had been fortunate in the weather for traveling. Although the breezes had been cool, they had had no rain. With the way the red dust of the road they followed was billowing up, Lucy was almost certain her brother's coachman would have preferred rain or a light mist. Her maid coughed and held a handkerchief to her face, her eyes squinched shut.

Lucy reluctantly dropped the curtain over the window and sat back. That morning the coachman had assured her that before evening they would arrive at their destination. "Fine directions, Miss Lucy. Nary a bit of confusion over which way to go. And the horses have made the trip easier," he had said heartily before she entered the coach for the rest of her journey.

Once Lucy had decided to marry Richard, he and Edward had taken charge of the details of the journey. At first Richard had insisted on sending a carriage for her, but Edward had changed his friend's mind, insisting that his father's carriage had been altered for more comfortable riding. Carefully, they had planned the exchange of horses and rest stops so that Lucy would have the easiest journey possible, with Edward providing horses for the first of the journey and Richard the last. By the time the coach made the return journey, the teams they had left behind would be rested. Then a groom could easily return them to their homes. Remembering the countless discussions she had been forced to listen to, the detailed instructions Richard had sent, Lucy sighed and wondered if she would be subjected to that degree of organization for the rest of her life. The thought had caused more than one qualm. Only the knowledge that the banns had already been read once caused her to hold her tongue.

Remembering the green hills and red earth outside her window made Lucy want to stop the coach, get out, and walk for a time. She was so tired of riding. Each night she ached more than the night before. Recognizing that there was nothing she could do about the situation, she did not complain. However, her maid, noting the paleness of her mistress's face, had had a word with the coachman at the last stop, and the next would be longer.

When a light mist blew in, settled the dust, and then disappeared, Lucy opened the curtains, gazing at the surroundings that would be near her new home. The raucous call of gulls told her they were not far from the sea. Richard too had told her that, commenting on how much his children enjoyed going out in the boat and how he would teach her to sail. She had been noncommittal about his offer, but the thought intrigued her.

The fresh air and the knowledge that her journey would soon be over revived her, sending flags of color into her pale cheeks. Betty nodded in satisfaction. "Will you be wanting me to help you change into another dress the next time we stop?" she asked.

"It will be just as rumpled as this one," her mistress said, looking down at the gray traveling dress she wore. After several days of traveling, nothing she wore seemed fresh.

"I ironed the blue you like so well this morning and packed it carefully on top. If it has a few wrinkles, I can quickly press them away. In every inn where we have stopped, the innkeepers' wives have had their irons next to the fire. Surely this one will be no different." Having served her mistress since Lucy was old enough to have her own maid, Betty was determined to ensure her mistress appeared at her best when she was introduced in her new home. When Lucy nodded her agreement, Betty sighed happily.

Had Lucy realized the visions that were running through her maid's head she would have been quick to challenge them. Betty, like the other servants in her father's house, had been intrigued by her mistress's engagement to a man she had not seen in almost eight years. The younger maids had speculated about whether Richard Blount had been the reason her earlier engagement had been called off. Even when Betty and the housekeeper had explained the circumstances that caused the broken engagement with the earl, their romantic notions had persisted. In spite of what she knew, Betty had secretly hoped that there was something to the rumors.

The last stop completed, Lucy, attired in a freshly pressed dress, felt her hands beginning to tremble. Richard had told her they would have only a few more miles to travel after this point. She tried to maintain her calm, recalling Richard's descriptions of his home. The village they had just stopped in was the closest one to his home, she knew. Having lived her life within reach of neighbors and friends, she was not certain how she would deal with the isolation. And here were no flat meadows through which she could walk as she wished. As lovely as the hills were, Lucy knew they would restrict her movements.

Before long Lucy caught sight of a large house surrounded by gardens and trees set up on a hillside. A long road wound up to it. Her breath caught in her throat.

Richard, alerted to the coach's approach by the groom he had had waiting at the inn for just that purpose, sent his servants scurrying about the house as though they had not spent the last few weeks cleaning. "Are there flowers for my wife's chambers, Mrs. Dawes?" he asked the housekeeper.

"Early roses, sir. I believe you mentioned that Mrs. Blount prefers white to any other color."

"She did as a girl." Richard stopped for a moment, a smile fleeting across his face as he thought of the way Lucy had insisted they stop so that she could pick flowers wherever they went. By the end of the day, the posies would have wilted, but Lucy would cling to her finds as though they were gold. A door slamming broke his reverie. He nodded to the housekeeper and hurried up to the schoolroom.

"Is she here, Da?" his daughter asked, her face alight with excitement, the books in front of her forgotten.

"Not yet, Caroline. But the groom has brought us word that she is at the inn." Richard looked around the room. "Do you all remember what you are to do?" he asked. The three children nodded. "Hurry now and change clothes. You want to make a good impression," their father said firmly.

"And we are to call her Mama?" Caroline asked, her brow wrinkled in thought.

"If you wish," her father said gently. "Remember I told you that you had a choice." He looked at the boys and raised an eyebrow. "If you do not hurry, you will not be ready to greet her when she arrives."

David muttered something under his breath. When his father stared at him, he sought for a diversion. "Are you changing too, Da?" David asked, looking at his father's rumpled hair. Although Richard brushed it into place each morning, the slightest hint of wind made it curl. His dashing about had made it even more unruly.

Richard caught sight of himself in a mirror on the schoolroom wall. "I am on my way. I will meet you in the hall as soon as you are ready." As he closed the door to the schoolroom, he sighed, wishing David were happier about the situation.

When he walked down the main staircase not long afterward, no one would have realized that his heart was beating like a drum. Every hair was in place, and the rumpled clothing of earlier had given way to fawn pantaloons, an elegant waistcoat, and a rich brown coat that hugged his shoulders. The only jewelry he wore was a heavy emerald signet ring on his right hand.

"The gatekeeper has signaled that the coach has started up the drive, sir," his butler told him.

"Thank you, Dawes." Richard took a deep breath. "As soon as Mrs. Blount has greeted the children, their tutor, and their governess, I will introduce her to you and your wife and let you present the servants to her."

The butler merely nodded and did not remind him that they had discussed exactly where each person was to stand and the order in which each was to be presented. They heard a noise on the stairs and looked up to see the three children and their entourage walking sedately down the stairs. At least Caroline, her governess, the boys' tutor, and the nurserymaid were walking sedately. His two sons were dashing down as though on their way to the stables.

"Is she here yet?" Robert asked, rushing to a stop before his father. He inspected Richard and nodded. "Much better, Da." His father bowed slightly.

David, a few steps behind, slid across the floor to the window. "I can see the coach." His voice was much more controlled than his brother's.

A few steps from the bottom of the stairs, Caroline gave a little hop and ran down the rest, completely forgetting her decorum. "Is she pretty?"

Her father gathered the three of them close. "She was as a girl. And you have seen the miniature she sent me," he said quietly.

"Miniatures!" his older son said indignantly. "The one you have of me looks like a baby."

"It was painted when you were less than a year old," his father reminded him, reaching up to smooth a wayward curl much like his own.

"And you let me go about with those long curls?" David asked, his eyes pained.

Before his father could explain that David's mother had insisted on keeping her son's curls until he was almost ready for short pants, the noise from outside told them the coach had arrived.

As though they had just realized the great changes that would be occurring in their lives, the children pressed close to their father, Caroline grabbing his hand as if afraid he would disappear. Richard smiled at them and tried to slow his own pounding heart. He nodded to Dawes, who opened the door for them. Together he and the children walked out onto the steps.

"Wait right here," Richard said softly to the three of them. Then he moved to the open door of the coach.

When Richard stepped within her view, Lucy could hardly catch her breath. Almost pretty when a boy and young man, his experiences had altered him, adding lines so that he had become a handsome, distinguished man. For a moment Lucy was afraid to move. He had not seen her since the accident. What was he going to think? Although most people were too kind to admit it, Lucy knew she was only a shadow of her former self. What if he were disappointed in her? Would he show it? Allowing her maid to get out first, Lucy gathered her courage and then slid forward.

Richard automatically put out a hand to help her from the carriage. Feeling nervous, she paused on the first step. The blue of her hat and her dress were echoed by the blue skies just peeping through the gray clouds that had covered the heavens that day. Smiling tremulously, she took her husband's outstretched hand and stepped cautiously to the ground, Betty standing anxiously by to help her if she should need her.

Safely on the ground once more, Lucy smiled at Richard, willing him to say something. Always known in diplomatic circles for his ability to handle difficult social situations, Richard was uncharacteristically silent. The last time he had seen Lucy he had known that she was a recognized Beauty, had even teased her on how well she had turned out, but had not been affected by her loveliness. Prepared for a tremendous change in her by her letters, he was stunned by her loveliness. She had changed; no longer the rounded porcelain beauty of her Season, she was more slender, more refined, an elegant lady who would be beautiful even in extreme old age.

The silence grew as Richard held her hand and smiled into her eyes. Lucy's cheeks grew warm. Before the quiet overwhelmed her, a boy's voice asked, "Is this our new mama, Da?" Robert pulled on his father's leg to get his attention.

Richard looked down at his youngest son and resisted an urge to tousle his hair. "Yes, Robert." Then he smiled at Lucy once more. "You will have to forgive my manners, my dear. Your arrival has us all at sixes and sevens." Fortunately, she did not have to answer. He drew her hand through his arm and turned to his children.

David, his eldest, stood on the top step, a set line about his mouth. The two younger children were on the bottom step right in front of him. "May I present my children?" Lucy smiled up at him, her nervousness hidden for now under the calm exterior she had worked so hard to perfect.

"This young lady is my daughter, Caroline," he said with a smile, taking pride in the picture his child made, her blond hair curling about her shoulders and her white muslin dress with pink ribbons still crisp and clean. The girl made a credible curtsy.

"I am happy to meet you, Caroline," Lucy said quietly, restraining her fears and excitement at the thought that she was now this girl's mother.

"And this is Robert." Richard held out his hand to his son, who was hopping up and down in his excitement.

"Robert." Lucy watched him bow and smile up at her. She glanced up at the oldest boy, standing on the top step, his hostile eyes almost level with her own. "And this must be David," she said quietly. Although she told herself that it was natural that the boy would resent the fact that she was taking his mother's place, Lucy could not help feeling hurt. Hiding her feelings, she turned to

Richard. "He was only a few weeks old when we met the . . ." Her voice cracked.

"The last time in London? Yes. David, come down here." In spite of the loving tone, his son knew a command when he heard it. He walked down the steps and made a bow. "Lucy and her brother Edward sent you that splendid horse you used to ride when you were in the nursery," he said, putting his arm over his son's shoulders and patting them. Of all his children, David had been the one to suffer the most at his mother's death. And Richard realized the boy would need time to accept the idea of his remarriage.

"Thank you very much. We have all enjoyed it very much." Both Lucy and Richard winced internally at David's carefully correct tone.

Robert gave another little hop up to the next step. "I used to ride him too," he said, smiling up at Lucy. "So did Caroline."

"How wonderful. I used to ride my brother's when he would let me," Lucy said in a confidential voice.

"You would ride anything," Richard said teasingly.

Lucy's face lost some of its bright color. Then she gained control of herself again. "That was long ago." For the last eight years, her family had avoided talking about her former love of riding, but Richard could not know that.

Richard had noted the change in her and cursed himself for ever bringing up the subject. "Here we are dawdling when I am certain that you are longing for a cup of tea. Let me present our staff."

In a few minutes, the awkward introductions were over, and Lucy was ensconced in a comfortable chair in front of a fire designed to chase away the chill that lingered in spite of the warmth of the day. The children sat quietly near her, their eyes moving from her to their father. Even Lucy had begun to be affected by the silence when the door opened and Dawes and a footman brought in tea and put it on a table in front of her.

"Do you still like your tea white and very sweet, Richard?" she asked, happy to have something to do.

"I still take the milk but take very little sugar," he said with a laugh. "It has been some time since I insisted on five lumps."

"Five lumps, Da? You only let us have one," Caroline said with a pout.

"One is quite enough. If I remember, Lucy does not take any sugar." He looked at his wife, taking pleasure in the picture she made. In spite of the awkward silence that had just fallen, Lucy's introduction into his household had progressed better than he had thought it might.

By the time the teacups had been passed around and Lucy had her own, the children were chattering among themselves. Richard, who was sitting next to her on the settee, took advantage of their inattention. "How was your journey?" He had noticed that the color in her cheeks came and went. "This is the first time you have traveled very far. . ."

"Since my accident?" Lucy tried to smile, but her efforts were not entirely successful. "You must not be afraid to mention it, Richard. I have lived with it for eight years now."

"I will remember." Then he inspected her carefully. "You have not answered my question." She shifted nervously as she used to do when she was going to try to bluff her way out of a situation. "And do not try to lie to me."

Lucy sighed. She looked at her stepsons and stepdaughter who seemed bursting with energy and good health and wished she were more like them. And the life bursting from Richard made her wonder why she had dared to accept his offer. Again, she sighed softly, resentful of his knowledge of her. Then as if to acknowledge the legitimacy of his demand, she said softly, "The coach was very comfortable."

"But?"

"Even the best of coaches cannot remove the jolts and

bumps that are part of every journey. And I have not
been accustomed to traveling so far," she added.

"I should have allowed you to go to your room immediately," he said with regret. His guilt at having subjected her to more activity than she could bear was
evident in his features. What was well hidden was his
disappointment in what he had planned for the evening.

"Nonsense. The children and I must have time to get
to know each other," she said with a smile that made him
forget how tired she was.

"That can come later," he insisted. "Although they
breakfast in the schoolroom, I have been permitting
them to join me for dinner since I rarely have guests. We
keep country hours here, but you can change that if you
wish."

"No. Gaining a stepmother is enough of a change
without changing time schedules too," she said, wondering what would happen once she took the reins of the
household into her hands. She had had control of her father's home since her mother's death, but the servants
there had known her most of her life.

Noting the boys had begun to tumble around like
young puppies, their father called to them. "It is time for
you to return to the schoolroom," he said firmly, ignoring their groans and complaints. "I will be up shortly to
see you. Now show Lucy that I have not let you run wild
but have taught you manners."

"They have excellent manners," their new stepmother
said with a smile. The younger children smiled back at
her. David simply gave a bow. Soon the door closed behind them, and a silence crept over the room. Lucy, who
had been more tense than even she had known, gave a
sigh and sank further back on the settee, slumping in a
way that would have brought her governess's immediate
disapproval had she still been in the schoolroom.

"And it is time that you were upstairs too," her husband told her. He stood up and held out his hand. Grate-
fully, Lucy allowed him to help her to rise, and then he
stepped back. She took a step, wincing involuntarily be-

cause she had stiffened while she was sitting. Richard took the two steps necessary to reach her side and swept her into his arms and carried her toward the door.

"Oh, you must not," Lucy said, flushing with embarrassment.

"Am I hurting you?"

"No."

"Then you must not tell me what to do, Madam Wife. I will have you in your room very shortly."

"I am too heavy," she protested as he carried her up the stairs. She glanced around to see if anyone was watching. Two maids stood transfixed, their eyes and mouths open wide. She closed her eyes, knowing that within minutes the household would be talking about the two of them.

"Nonsense. You are scarcely heavier than Caroline," he said firmly. Recognizing the futility of arguing with him, Lucy relaxed and put her head on his shoulder. "When you are rested, tomorrow or the next day, Mrs. Dawes wants to show you the house. It is not as large as your father's, as you will soon see."

He opened a door and carried her inside, trying to see the room with her eyes. "I did not know what colors you would like," he explained. "You can change anything that does not please you."

She looked around eagerly, noting the heavy rose silk hangings around the bed and at the windows. "These are lovely. Did your wife choose them?"

Richard's face froze. He forced himself to answer. "No, my mother did. My first wife never came to Devon. It was not fashionable enough for her." His voice was cold. He carefully put Lucy down. She stepped back a step or two, hoping that he never spoke about her in that tone.

"I do not wish to make any changes immediately," she said quietly, wishing she could take back her question. Behind them a door closed. Both of them jumped and turned around quickly.

"Shall I come back later?" Betty asked, her arms full of garments she had just unpacked.

"Arrange a bath for your mistress," Richard demanded. Betty, hiding her resentment at his tone, nodded without telling him she had already done so. Richard then turned to his wife. The anger that had overcome him for a moment was gone. He ran a finger down her soft cheek to her chin and lifted it up. "There is no need for you to dress for supper tonight. I have ordered that it be served in your room." Lucy sighed in relief. His next words, however, sent a frisson down her spine. "Enjoy your bath and a nap. I will join you later." Ignoring Betty, he lowered his head and kissed her softly on her lips. "I always wanted to do that," he said with an impish smile.

Lucy was still standing in the middle of the room, her hand pressed to her lips, when Betty opened the door for the other servants who had come to fill Lucy's bath. "Put the tub in front of the fire. Then move the screen," Betty told the maids who waited there. "Is the water hot?"

The conversation flowed around Lucy like water around a boulder in a stream. For eight years she had denied any feelings for anyone but her family, had determinedly set them aside. Now with one gentle kiss her impregnable defenses began to crumble. Reveling in forgotten sensations, she simply stood in the middle of the room, her exhaustion and aching forgotten. Richard, her brother's friend, the man against whom she had measured each of her suitors, had kissed her. The kisses she had allowed a few favored gentlemen and even the ones that George had given her faded from her memory before the gentle warmth of Richard's lips.

"May I help you disrobe?" Betty asked, her voice raised as though she were speaking to someone who could not hear well. She wore a puzzled look on her face.

Obedient as a child with her nanny, Lucy turned around. Richard had kissed her. Moving as her maid directed, she soon was up to her chin in hot water. The warmth caused her to sigh contentedly. "Do not let me go to sleep in here, Betty," she said with a smile.

"Hmmm. As if I would." The maid watched her mistress carefully, adding hot water carefully and handing Lucy her favorite soap scented with roses. When Lucy's eyelids began to droop, she whipped out a towel and helped her from the tub. "Just slip into this gown," she suggested. "I have turned the bed back for you. Rest for a while."

"Do not let me sleep very long. My husband is joining me for supper later," Lucy said dreamily.

"And for something else I don't doubt," her maid muttered under her breath. "You think he would have sense to let her rest. Men!"

Almost as soon as Lucy woke up, servants appeared to arrange a table with flowers and plates before the fireplace and small settee. Lucy took one look at the elaborate table setting and began to worry about what she should wear. "Get out the blue silk. Or should it be the rose?" she asked. "Have you had a chance to press it?"

"Mr. Blount asked me to tell you not to dress. In fact, he suggested a dressing gown," Betty said quietly. "I have laid out your rose velvet because the evening will be cool."

"A dressing gown. I am not ill," Lucy protested.

"But you have been on an exhausting journey," her maid reminded her, her voice sounding strained. Though her mistress might be innocent of the fact, Betty was certain she understood her new master's objectives.

Lucy looked at her strangely, noting the weariness in her maid's face. Guilt flooded her as she realized that Betty had been up at least an hour longer than she had and, instead of tea and a nap, had been unpacking for her mistress. Rather than give her extra work, she quickly acquiesced. "A dressing gown over my nightrobe will be fine. And put my hair into a single braid." She sat down in front of the mirror.

When Betty put the brush down and stepped back to check that every strand of Lucy's thick hair was in its place, Lucy looked into the mirror. The lines of pain in her face had eased, she noted, but she was still pale. However, when her maid offered her a pot of rouge, she shook her head and sighed. She might as well let her husband see firsthand exactly what he had agreed to marry. Lucy glanced at the mirror and stood up. "You have had a long day too, Betty. As soon as you have your supper, go to bed. Have you had a chance to see your room and unpack?"

"Yes, Miss Lucy. I will have a room of my own since I am your maid," Betty said proudly. A member of a large farming family in the neighborhood of Lucy's old home, she was more accustomed to sharing not just a room but a bed. Even though Lucy had been mistress of her father's home, her maid still had to share a bed with another woman.

"Let me know if you need anything," Lucy said softly, wondering what it would have been like to share a home with ten brothers and sisters. With her brother away at school or in London, she had often been lonely. "Now be off with you. I shall put myself to bed." She smiled as she took a seat next to the small fire.

You or someone else, Betty thought cynically as she gathered up Lucy's discarded clothing. "Shall I leave you a posset for pain?" she asked, even though she thought she knew her mistress's response. Lucy shook her head much as Betty had expected she would. Her work soon finished, the maid slipped out of the roon.

No sooner than the outer door had closed behind her than one Lucy had not noticed before opened. Richard put his head through the opening and asked, "May I come in?"

The trembling Lucy had felt before overtook her once more. It was all she could do to nod. Resisting the urge to find her heaviest cloak and wrap it around her, she walked to the settee. She glanced at him, very uncomfortable at having him in her bedroom.

When she had been ill, her brother had often stayed in her room to keep her company, but Richard was not her brother. No, he is your husband, Lucy reminded herself, feeling her cheeks grow warm. Husbands have the right to enter their wives' bedchambers. Remembering the talk she had had with Arabella's mother once the lady knew that she was serious about going through with the marriage, Lucy blushed even more, wondering if he would demand his rights that very instant. She looked at him from under her long, thick eyelashes. He had shed his coat, waistcoat, and cravat but still wore his shirt and pantaloons.

Richard, no stranger to a woman's bedroom, watched her change color. "Did you sleep well?" he asked casually, reminding himself that he would have to move slowly. Crossing to the bellpull, he gave it a tug. Then he filled two glasses with the wine he had brought with him and handed her one.

"Very well," she whispered after two unsuccessful tries. In spite of the excitement she felt, there was also a touch of panic. What if she did not please him? She took a sip of her wine and choked.

As though she were a child and he a nurse, he thumped her between her shoulders, almost knocking her off balance, causing her to spill the rest of the wine. When she continued to cough, he raised her arms over her head. As soon as she had stopped coughing, he refilled her glass and handed it to her. "Take only small sips." Lucy glared at him, brushing the wine from her skirts and wondering if it would stain.

"Do you still like peach tarts?" Richard asked, watching the vein in her neck pulsing. Lucy could only stare at him, her heart pounding wildly, wondering what he was talking about. "If you do not, please do not tell Cook. I insisted that she bake some for you for this evening. She said to tell you that she used the last of the dried peaches so that these will be the last until the new fruit is ready." He sat down beside her, noting her big blue eyes and the strained look around her mouth. She moved closer to the end of the settee, almost hugging the end.

"Lucy, I do not know what you have been told, but I

do not plan to make you the main course at this meal,"
he said, keeping his voice light and teasing. At least not
tonight, he added to himself. He smiled at her, willing
her to smile back. He longed to reach out and unravel
her carefully braided hair, but knew she would not let
him. Finally, as Lucy realized that he meant what he had
said, that he simply intended to sit beside her, she relaxed slightly. Then she started and sat up straight when
she heard the scratching at the door.

"Come in," her husband called. To Lucy's surprise
and pleasure, Dawes and two footmen presented the
meal and stayed to serve them. She noted with approval
that the clear soup was still warm, and the meats and
vegetables nicely presented, and she planned to compli-
ment the cook and Mrs. Dawes the next day. Richard
coaxed her to eat more than she had first intended, and
he kept her wineglass full. Although he only asked her
questions about her family, especially Edward, Lucy
struggled to hold up her end of the conversation. By the
time the remainder of the peach tarts had been removed,
the table cleared, and the servants dismissed, she was exhausted. Her eyes were beginning to droop once more.

"It is time for bed." Richard gave her his hand to help
her up. Wishing she were still as graceful as she once
had been, Lucy allowed him to assist her. But when she
tried to take a step, she almost fell for the second time
that day. Once again Richard swept her off her feet, this
time carrying her to the bed. In spite of her efforts to
prevent him, he helped her remove her dressing gown,
dropping it unceremoniously on the floor beside the bed.
When she was ensconced among her pillows, her face
burning with embarrassment, the covers pulled to her
chin, he said quietly but firmly, "Turn over." Her eyes
widened in panic. But his tone of voice, the same one he
had used long ago when he had decided that she was not
needed on one of her brother's and his expeditions, told
Lucy she did not have a choice. Richard was one of the
few people she had not been able to bend to her will. She

turned over, sighing as she did so. She closed her eyes, trying to be brave.

"Where do you hurt the worst?" her husband asked. Lucy tried to turn over to answer him, but he put his hands on her shoulders and held her in place. His fingers stroked the long braid that lay across her shoulder.

"What?"

"Where do you hurt the most?" he asked. "Here?" He began rubbing her back and legs. He pulled the sheet down, and Lucy wanted to sink into the feather mattress and hide her face forever, partly because she was feeling sensations that frightened her and partly because she was afraid he would be able to see the scars on her legs, scars she had hidden as much as she could. Long ago she had realized the necessity of having the doctor and her maid see them. But the idea that Richard also had that right was overwhelming. "What are you doing?" Lucy asked in a choked voice.

"Trying to ensure you have a restful night's sleep," he said soothingly, letting his fingers dig into the knot he had found in her back. Lucy gasped.

"Am I hurting you?" Richard asked, relaxing his grip on her.

"No," she whispered, wondering why her body seemed to pulse every time he touched her. She tensed, then relaxed as he found yet another tight spot. "What are you doing?"

"Something I learned when I was in Sweden. I took a fall when I was climbing the ice on one of fjords, and one of the guides did this to me. Later I had him teach me how. How does your back feel now?"

Lucy mumbled something, not wanting the warm sensations to stop. The heat of his hands on her back and legs helped her drift off to sleep. When she awoke the next morning after one of the few deep sleeps she had had in months, she was still warm and cozy, lying on her side, her head nestled on his chest.

Chapter Three

Breathing deeply, Lucy lay still, afraid to stir and waken the sleeping man. She heard the soft popping of the coal embers in the fireplace. Cautiously, she began to move. Richard's arm tightened around her shoulders. She froze, trying to remember just what happened the evening before. The last thing she remembered was his hands on her back and legs easing their cramped muscles. Surely if he had . . . She forced those thoughts from her mind and willed her body to relax, mentally taking stock. He was her husband, she reminded herself. She felt the muscles in her back begin to knot once more. Knowing that she must move, she tried to slide out from under Richard's arm.

"Are you trying to escape already?" his husky, sleep-roughened voice asked. Lucy started, pulled away from him, and drew the sheet up under her chin. She shook her head and moved to a sitting position.

"I get stiff," she explained, her blue eyes hidden by curtains of thick lashes. When she dared to look at him again, he had turned on one side, facing her, his gray eyes serious. She blushed. Then her eyes opened wide. He was still fully clothed, having discarded only his boots. He moved and dislodged the blanket over him, and she realized that he had slept on top of the covers. A soft "Oh" slipped from her lips. She covered her mouth with her hand and blushed again.

"I suppose that we will be the topic of conversation in the servants' hall this morning," he said ruefully. When he had decided to lie down beside Lucy, he had not thought about a blanket. Vaguely, he wondered who had had the courage to enter their room unannounced. He hoped that her maid, the most likely candidate, would keep her observations to herself.

Her eyes, already wide, opened even further. "We will," Lucy said in a matter-of-fact tone, just a hint of disapproval edging her words. "If you did not want people to talk about us, you should have been present for your own wedding." She was surprised by the amount of resentment she felt.

"I explained that I could not leave the children," he said firmly, his lips set in a stern line.

"You could have brought them with you."

"Lucy, I thought that I had made myself perfectly clear in my letters." He glared at her and sat up, disconcerted by her renewal of old arguments.

She glared back. "All your letters said was that you could not come. I do not consider that an explanation."

"You agreed to marry me by proxy. I thought that meant you understood." He slid off the bed and stood beside it, frowning down at her. His vision of the first morning of his marriage had not included a quarrel with his new wife.

"I understood that you absolutely refused to come to my home," she said quietly. When his letter telling her that had arrived, she had considered changing her mind. Then Arabella arrived to discuss plans for her own wedding. Reminded once again of how much her brother had had to give up, Lucy had reluctantly written Richard her agreement. But she had never understood his reasoning.

"We could have been married here. I told you to invite your family."

"And leave my father at home?" she asked angrily. "You have not seen him in years. Traveling for even a few miles causes him excruciating pain. Accepting your choice of marriage by proxy seemed the only way he could be present at my wedding."

"You could have refused to marry me," he reminded her, his gray eyes stormy and his voice cold. Was he doomed to suffer through yet another unhappy marriage, he wondered. Somehow he had expected more from the girl he had once known.

Recognizing something in his voice, something that she had heard in her own when she was determined to hide her pain, Lucy moved over to the edge of the bed next to him. "But I did not want to do that." She reached out and grabbed his hand, much the way she had when she was a child and he was trying to get rid of her. He stepped back. Her hand dropped. At that moment Lucy felt the same desolation she had known when the earl, her former fiancé, had accepted his dismissal.

"What made you decide to marry me? Did you think I would be a more complacent husband than your other offers?" His voice accused her of betrayal. He looked her over, contempt evident in his face.

"Complacent about what?" she asked bewildered. "Richard, I do not understand." She slid out of bed and stood in front of him, her blue eyes wide and hurt. Nothing in his letters had prepared her for his bitterness and anger. "What have I done wrong?"

He opened his mouth to answer her, then snapped it shut again. The sight of her standing there, her long braid hanging over the rumpled gown she had worn to bed, reminded him of Lucy, the young girl who was too busy living to have time to worry about the state of her clothes; he remembered happy times they had once shared. The thin line around his mouth began to soften as he remembered whom he was talking to. He took a deep breath, gaining control of his emotions once more. "We can discuss this further later. I believe Mrs. Dawes is waiting for you," he said quietly; then he walked away from her.

Lucy stared at him. When he opened the door to his room, she hurried after him. "Richard, we need to talk now," she protested.

"Later," he said firmly, closing the door in her face. Lucy stared at it for a moment and then whirled angrily, wishing she had something to throw. Then, almost as quickly as it had appeared, her anger was gone to be replaced by doubt. "What have I done now?" she wondered as she walked about the room.

When she finally glanced at clock on the mantel, she was horrified. Lucy moved quickly across the room to the bellpull, wondering why Betty had not yet been in to check on her.

When her maid arrived only minutes later, she asked, "Why did you let me sleep so late? I am keeping Mrs. Dawes waiting."

"The master gave orders that you were not to be disturbed," her maid explained as she laid out her mistress's clothes for the day. Betty glanced at the other maid who had followed her into the room and who was building up the fire and then back at her mistress. She held out a fresh chemise.

"Oh." Lucy's face flushed as she glanced at the young girl at the hearth, finally realizing what the staff must be thinking.

"Should I ask for your breakfast to be served here, or will you go down?" Betty asked, bringing Lucy back to the present.

Her mistress adjusted her garter to her satisfaction and stood up, letting her petticoat fall. "I will breakfast downstairs." She sat down in front of the mirror and let Betty pin her hair into place. Perhaps Richard was disappointed in the way she looked and had hidden his dismay under his angry manner. "Would I look better with a few curls around my face?" she asked, twisting her head from side to side, making her maid's work much more difficult.

Betty, her face carefully blank so that Lucy would not see her keen interest, went about her work, and then when she had the last pin in place, answered. "I think they would be very becoming. I have my scissors with me, and it will take only a moment to heat the irons. Shall I do it now?" For the last few months she had been trying to interest Lucy in the latest styles.

"Now?" Lucy tried to remember what she looked like

with short curls. During her Season she had had her hair cropped short, but it had grown long in the years since the accident. "Not today." Maybe it was not her hair; maybe Richard just did not like the person she had become. She had been a giddy young girl the last time he met. Then again, he might be disappointed in her lack of style. "Perhaps you can study the fashion plates and select some styles you think will suit," she suggested, noting the disappointment on Betty's face.

As she helped Lucy into the yellow cambric round gown, Betty suggested, "If you will be inspecting the house this morning, you should take your cane." When the last copper hook had been fastened, she handed Lucy a silver-topped stick. Lucy glared at it as though it were a snake but took it anyway. She might as well carry her symbol of defeat proudly; she knew her maid was right.

When she entered the breakfast room a short time later, Richard looked up in surprise. "I thought you would have breakfast in your room," he said as he seated her and called for fresh tea.

"Only when I am truly ill. I much prefer to be up and about, usually much earlier than this," she said firmly, motioning to the footman, who stood close to them. Soon he had disappeared with her request. She leaned forward, her face intent on the man across from her. "Will we have time to talk further today?" she asked bravely, not at all sure she wanted to hear his answer.

He looked around the room as though he expected someone to be spying on him. "The servants," her husband protested, his voice lowered to a hush.

"I am no little girl, Richard. I know that now is not an appropriate time. But I want you to find some time for me today." She surprised herself with the firmness in her voice.

"The children will join us for dinner," he reminded her, "and Mrs. Dawes is waiting for you now."

"Then may we talk tonight?" A footman walked into the room, and she fell silent. She sat back in her chair and nodded as the man placed a plate in front of her.

Richard did not answer her but finished the tea in his cup and held it out for more. Lucy sighed and refilled his cup. Too unsure of her own status in the household, she was afraid to press the issue.

After the tumultuous morning, the rest of the day passed rather quickly. By the time Lucy returned to her room from her inspection tour, she was using her cane. She breathed a sigh of relief as the door closed around her, the pain she had hidden so well now evident.

"Are you all right?" her maid asked anxiously. "I could prepare a posset."

"No, a little rest before dinner and I will be fine," Lucy said with a weak smile, wishing as she had often wished before that her body were stronger.

"The minute I saw those winding staircases I knew you would be worn down. Do you wish me to help you out of your gown so that you can lie down?" Betty bustled forward, her crisply starched skirts rustling around her. She glanced at her mistress's face and did not like what she saw.

In spite of the feeling that she was giving in to her weakness, Lucy nodded. A few minutes later she was once again prone. She sighed. "I think I will wear the blue figured muslin to dinner," she said in a voice only seconds away from sleep.

Betty watched in satisfaction as her mistress closed her eyes and relaxed. From the moment she had been promoted to be Lucy's maid, the woman had watched over her mistress as though she had been her own child. Before the disastrous accident, her work had been mostly picking up after Lucy and turning her into a pattern card that others would follow. Since then, she had kept watch over her when the doctor feared for her life, adding her strength when Lucy's determination to grow strong again had begun to crumble. When her mistress had refused to accept the doctor's statement that she would be an invalid for the rest of her life and began to try to walk, it was Betty's shoulder she had leaned on the first few times. Now her maid was just as determined to provide her support as Lucy explored the new path she had taken, one that would be rather bumpy if her new master's servants were to be believed. Betty herself wished to reserve judgment on her new master. When she had entered her mistress's room earlier that morning, she had been surprised to find him still there, his restraint obvious to her curious eyes.

After her short nap, Lucy woke refreshed if a trifle stiff. Gingerly, she began walking up and down the room. The day before she had been too excited to notice much about her surroundings. Now she walked to the mantel to inspect the clock there, an Italian one if she was not mistaken. As a girl she had been fascinated by clocks and had a collection of them. In fact, her brother had often teased her about her interest, declaring that she should concern herself with fans instead. But after the accident she had lost interest. Idly, she wondered what had happened to them.

The dressing bell broke into her musings. By the time she had finished dressing and gone downstairs, the children had already joined their father. Lucy paused in the doorway, noting their preoccupation with each other, and wondered if she would ever be a part of the group. She had hesitated on the threshold only a moment when Richard looked up. He got up, took her hand and raised it to his lips. She blushed, and the children giggled. Then he led her to a seat. The intervening hours had caused him to regret his words that morning. "The children were just telling me about their morning," he explained. He examined her carefully, pleased to see that the strain was gone from her face. "Come join us." He patted the seat beside him on the settee, a seat that David had just vacated.

Relieved that the tension between them was gone, she took the place he indicated. David glared at her when he thought his father was not looking and refused to do more than murmur his hello. Caroline and Robert were more welcoming. "I can spell my whole name," the little girl said proudly. "C-A-R-O-L-I-N-E, that's Caroline.

E-L-I-Z-A-B-E-T-H, that's my middle name," she added with a shy smile.

"Da, are you going to let her do it all again?" Robert complained. "I wanted to tell Mama"— David glared at him, and Robert quickly changed what he was going to say, "her"—he pointed at Lucy—"what I learned about Russia this morning." He leaned against his father, his face wearing a wistful look. He would have been more successful if he had not glanced up to see if his tactics were working. Lucy had to bite back a laugh, remembering how she had tried much the same technique when she was his age.

"Let Caroline finish. Then it will be your turn," his father said calmly, hiding his own amusement.

"But then it will be time for dinner. You know Dawes always announces it on the stroke of two, and Caroline takes too long," the boy complained. His father simply raised an eyebrow and looked at him, waiting. Realizing that he had reached the limit of his father's patience, Robert fell silent.

"Go ahead, Caroline," her father urged. Robert muttered something under his breath but quieted as soon as he saw his father looking at him sternly.

"B-L-O-U-N-T," the little girl said triumphantly. "My whole name is Caroline Elizabeth Blount, just like my grandmother's. She died before I was born, but there is a picture of her in the gallery at home." Suddenly, the memory of what had happened to their home returned full force. Caroline's voice grew choked, and a desolate look came over the little girl's face then. She ran over to her father, tears running down her face. "I forgot, Da. I forgot. It got burned up too, just like Mama, didn't it?"

Her father gathered her up in his arms and wiped her eyes, wishing, not for the first time, that he could erase the painful memories from his children's minds. David and Robert huddled around him, patting their sister on the back, their faces equally saddened. Lucy felt more of an outsider than before as she watched the scene. She took a deep breath, telling herself that it was natural that

Caroline wanted her father to comfort her. But as little as she wanted to admit it aloud, she wanted to be part of that group too, longed to have someone of her own to hold on to. Before she had decided to marry Richard, she had been able to hide from those feelings, to deny their existence. However, as she began considering his proposal, reading the passages he had written in his letters about his children had released some craving inside her.

Just then Dawes walked in and announced, "Dinner is served."

Lucy and Robert glanced up at the clock at the same moment. "And you thought I was exaggerating, Da," Robert said indignantly. "I knew I would not have time to tell her about Russia." His complaint released the tension of the moment. They all laughed nervously, and Richard stood up. David and Caroline fixed their eyes on the carpet as if embarrassed by the emotions they had just revealed in front of a virtual stranger.

"Perhaps during dinner," Lucy suggested, taking her husband's arm and allowing him to lead her to the dining room. David offered his arm to his little sister, leaving Robert to trail along after them.

Because he had been seated at the other end of the table and had been reminded to use his best manners, Robert could not share his information with Lucy. As soon as the meal was over, Richard shepherded his small group out into the garden for a walk. "Da, can I tell you now?" Robert demanded.

"It is 'may,' not 'can,' Robert," his little sister said, her tone so like that of her governess that everyone laughed. She glared at them indignantly. "Well, it is!"

"You are right, my dear," her father said, hiding his laughter only with effort. Lucy hid her laughter behind a handkerchief. "And so are you, Robert. Tell us about Russia."

Drawing himself up importantly, Robert opened his mouth and then shut it abruptly. "You made me wait so long I forgot it," he complained. He glared at them as his brother and sister burst into loud laughter. David walked closer to him and whispered something in his ear. Robert turned red and punched his brother. "Take that back!" he demanded.

Before either of the adults could react, the boys were rolling around the ground, hitting each other. Their father grabbed the back of their collars and held them at arm's length. "You will stop this immediately," he said in a stern voice. He forced one and then the other to look him in the eyes. When he was certain they had been properly subdued, he released them. The boys took several steps backward, still glaring at each other. "Now, what was this about?"

Caroline, her hand holding on to Lucy's as if it were a lifeline, said in a soft voice, "David probably called Robert a dummy. It is what he always says." Her older brother took a step toward her, his face set in angry lines. Caroline stepped closer to Lucy's side and hid her face in her skirt.

Before the older boy could move very far, Richard had moved between them. "David, go to my study and wait for me," he said quietly. The stern lines of his face told his oldest son that protest would do no good. Glaring at his brother and sister again, he turned and made his way toward the house. Robert let a small smile of triumph creep across his lips. "And you, sir, may wait in the hall until I am ready for you," his father told him. The boy's shoulders slumped. He nodded and turned to go. Richard watched him go and then sighed.

"Da, David has been very mean to Robert lately," Caroline said, her voice little more than a whisper.

"Has he, sweetheart?" Richard asked, kneeling so that he could look her in the face. "Why did you wait until now to tell me?"

"I did not want David to get in trouble," she said, her eyes filling up with tears. One ran down her cheek. She rubbed her nose with the back of her hand. "He will be mad at me." She began sobbing. Richard picked her up and held her close to him, patting her on the back. He looked over her head at Lucy, who was standing help-lessly by.

"Let us go into the house," Richard suggested. He sighed, dreading the interviews ahead. Nothing that he said to David seemed to do any good. He knew that the boy had been closer to his mother than the other two and had felt the tragedy of her death deeper. As a result, he had made excuses for David, hoping as the boy adjusted to his loss his behavior would grow better. Now he was not certain.

This last year had been a learning experience for Richard. In the past his wife had been in charge of the children. He had seen them whenever he was at home, had even taken pleasure in their company. However, he had not been involved in their day-to-day discipline. Often away from home, either in London or on trips for the government, he had never realized the care they needed. In fact, had he thought of that at all then he would have assumed that their governess and their tutor were all they needed. As he had discovered this last year, they required much more. And from what he could learn without asking too many direct questions, his previous wife had taken as little interest in Robert and Caroline's lives as he had, at least in the last few years before her death.

As soon as they entered the house, Richard put Caroline down. "Will you stay with her?" he asked Lucy. "I had not meant to force our problems upon you so soon," he said apologetically. After their words that morning, he had resolved to allow his wife more time to grow accustomed to them before he made any more demands on her.

"Nonsense. How am I ever to be a part of your family if you do not allow me to help?" she asked quietly, having stepped so close to him that the little girl would not hear what she was saying. Her next words were louder. "I am hoping that Caroline will have tea in my room and tell me which of the clothes I brought with me will be suitable for sailing. I have never been on anything larger than a punt."

"You haven't?" Caroline reached out and took her hand. "Da takes David, Robert, and me out with him whenever it is pretty. Someday we are going to sail to France and maybe to Wales. That is where Da was born," she said importantly. Lucy smiled at her and then at Richard.

As the two of them climbed the stairs, Richard stood at the bottom, watching them until they disappeared from his view. Then he squared his shoulders, and his face grew stern again. He walked down the hallway to his study. Robert, who was sitting in a chair much too large for him, his head down, and his eyes fixed on his clasped hands, looked up when he heard footsteps. When he recognized his father, he stood up, his face wearing a look of hope.

"I will see you in a few minutes, Robert," his father said quietly. The boy sat back down, his shoulders slumped once more. Richard opened the door to his study and walked in.

Chapter Four

Not until the afternoon was almost over did Lucy give up her hopes that Richard would come to her room and explain what had happened. She had kept Caroline with her as long as the little girl was happy inspecting her stepmother's clothes and chattering. At last, however, the child began to grow fussy and ask for her father or her governess. Reluctantly, Lucy returned her to the schoolroom.

When they walked in, the two boys were already there. Robert looked up from his plate of bread and butter with a smile, but David frowned angrily. He glared at Lucy and his sister and hurried from the room. "Was Da very angry with you?" Caroline asked as she hurried to Robert's side. "Did he punish David?"

"It was nothing," Robert said, blustering, trying to seem more brave than he really was. "I told Da just . . ." Then he noticed Lucy's disapproving gaze; his bravado disappeared. "He, ah, he . . . ."

"Caroline, I believe it is time for you to wash up before supper," her stepmother said sternly.

"But I want to know what happened," the little girl protested.

"Go and wash up, Caroline," Lucy said firmly. The little girl glanced at her again as though she wanted to argue. Then the child looked at Robert as though she were going to ask him a question; he shook his head. Caroline turned toward the door, crossing the schoolroom but stopping every few steps to glance at Lucy as if expecting her stepmother to relent. She halted at the door that opened on her bedroom, her hand on the latch. "Get ready for supper, Caroline," Lucy said, the tone of her voice stern.

When the door had closed firmly behind the girl, Lucy turned her attention to Robert. "I think your father would be very disappointed if you were to tell Caroline what he said to you in private," she said quietly.

"Well, but . . ."

"Did he tell you what he said to Daivd?" The boy shook his head. "Did David tell you?" Robert blushed and shook his head once more. "Then what were you about to tell your sister?"

Robert looked anywhere but up into her face. "Ah, well, ah . . ."

Remembering that he had been sent to wait in the hall until Richard had talked to David, Lucy bent over and lifted the boy's chin so that he was forced to look at her. "Robert, were you listening at the door?" she asked sternly. He blushed and moved away from her. "Were you?" she asked again.

"Well, ah, I wanted to know what was happening," he said, his chin beginning to wobble just a little. Lucy was reminded how young he still was, not yet seven.

She sat down in one of the chairs and pulled him close to her once more. She hugged him and then asked, "Did you know that it was wrong to listen?"

He hung his head, his face close to her shoulder. "Yes," he whispered. "Are you going to tell Da?"

"That depends. Are you going to do this again?" Lucy hoped that she was handling the situation properly. Obviously, there was more to being a parent than she had first thought.

"No." He wore a woeful expression on his face.

Once more she put a finger under his chin and lifted his face so that she could inspect it. The regret she saw there was the answer she needed. "I do not think this needs to go further than us. But, Robert, this is not to happen again. Is that clear?"

"Yes." Relieved that he would not have to face his father's displeasure once again that day, Robert hugged her, hiding his face in her shoulder. Instinctively, Lucy returned the embrace, feeling strangely satisfied.

When they heard a door open, Robert jumped back as though ashamed of the feelings he had been showing. He was the first to see his father. He simply stood there staring at him as if afraid his father had heard what they had been talking about.

Lucy turned around in her chair. Her heart began to beat faster. Her husband just stood there for a moment, taking in the picture she made with his son. Then he smiled at them both. "Where are David and Caroline?" he asked, taking his customary place in a large chair that was reserved solely for him.

"Caroline is changing, and David is in his room," Robert said hurriedly, his words spilling out so fast that Richard had to listen carefully to understand him.

"Have you finished your supper?"

"Almost. Mama and I were talking." Since his brother was not there, Robert did not hesitate to use the term for his father's new wife. In the few hours since her arrival, Lucy had given him more attention than his mother had bestowed on him during all the years they had been together. Lucy felt her cheeks growing warm with pride at the sound. She was his mother. Glancing at Richard, she smiled and silently vowed that no one of the children would suffer because of her presence in their lives.

Just then Caroline opened the door and skipped into the room. She caught sight of her father and ran over to him, climbing up on his lap. "Are you going to have supper with us?" she asked, tilting her head to the side and smiling at him. "I am not very hungry. I had tea with . . ." Like her brothers, Caroline was not yet sure of Lucy's role in her life. Although her governess and nurserymaid in addition to her father had told her that Lucy was her stepmother, the word was hard for her.

"Call her Mama," her father said with a smile.

No one had heard David enter the room. But they heard his words. "But she is not our mother. Our mother died in the fire. You let her die." All the anger and pain over his mother's death that the boy had held back for the last year came boiling over. Totally at the mercy of his feelings, David ran over to his father and began hitting at him, his hands balled into fists. "You let her die."

Caroline, frightened by her brother's words and violent actions, slid from her father's lap and ran to Lucy. Freed from the constraints of having to worry about her, Richard stood up and faced David. Rather than trying to curb the anger that boiled over from his eldest son, Richard took the blows. When at last David's swings began to weaken, he took him in his arms, lifting him off his feet and holding him as though he were a small child. Finally the boy burst into tears. His face white with the impact of his son's pain, Richard left Lucy to cope with the other two and carried David into his bedroom.

"What is wrong with David? Why was he hitting Da?" Caroline asked, her eyes filled with tears. Then her face grew even whiter. "Is Da going to punish him again?" Robert, trembling slightly, leaned close to his stepmother.

"No, sweetheart. He is only going to try to make him feel better," Lucy assured her. She pulled both Caroline and Robert in front of her so that she could see their faces. When she saw the pain there, she sighed.

"Did Da really let our mama die?" Robert asked, his voice quiet and his words mumbled.

"No, I am sure he would never have done that," Lucy said reassuringly, hoping she was saying the right thing.

"But you were not there," Robert reminded her.

"No, but I have known your father for a long time, longer than either of you have been alive. He would never do something that would hurt anyone," she said firmly. Both children stared at her as if they could read the truth in her face. Caroline sighed and climbed up into her lap. Robert was not as willing to give up his questions.

"Why did David say that, then?" he asked, his face showing a worry at odds with his childhood.

Desperately searching for some way to reassure him, Lucy took a moment to answer. Finally, she said, "Remember your fight with David this afternoon?" Already that seemed so far in the past Robert had to think a moment. Then he nodded his head. "You said you hated him. Do you really?"

"No." The word was said so quietly that Lucy almost missed it.

"Then why did you say it?" his stepmother asked. Caroline looked from one to the other of them without saying a word, her eyes wide.

"He made me angry. I am not a dummy!" The emotions the boy had felt during the fight threatened to overwhelm him again. His face clenched.

"I told Da that was what David had said," Caroline added at this point, pleased that her comment had been affirmed.

"Yes, you did, sweetheart," Lucy told her, smoothing the long curls back from her face. Once again she wished she had had more experience with the children before having to deal with this situation. She smiled at Robert. "Did you really mean it?"

"No." Robert raised his eyes from the floor. He had been staring fixedly at the toe of his boot as it made a circle on the floor. Now his eyes fixed on Lucy's face as if trying to understand what she was saying. "I don't understand," he said, his mouth trembling.

Although her lap was already full, Lucy reached out and pulled him up on it, ignoring the pain in her weak leg. When Caroline wrapped her arms around him, he did not try to pull away. Lucy put her arms around both of them. "David was angry," she said quietly.

"Why?" Caroline asked.

"He loved your mother very much, and he misses her," Lucy said quietly, hoping she was right.

"Oh." For a while the only sound was of the three of them breathing.

Then Robert asked, "But why was he so angry with Da?"

Before Lucy had time to think of an answer, Richard had walked back into the schoolroom. "Da," the children whispered and made a dash toward him, wrapping their arms around his legs, making it almost impossible for him to move. He knelt down carefully and hugged them, trying to give them some of his strength. After a few moments, Robert pulled away.

"Is David all right?" he asked, his little boy's face showing his worry.

"He will be. For the next few days, though, I would like the two of you to be especially kind to him." He hurried on when he saw the stubborn line of Robert's mouth. "I know that it will not be easy; he has hurt you. But do you think you could try?"

"I will, Da," Caroline promised. She wrapped her arms around her father's neck and gave him a big hug. Then she yawned widely. Lucy smothered a nervous laugh with her hand. All three of them watched Robert.

Finally, he sighed. "I will try," he promised. Like his sister, he hugged Richard's neck.

"Good. I am proud of you. Now I believe you two need to say good night to Lucy, finish your supper, and then go to bed. It has been an eventful day." Richard gave each of them one more hug and then stood up. He led them over to where Lucy sat and watched indulgently as they said their good nights. After seeing them seated at their table again with their nurserymaid close at hand, he held out his hand to his wife and led her from the room.

When the door closed behind them, he sighed deeply. Then he pulled Lucy's arm through his own and began to walk to the stairs. "I did not plan to present you with such high drama on your first day here," he said, trying to make his tone light. From the moment the boys had started fighting, he had dreaded facing her once more. She was already having doubts about the wisdom of their marriage; this last outburst might be enough to drive her away.

"Richard, I may not have been a part of the *ton* for

years, but I have not been locked away from the world. My best friend, Arabella, the one Edward is marrying, has several younger brothers and sisters and innumerable cousins who visit regularly. I am accustomed to childish quarrels that blaze one moment and are gone the next," she said, wishing she could smooth the lines from his furrowed brow.

"But I imagine that it is not every day that you hear your husband accused of deliberately letting his wife die," he said with a rueful laugh. Then before she had time to answer, he went on. "I can explain."

"You do not need to do that," she said quickly.

"I want to." Richard sighed once more. Opening the door, he ushered her into her rooms. Catching her maid's eye, Lucy motioned her to leave. As though he were unaware of anyone else being present, he led Lucy to the sofa and then sat down beside her. He leaned back, his head resting on the high back, his eyes closed. "God! How I wish I had been faster that night."

"I am certain you did all you could," she said soothingly, her face calm and her voice only a little louder than a whisper. The pain in his voice made her wish that there was something more that she could do.

He laughed bitterly. "All I could? I wish I were as certain as you." He sat up straight, squaring his shoulders. Then too restless to sit still any longer, he got up and began walking about the room.

Lucy, her face white, stared at him, silently willing him to explain. She remembered all too well the agony of holding her emotions inside her and the relief she had felt when Edward had forced her to discuss some of them. If he would only share those feelings with her, maybe he would begin to feel better. Somehow she knew that his guilt about the night his wife died had something to do with their quarrel this morning. If he would only confide in her, maybe she could help him forget. However, knowing better than to say anything, she merely smiled encouragingly.

"I wanted to take her and the children away, but she

would not hear of it," he said quietly, pausing to put his arm up on the mantel and to lean his face against it.

"Away? What do you mean? To London?"

Richard walked back to her and sat down beside her. He picked up her hand and held it within his own, his eyes fixed on it as though fascinated by the contrast between them. Lucy, using all the patience she had learned during the last eight years, sat quietly, waiting for an answer. He finally looked up. "David was right. Her death was my fault."

"I do not believe you."

"You should."

"Did you start the fire?"

"No!"

"Then how can you say it was your fault?" Lucy asked, reaching up to smooth back a wayward curl that had fallen over his forehead. He captured her hand again and brought it to his lips for a kiss. Lucy caught her breath as unfamiliar sensations burned down her arm and to the depth of her being.

"Thank you for believing in me," he said quietly, looking deep into her eyes. She was more beautiful at this moment than she had been as a girl. Then she had worn her beauty like a shield, holding off the unpleasant details of life. But now there was a depth to her, a depth he longed to explore. "I wish I were worthy of that faith." He closed his eyes, seeing once again the flames of that night, flames that haunted his dreams. He held her hand tightly as though it were a talisman that could ward off evil thoughts.

"Oh, Richard," Lucy said softly, reaching up with her other hand to caress his face. The strange emotions she had felt earlier grew stronger, made her long to throw herself into his arms, to beg him for additional kisses. Her cheeks burned with the excitement she felt. Somehow, she managed to resist, sitting quietly beside him, only her hands touching him.

Her silence was the goad he had been needing. As though she were a priest hearing his confession, he poured out the story. More than once Lucy had to bite her lip to keep from saying something that might have halted his words.

Before the fire, Richard explained, he and his wife had had one of their quarrels, quarrels that had been growing increasingly more frequent since Caroline's birth. Leaving his wife, he had gone to his study and started drinking. Unlike other evenings when they had quarreled, he had only had a few glasses. Then an uncontrollable urge to see his children had sent him to the schoolroom suite. He had stood by Caroline's bedside first, watching the easy rise and fall of her counterpane pulled up to her neck. Then he went to the bedroom that his boys shared. There he stood for some time just looking at them. Feeling somewhat better, he had left.

As he walked down the main stairs to his bedroom, he caught a whiff of smoke and then a curtain of fire swept across the landing in front of him. He had turned and run back up to the schoolroom. After that he was not certain what had happened. The servants told him that he had given the alarm, awakened the children, and seen that the children and the servants who slept on the floor above them escaped down the winding back staircase only a few moments before it too was engulfed in flames. When he had the children safely out of the house, he had ordered his butler to make sure everyone else was out. Frantically, he had searched through the small groups of horrified people, hoping to find his wife. When he realized that she was missing, he tried to dash back in through the walls of flame, but his servants had grabbed him and held him.

Thanks to his early warning, there were only two people who did not escape—his wife and her maid. The morning after the fire, the kitchen maid had remembered brewing a sleeping tisane for his wife, a tisane that usually made her sleep heavily for eight to ten hours.

"Had I been next door I could have carried her out," Richard said bitterly. He had gotten up sometime during his explanation and was standing by the fireplace, looking at the flames there with loathing.

"Yes, you could have. But what would have happened to the children and the servants?" Lucy asked, her voice breathless with horror at the pain and guilt he must have endured.

He looked at her in surprise as though he had never thought of that question. "Would they have escaped if you had not been there?" she continued.

"I do not know."

"You said the main staircase was in flames. Would they have thought to use the back ones instead?" she asked, trying to soothe him.

"The servants might have, but . . ."

"Then you must remember the lives you saved, not the ones that were lost. You did your best, Richard," she said, coming to stand in front of him. "As you once told me, that is all anyone can hope for."

He reached out and hugged her, feeling her warm body against his. "How did you get so wise?" he asked with a laugh. Then his body stiffened and his voice grew somber. "David will not understand that."

"Not now. As he grows older perhaps," she said, reaching up to smooth a wrinkle from his forehead.

"We, more especially you, may have a difficult time until he does. He does not approve of our marriage," Richard said ruefully. He drew her closer to him, the warmth and closeness of her body stirring his own emotions. He took a deep breath, enjoying the soft fragrance that clung to her skin.

"It is easier to be understanding if you understand the cause. Of course, he resents me. I am alive; his mother is dead. He will come around. You will see." She leaned back against his arms so she could look at his face. What she saw there made her catch her breath.

Richard bent his head slowly as though giving her a chance to pull away. She moved closer. Then his lips were on hers. At first he tried to keep the kiss soft and light; then as her lips answered his, the caress became more passionate. He urged her lips apart, his tongue teasing them. The light kisses she had exchanged with her former fiancé had not prepared her for the blaze of passion that had her tingling all over. But instead of pulling back, she wrapped her arms about his neck and opened her lips, letting him in. Richard immediately took possession.

His arms pulled her even closer to him, the hardness of his body evident through the thin layers of cloth that separated them. He kissed her again, his hands a source of fire on her back. Then he pushed her away a little. She bit back a cry of protest. He bent his head lower and kissed her neck behind her ear. His lips against her skin were hot and set her on fire. Lucy felt as though her heart were pounding so hard it would break through her chest.

Richard nibbled at her earlobe. She moaned softly. Then he moved lower, showering her shoulders with kisses. She tried to get closer to him. Richard smiled; then she felt his tongue tracing her collarbone. She moaned again.

The sound she made released something in Richard. He reached behind her and unhooked the bodice of her gown and pulled it off her shoulders, freeing her breasts from the dress. Too enraptured by the emotions she was feeling to protest, Lucy let the dress drop to the floor. He caught his breath at the sight of her creamy breasts held high by her stays. He reached up with one hand and ran his fingers across them, dipping under her stays and zona to touch her nipples. The fire that ran through her then startled Lucy. She tried to pull away, but Richard, his eyes dazed by passion, refused to let her go. She twisted in his arms.

The movement brought him out of the fog of emotion. He smiled at her, letting her move away although he did not let go of her. "Am I going too fast for you, little one," he asked, bending his head to kiss her once more.

When she could once more speak, Lucy said in a voice husky with emotion, "I am no child."

Richard glanced at her full breasts and then up at her. "That is very evident," he said with a smile. She blushed. "You are very beautiful."

Having compared herself unfavorably to her younger self for years, Lucy shook her head. "I am too thin," she whispered.

"Not where it counts." He bent her head and kissed the tops of her breasts. She caught her breath again. "Am I frightening you?" he asked, although he was not at all certain he would be able to let her go if she answered yes.

"No," she whispered, unable to keep her body from trembling. She was afraid, afraid of her own emotions, but she did not want him to stop.

"Good." Richard pulled her back against him, crushing her breasts against his chest. Once again he kissed her, sending fire surging through her veins. Standing on her tiptoes, she tightened her arms around his neck and returned the kiss. When he let his mouth wander once more down her neck and to her breasts, Lucy was panting, her lips parted and her eyes glazed by a desire that was strange to her. Her hands moved to his shoulders and then to his chest, trying to get closer to him. Following his example, she pushed his shirt out of her way so that she could touch him, running her hands over his shoulders.

Although neither of them ever remembered how it happened, soon they were standing there, he in his pantaloons and shoes, she in her zona. Coming to his senses enough to realize that a settee was no place to seduce his wife, not when a perfectly good bed was only a few feet away, Richard picked her up and carried her to her bed. She watched wide-eyed but blushing as he stripped off his pantaloons and shoes. When he reached for the waistband of his drawers, she closed her eyes. Away from the warmth of his arms, she shivered. Then she realized that even though the room was lit only by a few candles and firelight he could see all of her clearly. Panicked, she tried to get under the covers.

He climbed into bed with her and pulled them down again. "You do not need those," he whispered. "I can keep you warm." She shook her head and refused to let go. Thinking that she was shy, Richard bent down and kissed her. She did not resist, although she did not respond either.

Finally he realized that she was crying. "What is wrong?" he asked, one hand wiping the tears from her eyes and cheeks. "Do you want me to stop?" He pulled back a little, hoping that his control would hold. She shook her head. "Then what is wrong?"

She tried several times before she could get the words out. "My legs," she whispered.

"Am I hurting you? Why didn't you say something before?" he asked, moving farther away. Lucy made an effort to stop her tears. Since she had recovered from her accident, she had reserved her tears for those times when she was alone.

"Don't go," she begged, moving closer to him once more.

He turned on his side and looked down at her. Even though her lips still trembled, she was no longer crying. "I do not want to hurt you," he said anxiously.

"It was not you."

"I do not understand."

"I did not want you to see them." On the last word, her lips began to quiver. She closed her eyes, hoping she could hold back the tears.

"See what?" he asked, confused.

She took a deep breath and tried to control herself. "My legs," she whispered.

"What about them?"

"They are ugly," she said bitterly. From the moment she had been able to stand in front of a long mirror and inspect her body, she had been horrified by the deep scars she bore. The rocks that had caused her horse to fall had been between her and the ground. Their rough and sharp edges had gouged long cuts into her thighs and calves. Although most of her injuries had been internal or to her bones, her scars remained to remind her of that day.

"Let me see," Richard demanded. Once more she tried to hide beneath the covers, but he refused to allow her to do so. He stripped them back. Sliding out of bed, he picked up a candlestick and put it closer to the bed. Standing there, he inspected her carefully. Ashamed, Lucy turned over, hiding her face in her pillows. Her zona crept up, revealing her bottom to his interested gaze. He climbed back into bed beside her.

She lay there motionless, waiting for him to say something. When he said nothing, she turned back over. "They are ugly, aren't they?" she said, expecting to see disgust or pity in his eyes.

"What?"

"My scars."

"These?" he asked, moving so that he could kiss the fine white lines that marred the perfection of her skin. She caught her breath and froze as his kisses moved higher. His lips found a scar on the inside of her thigh. She gasped, wanting to tell him to stop but enjoying the sensations too much to force the words from her. He raised his head and smiled at her. "These are the marks of life." His finger traced the line his mouth had kissed. Once more Lucy felt as though she were on fire. She twisted nervously. "No one who truly lives is free of them. Perhaps later I will let you explore some of mine." He moved back to her side, his gray eyes stormy with emotion. She kept her eyes fixed on his. As he kissed her once more, he struggled to maintain his control. That kiss freed her. The fear that had held her disappeared. Her lips opened under his, her tongue caressing his lips. Her arms pulled him close, and he was lost.

Chapter Five

When she first awoke the next morning, Lucy almost convinced herself that the events of the previous evening had been a dream. Then she realized that she was not alone. Much as she had done the day before, she tried to slide out of bed without waking Richard. But her first movement brought a groan to her lips.

Yawning widely, completely relaxed for the first time in months, Richard sat up. "I am going to have to break you of trying to leave me in the morning," he said with a smile. He reached for her, planning to kiss her. Then he drew back at the sight of her pale face. "What is wrong?" he asked anxiously.

"Nothing. I will be fine in a few minutes," she said, trying to smile. Although she was often stiff in the mornings, especially once the weather grew colder, the stiffness soon disappeared.

"Was last night too much for you?" he asked, mentally berating himself for not remembering that he would have to treat her very gently.

"No." Remembering how she had wrapped herself around him, encouraged him, she blushed, her long eyelashes sweeping her cheeks. Then she looked up at him and smiled. Richard caught his breath, wanting nothing more than to pull her under him once more. The white line around her mouth brought him to his senses. He slid from bed and hurried to her side.

"Turn over," he demanded. She merely stared up at him. "So that I can loosen those muscles," he explained. Remembering the way he had eased her pain the night she had arrived, she did as he said, resting her head on her folded arms.

By the time he had finished, the pain in her back and legs had been forgotten. Lucy rolled over once more and looked up at him, wishing that it were night once more. The passion that blazed from his eyes made her catch her breath. She reached up for him. The invitation was what he had been waiting for. Climbing back into bed, he wrapped his arms around her and drew her once more into the flames of desire.

The next time they awoke the sun was high in the heavens. To her surprise, Lucy had no trouble moving. She looked down at Richard, who had chosen her breast instead of his pillow. She could feel his warm breath on her bare skin. She shivered. His eyes opened, and she could feel his warm tongue on her skin. Then, to her horror, her stomach growled.

Richard sat up with a laugh. Lucy wanted to tell him to stay, but she was too embarrassed. "Shall I ring for breakfast?" he asked, as though it were the accepted thing for them to wake up together. She nodded and snuggled back into the warmth of the covers. Richard, still nude, was reaching for the bellpull when Lucy sat straight up in bed. "The clothes we took off!" she said in horror, remembering the way they had discarded them the previous evening.

"Already gone," he said, looking around.

"Gone?" she asked in horror. What would the servants think, she wondered. Her face turned red as she realized exactly what they must be saying.

"I suspect your maid," Richard said calmly. Lucy breathed a sigh of relief. "Perhaps you should have a word with her today."

"About what?" Lucy asked innocently.

"About waiting until she is called before she enters your room, Madam Wife. You need more privacy now that you are a married lady," he stretched and then walked back to the bed and kissed her lightly. "I will return shortly," he promised. She watched him walk across the floor to his own door, totally unconcerned over his naked state. Although her cheeks blazed with emotion, she could not look away, enjoying the lean hips and trim buttocks that looked as good unclothed as they did in his knitted pantaloons.

When the door closed behind him, she slid back down in the bed, bringing the covers first to her chin and then over her head. She could still smell his scent on the sheets. "Oh my," she whispered. "Oh my."

In the days that followed, Lucy began to feel at home in Richard's house. The afternoons belonged to the children, but her evenings and early mornings were shared only with Richard. After the year of celibacy and the uneasy relationship he had had with his wife before that, Richard reveled in introducing Lucy to new sensations. For her part, Lucy was an eager learner.

To her surprise, she remembered how to flirt. When they were having dinner with the children, she would look up at Richard through her long eyelashes and smile sweetly. Then she would run her tongue around her lips as though pursuing a crumb. He would shift as though he were uncomfortable, but she could see a gleam in his eyes that promised retribution when they were alone, a retribution that she hoped would not be long in coming.

From the moment she had agreed to marry him, Lucy had known that Richard expected her to be his wife in all senses of the word. What she had not known is how much she would enjoy their physical relationship. No matter how many times they had made love, he could touch her, and she would be on fire once again.

Gradually, she took her place as mistress of the house. Only David resisted her overtures of friendship. Caroline and Robert were her devoted followers, turning to her with stories about their day as often as they turned to their father. David only glared at her and answered in monosyllables when she asked him questions.

The only time he seemed to forget his anger was when they were sailing. Richard had taken her for a sail alone the first week she had arrived, telling the children that he must make sure she would not be sick before he trusted her in the boat with them. To his delight, she was a natural sailor, following his instructions carefully. When he anchored off the point, out of view of the house and its inhabitants, she asked curiously, "Why are we stopping here?"

"I have something I want to show you," he said with a leer. He moved carefully toward her, a look on his face that she was quick to recognize.

"Richard! We can't. Not here," she said, her eyes wide. She backed up a little.

"If you do not want to have to go swimming, I would not move back any further," he told her, capturing her hand and pulling her toward him. She did not try to resist but moved forward into his arms. They kissed. "I could not resist you another minute," he whispered against her ear.

She put her lips on the pulse that throbbed in his neck and heard him catch his breath. Growing bolder, she kissed his chest and then his mouth, letting her tongue slip between his lips. Richard pulled her into his lap, sending the boat rocking. She drew back in fright. "We will not have to swim home," he promised. "And even if someone were to sail by, he would not know what we are doing. Let me show you?" Too breathless to say anything, she nodded, wrapping her arms around his neck, her golden brown skirts pooling around them. Before long, Lucy had forgotten where they were. All she cared about was Richard and what he was making her feel.

When he was certain she was ready, Richard folded his legs, adjusted his clothing, and then lifted her gently. Holding her skirt and petticoat out of the way, he put her back on his lap. When she felt him hard and hot beneath her, Lucy's eyes opened wide. Then she smiled and settled down on him more firmly. The waves lapping the boat provided the only motion they needed for a time. Untying the ribbons at her neckline, Richard pulled her bodice open so that he could kiss her breasts. She reached inside the open neck of the shirt he wore to run her fingers over his chest. He pulled her toward him. The action was the trigger that ignited both of them. Much later, pink from the sun but laughing and relaxed, they had returned to the house.

"Well, can she sail with us, Da?" Robert wanted to know as soon as he saw his father. David frowned.

"That she can," Richard tousled Robert's hair and put an arm around David. David stiffened.

"Can we go out today?" Caroline asked, her eyes bright. "I wore one of my oldest dresses. Mrs. Stanhope says a lady must be careful of her clothes."

Lucy looked down at her own wrinkled dress and laughed. "I wish she had given me that advice before I went out today." She smiled at Richard mischievously. "I had no idea that sailing was so hard on clothes."

He returned the look, sending her senses reeling. Only her determination to hear what Caroline was saying kept her from melting on the spot. "It is the salt," Caroline explained seriously. "Mrs. Stanhope says that salt is not good for clothes."

"I am certain she is correct," Lucy told her. "But I do not think I am ready to go out again today. Why not come for a ride with me in the pony cart?" Richard had insisted that she not try to walk the hills around the house. Even though she had protested when he first introduced the idea of the cart, she now enjoyed the freedom it gave her. And after her experiences in the boat, she was not certain she could have walked up the hill even with Richard's help.

"You boys can come to the stables with me," Richard told them, putting a hand on each of their shoulders. "I am so old I will need your help." Robert laughed. Even David let a smile creep onto his lips as he watched his father stoop over and take one or two wobbly steps.

"I will be there first," Robert shouted, taking off as fast as his legs would go.

David followed him, his longer legs quickly closing the gap between them. Richard simply watched them go and then turned back to Lucy and Caroline. "Enjoy your ride," he said as he followed his sons. Deliberately, Lucy let Richard and the boys disappear around the side of the house before she set her pony into motion again. "Those boys think they are so smart," Caroline said, raising her chin in the air. "All they care about is running races, being first."

"They are not competing with us, just with themselves," Lucy reminded her. "But if you want I can drive you to the stables. You can join them there. Maybe they will race with you too."

"All they will want to talk about is who won. And I know one of them will always win. My legs are too short. They will always beat me," the little girl said with a sigh. Then her face brightened. "Of course, you did not ask them to ride with you," she said proudly. "Do you think Da will let me have a pony cart too?" she asked.

"Perhaps you should ask your father," Lucy said quickly, recognizing the gleam in Caroline's eye. She did not intend to be played the way she and her brother had manipulated their unsuspecting mother.

Following that afternoon, the family sailed whenever the day was clear with a light wind. Neither Lucy nor Caroline liked sailing when the wind was stronger, although Richard often took the boys out with him on those days. They would come home windburned, their hair tousled, and filled with excitement. On those days David seemed an ordinary young boy, filled with the excitement of living.

Even with David's sullen silences, Lucy enjoyed her new life. Every day presented a new adventure. At first it was strange having another person always at hand, the first thing in the morning and the last thing at night. But Lucy would not have wanted anything different. Richard's touch reminded her that she was alive, that someone thought she was attractive. After eight years of thinking herself worthless as a woman because she could not bear children, she was delighted in her new roles of wife and mother.

Richard too was happier than he had been in a long time. Sending Edward the letter that had led to Lucy's acceptance of his offer had been the perfect solution to his problems. Despite David's refusal to accept Lucy as his stepmother, she was exactly what his children needed. She was just what he needed. The young girl who had been such a good companion was just as successful as his wife.

His contentment with his marriage lasted almost a month. Then one morning shortly after the post arrived Lucy was called to his study. Fully expecting to be pulled into his arms and kissed breathless, she opened the door, a wide smile on her face, her soft blue muslin gown obviously chosen to capture his attention. She took one look at him and stopped in her tracks. "What is wrong?" she asked anxiously. "Is it one of the children? My father?"

Richard laughed harshly. "You might say that." He glanced down at a newspaper that lay crumbled on his desk. "Did you know what he was going to do?"

"Who? What are you talking about?" She circled his desk, her hands raised as if to clasp her arms around his neck. He backed away, his face as angry as storm clouds. "Richard?" Her face revealed the hurt and confusion she felt.

"You have been so agreeable I should have suspected something. Did you think I would not notice?" he asked, his teeth clenched. The moment he had seen the article in the paper thoughts of the way Lucy must have tricked him had popped into his head. She was as untrustworthy as his first wife.

"What are you talking about?" Lucy asked. Her eyes were shadowed by an unknown fear, and her voice trembled.

"Nervous are you? Did you think I would not care? I believe I made my views perfectly clear. You agreed and then did exactly what you wanted." He picked up the London paper and waved it in her face.

She took it from him and sat down, smoothing the

creases from its pages. When she had read it, she looked up. "This is what you are angry about? The announcement of our marriage?" she asked, more bewildered than ever.

"What kind of reaction did you expect? I told you that I did not want any kind of announcement." He sat down behind the desk and leaned forward, glaring at her.

His tone of voice was more than she could bear. She stood up, straightening her spine until she had reached her full height. Then she leaned on the desk, staring down at him. Even in the state he was in, Richard admired the way the deep neckline of her dress framed her breasts. Her eyes blazing, Lucy asked, "And did you expect to keep our marriage a secret forever? I know that I am not the wife you would have selected had you been in London, but you chose to marry me." She stopped for a moment, her face thoughtful. Then she grew angry. "I suppose you are afraid your ladybird will read about our marriage and fly your coop. Or do you think you are too good for me?"

Startled by the line of her questions, Richard moved back. "No. Of course I do not." He cleared his throat as though he could clear the air as easily, wondering how she had twisted the situation to her own ends. "And I do not have a ladybird. Stop trying to change the subject."

"Change the subject? I cannot even find out what the real subject is," she said angrily, hitting the desk with the newspaper and her palms.

He stood up and leaned forward too, his gray eyes staring into her blue ones. "The subject is this announcement that appeared several days ago. Did you approve it before it was sent in or is it as much a surprise to you as it was to me?" His tone of voice cut through her with its sarcasm. Inside he was a mass of fear. What if the situation he had run from started again?

As though the wind had abruptly stilled, Lucy felt her anger rushing from her, leaving her limp. Hurriedly, she sat down. "This really is about the announcement," she said in amazement. As though she could hardly believe her own words, she said it again, "This is about the announcement."

"Of course, it is about this, this betrayal," Richard said angrily, not at all swayed by her sudden loss of anger. "I thought better of you, madam, than this. After all, you did promise to obey me."

"Richard, I had nothing to do with this information appearing at this time."

"Time? What does that have to do with anything? Did I mention a time limit when I asked you not to make any announcement?" he asked. His eyes blazed with such cold fire that Lucy felt a shiver run up her back.

She closed her eyes and took a deep breath, trying to gain control of her swiftly changing emotions. Nothing is ever accomplished by anger, she repeated silently to herself. The familiar saying she had learned from her own governess steadied her. She looked up, her face calm. "The only announcement I remember discussing in our letters was the announcement of our engagement. I can go get your letters, and we can check them to see if I missed any details," she said quietly, her voice as soothing as when she wanted to calm her father or one of the children.

At first Richard opened his mouth to contradict her memories. Then what she had said hit him. "You saved all my letters?" he asked, his face softening. He sat on the edge of the desk closest to her and started to take her hand. Then as if remembering his grievance, he straightened his spine and hardened his heart. "I do not need to consult them to remember what I wrote," he said as though he were the emperor and she a worthless peasant.

Lucy just stared at him for a moment. Then her own eyes began to blaze. "And I do not believe that I need to continue this conversation." Before Richard had a chance to stop her, she stood up and walked to the door, only the faintest limp revealing the tension she was under. "When you decide to reenter the world of reason, please let me know. Until then I have work to do."

The heavy door closed behind her, the quiet click of

the latch more startling than the slamming of the door Richard had expected. He sat there for a moment just staring at the place where she had been. Then he glanced down at the newspaper on his desk. For a moment the panic he had felt when he had seen the announcement with its statement of his address threatened to overcome him. He closed his eyes, taking deep breaths, reminding himself that for over a year he had been free of those life-threatening unexplained accidents. Just because a newspaper listed his home was no reason to believe that they would begin again.

Chapter Six

Although Lucy tried to appear as though nothing had happened, dinner that day was a strained affair. When David appeared dusty and disheveled, his face alive with excitement, Richard glared at him and then ordered him from the table. "No son of mine will appear for a family dinner, looking as you do," he told him angrily. The boy got up, his excitement gone and a white line around his mouth, and left the room. The other two children simply stared at their father, their eyes wide. Lucy kept her eyes on her plate, wishing she could do or say something to soothe either Richard or David but afraid to try.

As soon as David left the room, Richard wanted to call him back, to tell him he was sorry. But he sat there, his face a mask behind which his emotions swirled.

Instead of demanding that they go sailing or exploring the countryside, Caroline and Robert quickly found something else to do that afternoon. Lucy too escaped, calling for her pony cart and going for a drive alone. She had not gotten far from the house when she saw David sitting on a rock beside the track she was following. She stopped. He looked up and then looked away as though he did not want her to see that he had been crying.

"David, would you like to go for a ride with me?" she asked, thinking that he had never seemed so much like the little boy he truly was. Startled, he looked at her, his eyes so like his father's that she felt her heart in her throat. "Please."

At first he wanted to tell her no. Then he glanced back

toward the house. His father was standing outside on the steps looking down the hill where they were. "Yes," he said defiantly, tossing his head. His curls were tousled from the light breeze that was blowing.

For a time Lucy and David said nothing as they drove slowly across the hills. When they had reached a spot where they could look across the Channel, Lucy stopped. They stared out into the distance. Then she asked, "What have you been doing today?"

"Nothing." The boy stared at her defiantly, daring her to ask him more questions. She simply smiled and then returned her gaze to the waves. The silence between them grew. Lucy was determined that if the silence was to be broken, David would break it. David twisted uncomfortably. "There are new puppies in the stables," he said finally.

"How exciting. How many are there?" Lucy asked, turning so that she could face him. She wanted to brush the curls from his face but knew he would not let her.

"Six. Brian, one of the stable boys, sent word to me. I got to see four of them being born," he said, trying to appear less excited than he was. "Da said I could have one for my own." The inadvertent mention of his father chased his joy from his face. "That was before you came," he said bitterly.

"I am certain he will not change his mind," Lucy said, hoping she was right.

"Why not? Everything else has changed. We never see Da in the mornings now," David said, climbing from the cart and going to the edge of the cliff.

Lucy wanted to get out, to follow him, to put her arms around him and assure him that everything would be fine. Looking at the uneven ground and his angry stance, she decided to remain where she was. Wisely, she held her tongue. Finally, he turned around and walked back to the cart, his shoulders slumped. "Are we going home now?" he asked, his voice ragged with his suppressed emotions.

"We can," she assured him. "Is that what you want?"

"I do not care," he said with a shrug.

"Would you show me the puppies when we get back?"

"You like puppies?" He looked at her as though he had never seen her before.

"My brother has always had hunting dogs. I have missed them here," she said with a smile. "What kind of puppies are they?"

The details about the puppies and their mother filled the ride back to the house. When they pulled up at the stables, David hopped out eagerly. "Let me go find them," he called, running into the building. Lucy handed her pony and cart over to a groom and allowed him to help her down. She stood for a moment to be sure she was steady on her feet and then followed more slowly.

The contrast between the bright afternoon sun and the dimness of the building blinded her for a moment. In her confusion, she walked into someone. Apologizing, she looked up. Richard stood before her, David at his side. "I brought Caroline and Robert to see the puppies," he said quietly, his hands on her shoulders. She longed for him to pull her closer, to tell her he regretted their argument that morning. He stepped back, letting his hands fall. "David says you want to see them too." She nodded, hoping her disappointment was not apparent. "They are this way. We will have to be quiet, or their mother will be angry." David and Lucy exchanged knowing glances. They had agreed with that plan while they were returning to the house.

After the successful visit to the puppies, everyone returned to the house. Realizing that no one had eaten much for dinner, Lucy called for tea. Grateful for a return to what they considered normal behavior, the children chattered about the puppies until it arrived. Then they hungrily devoured the bread and butter, finely cut sandwiches, and cakes. Lucy noticed that Richard ate almost as much as his children. By the time the tea tray was empty, the children, at least, seemed to have forgotten the anger of earlier.

For Lucy and Richard, however, the morning was not

so easily forgotten. But only someone who knew them well could have read the tension between them. When the children returned to their rooms, Lucy too made her escape, giving orders that her supper be brought to her room. Richard dined in solitary splendor, feeling more isolated than he had ever felt before.

When he entered her room later that evening and slipped into bed with her, Lucy froze. He did not try to talk to her or to touch her but only lay there, his eyes fixed on the canopy above the bed. He wanted to explain but did not want to burden her with his fears. The silence between them grew.

At first, Lucy was so tense she could not relax. She wanted to discuss what had happened earlier that day, to find some explanation. But she had no intention of being the first to reopen the subject. She lay there rigidly. Then, listening to his regular breathing, she realized that Richard was asleep. She raised up on one elbow and stared at him, wanting to throw something at him, to push him out of bed. Instead, she lay back down and closed her eyes. Before long she too was asleep.

Sometime in the night she awoke to find herself in Richard's arms. As usual, his touch set her on fire. She pulled him closer. Without a word, he began to make love to her, frantically, hungrily, as though he were afraid of losing her. Wordlessly, she responded.

In the days that followed they fell into a pattern. During the time they spent with the children, Lucy and Richard tried to pretend that nothing had happened. When they were alone together, something they tried to avoid, they behaved with civility but with no warmth. Only at night did the passion they tried so hard to deny erupt, searing them with its flames, leaving them feeling empty when it had passed.

In spite of the animosity it created between Lucy and Richard, the announcement had a positive result. A short time after it appeared, Richard began receiving letters from friends anxious to renew their acquaintance. But the messages he had been afraid he would receive did not come. Nothing out of the ordinary happened. Gradually, he relaxed.

As he was going over his books one morning, Lucy sought him out. "Richard, did you receive a letter from Edward this morning?" she asked, looking at the letter in her own hand. "Arabella says that he was writing you."

Never sure of what the post might bring, Richard usually avoided his mail, waiting until he had finished other tasks before opening it. "It may be here somewhere. Why?"

"She writes that Father wishes to give an engagement party in London for the two of them and wonders if we can come. She must have the place wrong. Father has not been to London in years; he says he cannot travel that far." She sank down in a chair before the desk and glanced at the desk. Ledgers covered every inch of its surface.

Richard closed the book in which he had been checking figures, gathered the other ledgers, and stacked them on the floor beside him. "This is your father who refused to travel so that we could marry here?" he asked, his voice bitter. Lucy began to stiffen. Realizing his mistake, he quickly turned her attention to something else. "The post should be here somewhere. Dawes put it down not long ago."

Lucy glanced at the desk but did not see anything that looked like letters. "Did he put it on the desk? Could it be in one of the ledgers?" she asked. The only paper on the desk seemed to be a sheet on which Richard had been working.

"No." He frowned, trying to remember what he had said when his butler brought the post in. "I told him to leave it. Look around. It must be here somewhere." He picked up the ledger he had been working on and opened it again.

Realizing the futility of gaining his attention, Lucy got up and began searching the room. Before long she found the silver salver and the morning post on the mantel. "Here it is," she said, bringing his letters over to him.

"You open them," Richard said, more interested in balancing his books than in someone who had either deliberately or not been a party to giving away his current residence had to say.

"I cannot. They are yours. Oh, here is one from Edward," she said, picking it up from the stack.

"I thought you said you could not open it," he said teasingly, putting down his pen and stretching.

"It is his handwriting. I would recognize it instantly," she said impatiently. "Open it."

He took the letter from her and leaned back. He looked at it and then shrugged his shoulders. "It can wait."

"Richard!" his wife almost shouted.

"Oh, you want to know what he says?" her husband teased, enjoying Lucy's reaction. Since the day when he had discovered the announcement in the paper, the only emotions they had shared had been an icy disdain and the passion late at night. He deliberately kept her waiting to see what she would do.

She leaned forward as though to snatch the letter from him, giving him an excellent view of her breasts. He smiled and moved back. "I thought you would not open my mail," he laughed.

"Please, Richard. See what he says," she begged.

"And what kind of forfeit will you pay if I do?"

She eyed him warily, unsure of his reactions. Since the confrontation over the announcement, she no longer knew how he would react, and her old doubts about her attractiveness had surfaced. "What?" she asked, settling back in her chair.

He thought for a moment. Then he smiled. "Come here, and I will explain," he coaxed, waving the letter in front of her.

Slowly, she got up and walked behind the desk. As soon as she was close enough, Richard grabbed her and pulled her onto his lap. Lucy stiffened; then she went limp, one arm going behind his neck. "And is this my forfeit?" she whispered.

"No." He settled her more comfortably on his lap. "I need a kiss."

"A kiss?" She pulled back away from him so that she could look him in the face. After the coolness between them, she was not certain if he was teasing or serious.

"You know. You put your open lips on mine," he said with a smile, putting his arms around her and pulling her closer. He took a deep breath, enjoying the clean scent that was so much a part of her.

"I fear I do not know you well enough for that," she protested. Her words, though teasing, held a ring of truth in them.

"Then why did you allow me to . . ." he nuzzled her neck and whispered in her ear. She blushed and tried to pull away, but he would not let her go. He tightened his arms around her. "Just one kiss," he whispered enticingly. Slowly, as though she was not sure of what she was doing, she bent her head and put her lips on his.

After they had finished rearranging their clothes sometime later, Richard picked the letter up from the floor where he had dropped it. Breaking the seal, he spread it open. "Arabella was right. Your father has insisted that the engagement party be held in London. He is opening your townhouse. Edward asks that we come to town immediately to help. He is afraid your father will exhaust himself." With effort he kept the anger he felt toward her father from his voice. How dare the man refuse to travel to see his daughter married and then go up to town simply for a party. Then another thought struck him. He looked at his wife. She had refused to return to London for eight years.

Lucy surprised him. "When Father makes up his mind, no one can stop him. Can you spare me?"

"Spare you?" he asked, confused.

"You will not want to go with me, will you?" she asked, remembering his adamantine refusal to leave his home long enough to marry her.

Richard got up and crossed to the window, looking out but not seeing the Devonshire countryside. "I do not want you to go alone," he said. She held her breath, hoping that he would not refuse her permission to go. Then he surprised her. "We will all go."

"All?" she asked, not really understanding what he meant. She glanced around as if something in the room could give her a clue to what he meant.

"The children will enjoy the sights." He turned around to look at her. "Will your father have enough room for us? My townhouse has been closed for over a year, and I let the servants go. But if you prefer to stay there, I will notify my man of business and arrange for him to hire new ones and open it up."

"The children too?" she asked, still amazed by his easy agreement.

"They deserve a holiday." She raised her eyebrows. "Oh, we will take Mrs. Stanhope, Mr. Avery, and the nurserymaid," he assured her. "But there will be times when we can get away for a family outing."

"Why now?" she demanded, remembering how only a few short months earlier he had refused to consider leaving Devonshire.

He had the grace to look uncomfortable. He turned around and looked out the window again, his back stiff and straight. The guilt he still felt over denying her the wedding she wanted tore at him. "Things have changed," he said quietly, hoping she would not question him further.

"What things?" she demanded, determined to get an answer from him.

He turned around and glared at her. She took a step back. He gained control of himself once more. "Nothing that concerns you," he said quietly, hoping that he was right. He saw her flinch as though taking a hit and cursed silently. Knowing that he had destroyed the playful mood that had done so much to soothe her ruffled feelings, he walked toward her, mentioning the sights they could take the children to see. Everything that he said simply made her more angry.

As she had done so often since his unreasonable behavior had begun, she held her tongue. Although the idea of returning to London frightened her, she knew she had no choice. She would do anything to help her brother find the happiness he deserved.

Finally, he grew quiet. She stared at him, wishing as she had done so often in the last few weeks that she understood him better. Growing restless as the silence between them stretched uncomfortably for some time, she suggested, "Write to Edward. Tell him we will stay with Father and him. If we decide that there is not enough room, we can make other arrangements in London. When do you want us to be ready to leave?" Her voice was calm and low, revealing none of her hurt or confusion. Why would he go to London for her brother but not travel to her home for their wedding? The old feeling of worthlessness began to overtake her.

Richard closed his eyes for a moment, thankful that she seemed to be accepting the situation without creating a scene. He took a deep breath. "Edward says Arabella is already in town."

"She went for the Season," Lucy said quietly.

Richard continued, "Your father plans to arrive at the end of next week. Do you want to arrive at the same time or before them?"

"Before if we can." She looked up, her face serious, determined not to let him see how his decision had devastated her. "You do not have to accompany me if you feel uncomfortable, Richard," she told him quietly. "I will understand." After the strain of the last weeks, she would appreciate some time away from him, she admitted to herself. But at the same time the thought of being separated from him made her feel suddenly empty. Not for anything would she have admitted that she longed to have him support her during her return to London.

"How long do you think we should stay?" he asked, ignoring her last comment.

"Not long. When did Edward say the party will be held?" Richard looked at the letter again and then shrugged his shoulders. He handed it to her. Lucy read through it quickly and looked up annoyed. "Men. I suppose he has not put the party on the calendar. Can you spare a groom?" she asked, her brow creased.

"A groom? Whatever for?"

"Someone has to take a message to my father. We must settle on a date immediately before everyone starts leaving London. And he needs to have fresh fruit, vegetables, and other produce sent to town. Why buy wilted or stale things when the home farm can provide what we need?" She paused a moment. "Perhaps the servants should go ahead to open the place. A man on horseback will get my suggestions to him much faster than the post." She glanced at Edward's letter again. Then she put it on the desk. "I suppose he thinks a party arranges itself, or did he think Arabella would arrange it? Men!" Not waiting for his answer and still muttering under her breath, Lucy hurried from the room.

Richard watched her go, hoping his decision to accompany her to London had been the right one. Surely if incidents like those that had been happening before the fire were going to start again, they would have already begun. Uneasy, he followed Lucy out of the room and headed to the schoolroom to assure himself of his children's safety.

As they prepared for their trip to the city, Richard and Lucy had to work very hard to keep the children's enthusiasm in check. Both Robert and David had made lists of the attractions they wished to see. Caroline simply listened wide-eyed to the glories they promised her. Even if they had months in London, Richard and Lucy knew they would never have time to take the children everywhere they had thought of.

"A trip to Astley's," Richard promised the afternoon before they left, "and maybe to see the menagerie. You must leave something for later trips."

Although the children frowned, they hesitated, perhaps realizing that if they protested too much they might lose all privileges. Their governess and their tutor con-

stantly reminded them that they were lucky children.
Many parents might have left them in the country.

To Lucy's amazement, they left almost at the hour
they had planned. The sun was just creeping over the
hills as their entourage pulled away from the door. Betty
and Richard's valet had left two hours earlier with much
of their luggage. The boys, Caroline's governess, and
their tutor were in a second coach only a few minutes
ahead of them. To his coachman's disgust, Richard had
chosen to follow the children, ignoring the dust that
would inevitably be thrown up. Remembering the threats
he had received before the fire, he was determined to
protect his offspring. If they were in front of him, he
could keep a more careful eye on their safety.

Caroline, Richard and Lucy's companion for the early
part of the trip, was so excited she bounced up and down
on the seat until it was time to go. Lucy too felt her heart
pounding so hard she could hardly catch her breath. She
smiled at her stepdaughter and her husband, hiding the
fear that threatened to overtake her, a fear that she had
not felt on her last trip to the city. Remembering the
cruel smiles and wicked comments of the *ton* whenever
someone did not meet society's expectations, she wondered why she had agreed to return. She felt a shiver go
up her spine.

Although Richard had planned the trip carefully,
building in more stops than he would have made on his
own, the trip was still hard for Lucy. His carriage though
well built had not been designed especially for someone
for whom each bump was a discomfort. At each stop she
would painfully climb down and walk haltingly around
the innyard. During the first day, Richard practically had
to force her into the inn and to a room to rest because
she was afraid she was slowing their progress.

As he watched a white line form around her mouth as
she kept Caroline occupied, Richard made up his mind.
No matter what they had told the children, Lucy did not
need their companionship. When he told them of his decision at the next stop, everyone was displeased.

"It is my turn, Da. You promised," Robert argued, his shoulders square. After playing and fighting with his brother for several hours, he was ready for a change of scenery. Also, having the tutor and governess in his carriage had seriously hampered his activities.

"Let him ride with us," Lucy pleaded. Richard ignored both of them. Wondering if he had decided that she was not a fit mother for his children, Lucy wanted to cry. She looked at him, wanting to protest. Then realizing from the set lines of his face he would not change his mind, Lucy climbed back into the coach, her spirit hurting as badly as her back and legs. She had hoped to keep her fears away by playing games with Robert just as she had done with Caroline. As the door closed behind Richard, he took his seat beside her, putting his arm around her to cushion her from the jolts as they continued on their way. His arm, however, was not enough to banish her doubts.

The closer they came to London, the more Lucy's doubts about her ability to function in society grew. Besides providing her a chance to escape her family, marriage to Richard had promised a permanent home in the country. "How did I get myself into this?" Lucy whispered as their coach rumbled into London.

"What?" Richard, who had been dozing, sat up straight. "We are here," he said, smiling widely. He stretched. Then he looked at his wife, noting her pallor. "You are to go immediately to your room.. Have Betty put you to bed," he said firmly. He gave her a quick hug. "This trip has been harder on you than I thought it would be. We will travel fewer miles each day on the way home."

"No." Lucy took a deep breath and then tried to soften her tone. "If we were to spend more nights on the road, I would be more exhausted. The faster we can travel, the better."

"We shall see," he said quietly. He watched as she put on her bonnet and reached up to tuck a lock of hair behind her ear. He stroked her cheek. She kept her eyes on her hands, wondering how she had ever thought herself ready for this ordeal. "Try not to exhaust yourself," he added, worrying about her strength. The short time they had been married had taught him that she refused to pamper herself even when she was hurting.

His words sent prickles of fear through her. Did Richard have as many doubts about her return to London as she did, she wondered. Resolutely, she put those thoughts away from her. Reminding herself that ensuring her brother's happiness must be her first consideration, Lucy smiled and nodded. "Father will so love the children," she said brightly. Then her mask slipped a little. "He never thought I would give him any grandchildren." Remembering the pain of knowing she would never be a mother, Lucy could not maintain her smile. A tear slid down her cheek.

"Well, I hope he is prepared for mi—ours." Richard's slip of the tongue was like a dagger being plunged into Lucy's heart. "After days cooped up in a coach arguing among themselves, they need new vistas to explore," Richard said in the brightest voice he could summon. He tried to wipe away her tears with his handkerchief, but Lucy turned her head away. He sat back, his face bleak. He had hoped that the enforced isolation of the journey might give them a chance to recapture the easy friendship they had shared during the first weeks of their marriage. Instead, they seemed further apart.

When they finally pulled up to her father's townhouse in Grosvenor Square, Lucy was smiling sweetly. She allowed her husband to hand her from the coach and then smiled in surprise. She hurried to her father's side as though nothing had disturbed her. Richard, his lips set in a hard line, noticed that her limp was more pronounced.

Richard forced himself to be polite, greeting Lucy's father with a smile that never reached his eyes. It was Edward who brought out his warmest greeting. "Soon you will follow me to the altar," Richard said, pounding his friend on the back.

Edward stepped back. "Not soon enough for me," he

said with a smile. He inspected the gentleman before him. Although it had been less than two years since he had seen Richard, Richard seemed to have aged five.

"Growing impatient, Edward?" Lucy asked with a smile as she crossed the room to give him a hug. As he had inspected Richard, so he now looked his sister over carefully, not completely happy about what he saw.

"How was your trip?" her father asked as he moved closer to her so that he could take her hand.

"Long," she said quietly. Then she quickly changed the subject. "I did not expect to see you so soon." She smiled brightly at her father, determined that neither he nor her brother would see her fears.

"Father decided he must be here to greet you. And here we are," her brother said with a smile. "Where are those children you have been writing us about?"

"They should be along shortly. They left a short time later than we did from the last stop," Lucy said, casting a glance at her husband.

"A slight mishap with a stream and two boys slowed them down," Richard told them. He and Edward exchanged a smile as they remembered some of the scrapes they had gotten into. Fortunately when the mishap occurred, they had been close enough to London that he did not have to worry about the possibility of danger.

"Let us wait in the salon," Mr. Meredith suggested. He frowned at his son and his son-in-law as if he expected them to protest. Neither did, although Richard wanted to demand that Lucy go up to her room immediately. The way she beamed at her father, following his bath chair into the large room where a fire roared even though it was warm outside, told Richard that she would not go without a protest.

By the time they had found seats and a tea tray had arrived, they heard the obvious sounds of new arrivals, the children in the hall. "I do not want to go upstairs now. I need to see my father," David's voice said angrily.

Richard hurried to the door. As he opened it and stepped into the hall, he saw his son in the grasp of a tall footman, his tutor following along behind. "Let the children come in here to meet their uncle and grandfather," he said clearly, forcing himself to maintain at least a semblence of calm. When he got close enough to be heard without shouting, he said through clenched teeth, "You let my son go." The footman released his hand and stepped back, his heart beating faster.

When the man had melted away, Richard turned to the tutor. "What is going on here?" His eyes bored into the young man.

"Nothing. Just a misunderstanding," Mr. Avery said with a stammer he thought he had lost forever. The knowledge that he might lose his job over the incident was evident from his face.

"Da," David said, standing up with his back stiff. "I do not want to stay here." The long journey had erased any kindness he had felt for Lucy and had left him time to brood over the past.

"And where do you plan to stay?" his father asked, wondering what idea had crept into his oldest son's head this time.

"With Mama's parents, my real grandparents," the little boy said. His chin jutted out stubbornly as if daring his father to cross him.

Both Richard and Caroline had been interested observers to the scene. Now Caroline began to jump up and down and pull at her father's leg. He kept his eye on his son but bent down to hear what she was waiting to tell him. When he stood up again, his face was rueful. "Mrs. Stanhope will take care of the problem," he said. Quietly, he explained his daughter's urgent needs. When the governess and a maid led his daughter away, he turned back to his sons. "You do know that they are in Yorkshire. Your grandfather has been very ill." The boy shook his head.

Robert asked, "Then they won't be able to take us anywhere, will they? David said they would take us to see the Puffing Billy," he said in a rush of words. "You said you would be too busy to take us everywhere."

"Ah, so that is what this is about?" Richard said, pleased to discover such an ordinary reason for their behavior.

"Even if Grandpapa is ill, I want to visit him, not stay here," David said, glaring at his brother.

His father fixed him with cold, gray eyes. "Where I stay you stay," he said in a quiet but firm voice. He looked up and realized that the tutor was still nearby. He smiled at the man, realizing what must have happened. "And I am certain you would be happy to have some time to yourself, Mr. Avery. Perhaps the large young man could show you to your quarters and then bring you some tea. The boys can stay with me for a time." Instantly, the servants who had been hovering in the background whisked the tutor away. "When my daughter returns, send her to the salon," he called after them.

Lucy, who had grown worried when Richard did not return with the children and had followed him into the hall, did not say anything. When he realized she must have heard everything, her white face and hurt eyes made Richard's lips thin into a white line. Even David hung his head. Lucy squared her shoulders and put a smile on her face, wondering what had ever made her think she would be a success as a wife and mother. She should not have married.

"I expect you to be on your best behavior," Richard told the boys as he opened the door for Lucy to reenter the salon. Silently, they nodded. Still frowning, he walked back into the salon. The look in Lucy's eyes hurt him. He watched her put on a happy smile for her family and wished he could take her in his arms, tell her to disregard David's words.

After the initial outburst in the hall, David and the others were subdued. Finished with their tea and intrigued by the bath chair, they left the safe confines of their father and Lucy to approach Mr. Meredith, who had been trying to gain their attention for some time. Caroline asked the question they had all been wondering about. "Why does your chair have wheels?"

Richard sat up straight. "Caroline, you are not to ask personal questions," he said with a frown.

"Nonsense, my boy. How is she ever to learn if she does not ask," Mr. Meredith said. He smiled at the little girl and then glanced over to where his daughter sat beside the man who had married her. He frowned when Lucy moved a little further away from her husband.

"Why does it have wheels?" Caroline whispered, leaning close to him and patting his chair. She looked at her father to see if he was going to reprimand her again. Richard merely shook his head.

"I cannot walk."

"Not ever?" Robert wanted to know, his eyes wide. He took his place beside his sister.

"Not much. My chair allows me to get around. Of course, I need some strong young men to help push it," Mr. Meredith said, smiling at them. He looked at David and winked. The boy took a step toward him, intrigued, and then remembered his anger. He sat back down. His mouth was set much like his father's had been only a short time earlier.

"Can we push you?" Robert asked. Caroline nodded.

"I think it will take all three of you," Lucy's father said. "David, would you like to help?"

"Come on, David," Robert begged.

"Please come help," his sister said, running to his side and pulling on his coat. David twisted away from her, but he stood up. Reluctantly, as though he were being pulled by some invisible string, he moved toward the back of the chair.

"Be careful," Richard begged, having visions of his children tossing Lucy's father out of the chair and onto the floor.

More relaxed than she had been all day, Lucy said, "I think the hallway might be a better place for this experiment. Edward, if you will?" She stood back, waiting for her brother to push her father into the hall.

A few minutes later they watched as the three children pushed Mr. Meredith from one end of the hall to another, carefully at first and then more vigorously. "They are truly enjoying themselves," Edward said. "This may keep both Father and them busy for hours."

"Unless they toss him on the floor," Richard said, watching his three children with worried eyes.

"I doubt that will happen. Arabella's cousins, the oldest ones, have been trying to do that for years. Somehow he manages to hang on," Lucy said, smiling indulgently. Other than her welcome for her father and brother, it was the only true smile Richard had seen on her face that day. "By the way, Edward, I thought you would be dancing attendance on Arabella. Why are you at home? You have not grown bored with her already?" She did not look at her husband, fearing that he might agree that marriage could be boring.

"Never! Some of her aunts and cousins arranged to call this afternoon."

"Smart man to stay away," Richard said, slapping his brother-in-law on the back.

"Coward." His sister made a face at him.

"I am to call for her later this evening to take her to a ball. We have invitations for you," Edward said.

"A ball?" Lucy grew pale once more. She tried to say something else, but no sound would come out.

Casually, as though he had not noticed her reaction, Edward added, "Of course, after your journey you may not want to go out tonight. Arabella says if that is the case she will see you in the morning. I believe she plans to take you shopping. Richard, that outing may be expensive."

"Maybe I should go along to oversee. I have definite ideas about what I like my wife to wear," Richard said with a wicked smile.

His wife blushed. More than once he had complimented something she wore. But he had always added that she looked best in nothing at all. She glanced up from under her long eyelashes and then let them fall quickly. The remembrance of passion that she saw in his face made her feel warm all over, pushing her doubts aside.

"Well, are you going to the ball with me tonight?" her brother asked, looking from one to the other. Though he had not been pleased with the way they had treated each other earlier, their recent exchange of glances had eased his mind.

"No." The word issued from both their lips. They looked at each other and then away quickly.

"The trip was difficult for Lucy," Richard said, wanting nothing more than to see her safely in bed, a bed he planned to share.

"And I have nothing to wear," Lucy added, her insecurity forcing her to wonder if her husband was thinking of her comfort or if he was embarrassed to have his choice of a wife made public. Probably the latter, she thought bitterly. Like David, he was probably regretting that he could not get away, away from someone who had betrayed him.

Richard watched the emotions race across her face and sighed.

Chapter Seven

Despite a night in an unfamiliar bed, Lucy was ready when Arabella arrived the next morning. Dressed in a pomona green muslin that Arabella had insisted she purchase before her marriage, she stared at herself in the mirror, hoping her dress was not too out-of-date. When Arabella entered a few moments later, Lucy felt her hope disappear.

"A country cousin as well as a freak," she muttered to herself.

"What?" her friend asked, giving her a kiss on the cheek.

"Nothing important." Lucy returned the kiss. "I can tell that having the world know you are engaged must be very pleasant." She stepped back and inspected her friend. "All of this finery to entice Edward?" she asked, raising one eyebrow.

"Nonsense. I dress to please myself," Arabella said haughtily and then spoiled everything by breaking into a giggle. Lucy laughed with her. When they were calm once more, Arabella made a face. "I suppose I do dress with him in mind," she admitted. "Of course, Mama makes certain demands too. What about Richard?"

Lucy's face grew still. "What about him?"

"Does he make comments about your clothes, tell you what he does or does not like?" Remembering his comments about liking her in as little as possible, Lucy blushed. Arabella laughed. "I can see he does. What is it like to be married? I can hardly wait."

Once again Lucy grew still. Fortunately, just then the

door opened, and Richard walked in. "Richard, do you remember my friend Arabella," Lucy said quickly. "She has come to take me shopping."

Richard greeted her guest and at the same time tried to gauge his wife's temper that morning. Although they had shared the same bed, for the first time since he had introduced her to making love, she had not responded to his caresses, would not let him touch her even to rub the pain from her legs and back. "Buy what you like," he said pleasantly. "Have the bills sent to me here."

Remembering the comfortable allowance he had agreed to give her, Lucy shook her head. "I am well ahead of the world. I will pay for them out of my allowance."

His eyes grew darker, signaling his displeasure. She waited for his outburst but it never came. "Send the bills to me," he said again, this time through clenched teeth. Lucy said nothing.

As though sensing that the situation was more volatile than was comfortable, Arabella clapped her hands and smiled. "How kind of you. I hope Edward is as generous as you. Lucy, do you realize how lucky you are?" Her friend looked at Arabella blankly. "You can buy anything you like."

"Anything within reason," Richard said with a false smile. "While you are out shopping, I am going to take the children to the menagerie if it has not closed since I have been away. Have you been?" he asked Arabella.

"Once. I felt sorry for those beasts in their small cages," Arabella said. Her eyes darkened as she remembered how they had just lain there, listlessly.

"But I wanted to go with . . ." Lucy began before her voice drifted into silence. Neither Arabella nor Richard was listening to her. Feeling as though she were a shadow on the wall, Lucy wanted to scream, to cry out for attention. When the other two had finished what they were saying, Lucy smiled bravely. "Tell the children that I will see them later. I will have tea with them."

"Oh!" Arabella covered her mouth with her hand, her

eyes wide as if in surprise. "I forgot to tell you that my mother has insisted that you must join us for tea today. I suppose I can tell her you have other plans." Her tone left no doubt in anyone's mind what Arabella thought of that plan.

"You have tea with your friends," Richard said firmly. "When we finish dressing for the play tonight, we will go up together to see the children."

"The play?" Lucy asked.

"Your brother has arranged a family party; Arabella and her parents are to share a box with us this evening. I assured him that you would be delighted to attend," Richard said, leaving out the fact that he had protested such an outing before Lucy had had an opportunity to rest from the trip. Edward had finally convinced him that it was important for the families to be seen together united in support of the marriage. Although no formal betrothal had been announced, people had already begun to speculate about Arabella's second choice. Recognizing Edward's insecurities because they were so much like his own, Richard had agreed. He hoped the decision would not drive another wedge between them.

The moment she heard the plan, Lucy wanted to refuse to go. Then she sighed, plastered a false smile on her face—a smile that fooled no one, and said, "Of course, we will go. I hope I can find something to wear. My clothes are definitely not the latest crack."

"Come with me to my dressmaker. She will have something. Or maybe she can make you something," Arabella said. She checked her bonnet in the mirror to make sure the bow she had tied earlier was still crisp and jaunty.

"In one day?" Lucy said. "Arabella, I may have lived most of my life in the country, but even I know it takes time to make a garment."

Richard saw them into the carriage. "Buy whatever takes your fancy," he told his wife. He watched as they drove away. Then his shoulders slumped. He turned and walked into the house, feeling as though he had just been deserted.

Hours later as they moved through the crush in the corridors of the theater during the interval, that feeling of desolation still remained. If he had been able to do so, he would have picked up his wife and taken her home where they could be alone together. Instead he greeted one acquaintance after another, smiling pleasantly and inquiring about their families.

Lucy too stopped often to exchange greetings with former acquaintances. As Arabella had promised, she had found a dress that gave her the courage to smile and to talk naturally. When the modiste had shown her this gown in a rich peach with blond lace, it had lacked only the hem and a few alterations to fit her perfectly. The warm color was a perfect foil for both Arabella's white embroidered muslin and the chocolate brown coat that Richard wore.

She had been finishing dressing a short time before they were to go to the schoolroom to see the children when Richard had entered her room, a long black box in his hand. Silently, he had handed the package to her. She lifted the lid almost as if she were afraid it might contain something terrible. Lying on the white satin inside the case was a pearl and diamond necklace with matching earrings. She stared at them as though she were mesmerized. "If you do not like them, the jeweler has said he will take them back," he said, trying unsuccessfully to read her reactions. "This is the first opportunity I have had to buy you jewelry of your own." In his letters before they were married, Richard had explained that his first wife's jewelry had never been recovered after the fire.

Lucy ran her fingers over the cool stones. Then she looked up, her eyes wide. "For me?" she asked breathlessly. She had received jewelry from her parents during her Season, but nothing like this. He nodded. She quickly removed the pearl necklet she wore. He opened the clasp and put the new creation around her neck. Then he turned her around so that he could see.

"I wanted to find something that would complement your skin," he whispered, drawing her slowly toward him. Her hand wrapped around the pearl and diamond drop that hung from the center of the necklace, and she moved into his arms. The kiss they shared deepened.

He was ready to sweep her off her feet and carry her to the bed when the door opened. "Here is your cloak . . . oh," Betty stammered, turning her back and covering her burning cheeks with her hands. She slipped into the corridor.

"I thought I told you to have a talk with her about coming in without permission," Richard said sharply as he stepped back.

"I did. But you were not here when I sent her to press my cloak. I simply forgot she was coming back," his wife said as she tried to still her beating heart. She sighed with regret.

"Forgot, hmmm." He smiled. "If we do not hurry, we will have to forget our visit to the children."

Now that they were in the thick of the crowd, Richard wished that they had been able to forget the performance. Neither the actors nor the plot was outstanding. And they had been besieged by visitors. He looked up, trying to find Lucy, who had taken Edward's arm. When he found her again, his eyes narrowed. A tall, dark-haired man about the same age as Lucy was staring at her as though he had seen a ghost. Lucy, talking to an older lady, did not appear to notice him.

Fighting his way to Edward's side, Richard leaned over and asked angrily, "Who is that man?" His voice was so low that neither Arabella nor Lucy could hear him.

Edward looked around. Then his face froze. "We are going back to the box," he announced. The tone of his voice was enough to tell his fiancée and his sister not to argue with him.

When they were safely out of the crowds, Richard asked once more, "Who was that man?"

"What man?" Arabella asked. She tried to stop and

look around, but Edward kept walking. "Well!" she said indignantly, brushing past a man who though well dressed seemed out-of-place. No one noticed when the man stopped and stared at them as they walked away.

"Lucy is growing tired," Edward explained. One look at her friend's face told Arabella that what Edward said was true.

"I am a heartless creature to drag you all over town today and then expect you to join me tonight," she said. "Forgive me?"

Only too happy to find the relative comfort of their box, Lucy simply nodded. The men seated the ladies and then retired to the back of the box. "Tell me," Richard demanded, his voice pitched so low that the ladies would not be able to hear.

Not really certain how Richard would respond, Edward said simply, "That was George."

"George?"

"The Earl of Haversham, Lucy's first fiancé. I had no idea he would be here this evening. Heard he had taken his wife home to the country. She's increasing again."

"I shall not permit anyone to stare at her the way he was," Richard declared. The threat in his voice was apparent. He was amazed by his own reactions. Even when Julia, his first wife, had encouraged her cicisbeos to be underfoot constantly, he had only remarked that he was happy she had someone to escort her when he was gone. Now he wanted to hide his wife away from prying eyes.

"Imagine he was as shocked to see her as I was to see him," Edward said quietly. "Next time you see him he will be in control. I am glad that Lucy did not notice him, though."

"He had better be. I do not want anyone upsetting my wife." Richard took a deep breath. The jealousy he felt was new to him. "She is mine," he whispered so softly that even Edward could not hear him. "Mine." He took his seat beside Lucy once more and took her hand in his, his fingers tightening possessively. Startled, she looked at him. He smiled and forced himself to relax.

When the play was over, Edward and Richard escorted the party to the waiting carriages. Neither noticed the man Arabella had brushed against earlier waiting in the corridor outside their box. Following as closely as he dared, the man watched the carriages pull away and followed on foot, an easy task since the street was crowded and narrow and the coaches could not move very quickly.

By the time the coaches turned into a wider, less busy street, he had hired a hackney. When the two carriages turned in different directions, he cursed briefly and then gave orders to follow the last one.

As he watched Edward escort Arabella and her mother into their house, he cursed again. Discharging the hackney, he started to walk away. Then remembering that the two men had been in the same party, he smiled wickedly. Opening the gate to the park in the center of the square, he took up a spot where he could see the front door. Before long, his watch was rewarded.

Edward stood on the steps, smiling broadly. Since their engagement was soon to be public knowledge, Arabella's parents had begun to give them more privacy to say their good nights. He stretched and then walked off whistling, remembering the kisses he and Arabella had just shared. The watcher followed him, letting him get far enough ahead so that Edward would not be suspicious.

When Edward walked up the stairs to his father's home, the man was just in time to hear Edward ask the footman who opened the door, "Has Mr. Blount already gone to bed?"

The watcher's eyes blazed. Making careful note of the location of the house, he hurried on his way to one of the less fashionable parts of town.

While the watcher sought his own lodgings, Richard and Edward discussed the reappearance of the Earl of Haversham. "Do you want to tell Lucy that he is in town, or should I?" Edward asked. He filled two glasses with the best brandy and handed one to his friend.

"Why should we tell her?" Richard asked. He twirled the brandy around the glass and stared at it intently.

"Dash it all, man! Do you want to give her that kind of shock. No telling what she would do."

"Do? What are you talking about?"

"Think about it, Richard. George allows her to break her engagement. As a result, she refuses to return to town. This is her first visit in over eight years. How do you think she will react?"

"She is my wife. She will react with decorum," Richard said. "Besides that was eight years ago." He wished he were as sure as he sounded.

"She will have a better chance if one of us tells her she may run into him," Edward said practically. He had always been less willing to take a risk than his friend. "The first time I saw him after he left I had a hard time not running him through myself." He emptied his glass and got up to fill it once more. He held up the decanter. "Are you ready for more?" he asked.

Richard shook his head. "Surely he means nothing to her now," he said quietly. Lucy could not respond to him the way she did and still long for Haversham. Despite that thought the muscles in the back of his neck were as tight as bowstrings. Why had he agreed to come to town, he wondered.

"Probably not. I hope not. How could she care for someone who deserted her when she needed him most?" Edward asked indignantly. "Still, I think I should tell her."

"You? Why you?"

"I know the man. Do you? Think about how she will feel if she knows we have been discussing her in this way." Richard cut off what he had started to say and nodded, struck by Edward's argument. "I promise I will talk to her first thing in the morning," Edward said. He yawned widely. "Dash it, all this racketing around town is wearing me out."

"As soon as the engagement party is over, you can return home," Richard reminded him.

"No, that is your plan. But I have promised Arabella's parents that I will accompany them on several family visits. Lord, I never knew someone could have so many relatives. Fortunately, Lucy and I have only a few cousins and an elderly aunt who refuses to receive company."

"You are indeed lucky. I must still deal with Julia's family," Richard said with a grimace. David's demands that he be allowed to stay with his mother's parents had introduced another problem into his life.

"Have they created any difficulty?" Edward asked.

"No. They were as shocked as I about the fire and Julia's death. But they were very understanding when I wrote them about my upcoming marriage. I suppose I must arrange for the children to visit them."

"Why so glum about it? It will give you and Lucy some time to yourselves. If I were as newly married as you, I would enjoy that," Edward reminded him.

Richard smiled at the thought. Then the threats and fears he had so deliberately pushed out of his mind crept back in. "I would rather have my children in my care," he said firmly.

"Lord, deliver me from such responsibility."

"I give you nine months after you are married to change your mind," his friend said. He picked up his glass and made a toast. "To responsibility."

Edward laughed, his eyes sparkling. "To responsibility," he echoed.

The responsibility that he had toasted so blithely the evening before hung heavy about Edward's heart the next morning as he tried to find some time alone with his sister. Although she was up early, Edward was not. By the time he came down, she was closeted with the housekeeper, going over the menus and the decorations for his engagement party. By the time she was finished there, it was time for her to join the children and Richard for their trip to Astley's Amphitheater.

The trip was a respite to both Lucy and Richard. Even though they both had seen the children at separate times, this was the first time they had gone on a family outing in London. Caroline and Robert vied for their attention. And even David smiled occasionally.

Lucy could not keep from smiling either. After the tension of the last few days, she felt she was a member of a family again. She glanced over Caroline's head at Richard and smiled, including him in her happiness. He felt his heart begin to beat faster. Hope stirred within him. By the time they arrived at the performance, everyone was in excellent spirits.

Watching the trained horses and the people who performed on them, the children grew wide-eyed. "Do you think they have forgotten how to speak?" Richard asked quietly, his mouth close to Lucy's ear. She trembled.

"If I remember my first visit here, I too was quiet. Of course, I was trying to figure out how I could do the tricks at home." She had turned her head slightly toward him, and her breath was soft on his cheek.

"They would not dare!" She raised one eyebrow as if mocking him. He sank back in his seat and closed his eyes. "And this was my idea?" he asked weakly. His pose was spoiled by the wicked twinkle in his eyes.

"Richard, you probably did the same thing," his wife said, letting her gaze wander from the children to him, enjoying the sight of him in his dark blue coat and fawn pantaloons.

"Maybe they will have forgotten by the time we return home," he suggested hopefully.

"Did you?" she asked. She leaned forward to keep Caroline from leaning too far over the edge of the box.

The trick they had been watching finished. As they waited for the next group of performances to enter the amphitheater, David turned around. "There is a man who is trying to get your attention," he said. Then his eyes went wide as he caught sight of a woman in tights riding on top of her horse.

"What man?" Richard asked. David, his eyes fixed on the ring, pointed to his left. Richard turned his head; his eyes widened. Before he could prevent it, Lucy too had turned to look. Her face grew as pale as fresh snow on a cold winter's day. "Lucy?" Richard whispered. She did not answer, nor did she tear her eyes away from the man who was seated so close to them. "Lucy!" This time Richard's tone was more insistent.

She closed her eyes, mentally and physically bringing herself back to the present. "I—I," she began. Then she had to break off because her voice was so weak and shaky.

"Do you want to go?" her husband asked, trying to ignore the man who was staring at his wife. He wanted to pummel the man for destroying the happiness of the afternoon.

"Go? Da, there are several more acts," Robert protested. His older brother, realizing that more was happening than they were aware of, tried to make him be quiet, but Robert refused to be silent. Soon Caroline had puckered up her lips and had begun to cry.

Lucy silenced them all. Gaining control of her voice again, she asked "Go before the performance is over? Richard, what are you thinking of?" She smiled at the children, a rather shaky smile but still a smile. They clapped their hands and turned back to the excitement in front of them. Determined that she would not betray the confusion she felt, she too concentrated on the performers. Only Richard was aware of how often she glanced at the man who stared at her.

Her initial shock at the sight of her former fiancé began to disappear, replaced by anger and pride. How dare George make her the object of everyone's gossip by staring at her, by trying to capture her attention! She tried to look around to see who was there without being too obvious about it, but her efforts were unsuccessful. Finally, she stuck her chin in the air and put her hand on Richard's arm. He covered it with his own, pleased that she had reached out to him.

By the time the performance was over, Lucy had herself well in hand. When her former fiancé appeared before her, a small boy with dark hair beside him, she was able to greet him casually and introduce him to her husband and children. "How do you do, Haversham," Richard said politely, wishing him at Jericho.

The few moments of casual conversation were an effort for Lucy. The children, excited by what they had seen, provided the excuse to escape she was looking for. She smiled at the little boy beside her former fiancé. "Are you as anxious to go home and practice those tricks as my three are?" she asked. He nodded but did not get a chance to say anything. "Then we must not keep you," she said firmly. Saying good-bye to the earl and his son, she waited for Richard to take her arm, taking strength from his presence. "Perhaps we shall see you again while we are in town, George," she said politely. She looked at his weak chin; then she looked at Richard. How could I have chosen a man like that, she wondered.

As he escorted his small party to their carriage, Richard too wondered what she had seen in him. The jealousy that had devoured him the evening before boiled within him once more. He glanced at his wife, trying to read her feelings on her face. But she had learned to hide them. The only time when he thought he knew what she was feeling was when he held her in his arms.

While they were waiting at Gunter's for their ices to be served, Caroline pulled on Lucy's sleeve to get her attention. When Lucy turned to look at her, the little girl, her face set in a frown, whispered, "Will we have to talk to that man again?"

"What man?" Lucy asked, her voice as soft as Caroline's.

"The one who was staring at you. If I had done that, Mrs. Stanhope would have said I was being impolite," the little girl said. Recently, she had begun to quote her governess as though she were the supreme arbiter of fashionable life. Usually, the family simply accepted these grains of wisdom with a smile.

Lucy did not feel like smiling now. She took a deep breath and looked at her husband. He seemed to be concentrating on what David and Robert were saying. "Probably not. Why?"

"I do not like him," Caroline said firmly, letting her voice rise.

"Do not like whom?" her father asked, turning to her. He smiled at the picture she made. Her crisp white frock and white bonnet made her look like a fashion plate.

"That man. He should not have stared at Mama. That is not nice." Her little voice was very firm.

Her father wanted to reach out and hug her but restrained himself. "I agree," he said quietly. He smiled at her.

"Who is he?" David wanted to know. Now that they were settled, he was happy in London. As much as his father and his stepmother, he simply did not like change.

"Someone I knew a long time ago," Lucy said quietly, wishing she could introduce some other subject. Fortunately for her composure, their ices arrived, and the children's attention was diverted. The look on Richard's face told her that he could not be swayed as easily as the children.

As soon as they had arrived in Grosvenor Square and the children had been handed over to their attendants, Lucy made an excuse to return to her room. Then she asked Betty to find out where her brother was.

"Mr. Edward is in the study," Betty said. Before she could finish, Lucy swept out of the room. "With Mr. Blount," Betty added, looking at the empty doorway.

Richard too had run his brother-in-law to ground. Discovering that Edward was at home, he had found him with little trouble. The rage that he had been suppressing over the way Haversham had stared hungrily at Lucy spilled over when he saw Edward, his eyes closed, leaning back in a chair. He deliberately let the door slam behind him. Edward opened his eyes sleepily. "How was Astley's?" he asked, covering his yawn with his hand.

"I thought you were going to tell her about Haversham," Richard said angrily. He glared at his brother-in-law, but Edward was not looking at him.

"What?" Edward shook his head as if that would clear his thoughts.

"Haversham. You said you were going to talk to Lucy about him this morning."

"I was. Never could find her. Closeted with the housekeeper at first and then gone. Thought I would do it before dinner." He yawned again.

"Think again. We saw him this afternoon," Richard said through clenched teeth.

His words brought his brother-in-law out of his chair. "The devil you say?" Richard nodded. "How did she react?"

"How do you think she reacted? Just as you said she would."

Neither of the men had heard the door open behind them. "As you said who would?" Lucy asked quietly. Do not lose your temper, she told herself. But her admonition was not working.

Her brother and her husband turned around to face her, their guilt written on their faces. "Ah, eh," Edward stammered, trying to find the words. He glanced at Richard but found no help there.

"Do not try to fob me off with some lie, Edward. I know you better than you think. Who were you talking about?" When he did not answer, she faced her husband, firing her question at him.

"You," he said quietly, wishing he had a better explanation than the truth.

"Me? What about?" She looked from one to the other. Then an idea struck her. She looked at her brother again. "Edward, you knew he was in town," she said incredulously. He did not reply. "And you did not tell me." She glanced at her husband, accurately reading the guilt in his eyes. "And you knew too, Richard," she said angrily. "When were you planning to let me know?" she demanded.

"I tried to tell you this morning," her brother said defensively. "But I never could find you when you were free."

"You knew." She glared at Richard. "We were together all afternoon. You could have told me."

"I thought you knew. Edward had made me promise to let him tell you," Richard said defensively.

"How long have you known? When did you find out?" She turned back to face her brother, her back stiff.

"Last night," Edward said. His tone was apologetic.

"At the theater." Lucy glared at both of them. "And you did not tell me then or when we first reached home? Or were you afraid I would fall to pieces?" she asked. She picked up a figurine that stood on a table next to her. Richard, who was not accustomed to her temper, simply watched her. Edward, who had been witness to more than one of her explosions before her accident, took a step or two backward.

Gaining control of her emotions, Lucy put the figurine down once more. She smiled, but her emotions did not reach her eyes. "Well, I am sorry to disappoint you gentlemen." Her voice made the last word sting. "I did not fall apart. But if you ever do that again . . ." She paused. Then leaving her words hanging in the air, she walked out of the room.

As soon as the door closed behind her, Edward collapsed into a chair. "Whew," he said.

"That's all you can say?" his friend asked.

"All? I have not seen Lucy in such a temper in years," Edward said. "Eight years at least."

"How long will it last?" Richard asked, walking over to the side table where a bottle of wine and glasses had been placed. He poured himself a glass and drank it immediately.

"It depends?"

"On what?"

"How long she remembers why she is angry with us."

This time it was Richard who sat down as though he no longer had strength in his legs.

Chapter Eight

Although Lucy accompanied Richard and Edward to a ball that evening, it was apparent at the beginning of the evening that she had not forgotten. Dressed in a celestial blue silk gown with netting of the same color that had arrived during their absence that afternoon, Lucy was stunning. Once again she wore the pearl and diamond set Richard had given her the previous evening, but there was no warmth in the way she greeted her husband and her brother.

Stopping by the salon where her father sat before a blazing fire, she kissed his cheek. "Are you certain you will not accompany us?" she asked.

"And have to be carried up those stairs to the ballroom. Not likely, Daughter. Besides never did like the things. Went because of your mother. Now I do not have to," he assured her. "You go and have a good time." He looked from her to her brother. "And make sure your brother does not make a cake of himself over Arabella. No demanding she dance every dance with you or disappearing into an adjoining room like you did here the other night."

To both Lucy's and Richard's amazement, Edward turned red. "Father!" he protested.

"Hmmm. Do not 'Father' me. I know what is like to be young and engaged." Then he turned his gaze on his son-in-law. "Much better to be wed. Wouldn't you agree? Then do not have to say good night."

Richard did not know what to say. Therefore, he remained quiet. He did look at Lucy and caught her eye, giving her a smile that reminded her of evenings they had spent much more pleasurably alone. Like her brother, she blushed. Then remembering that she was angry with him, she straightened her back and hardened her glance. Richard sighed, wishing that they could talk and resolve their differences.

As they made their way up the staircase to the ball-room, Lucy felt ill. Although everyone had been kind to her the evening before at the theater, she knew that the gossips among the *ton* would be watching her to find the smallest chink in her armor. And if George showed up here. The thought made her tighten her grasp on Richard's arm.

"Are you all right?" he asked, putting his hand over hers. All the color in her face had disappeared.

"Fine," she said quietly. Then she shivered. "No, I am not," she whispered so softly that he could barely hear her.

"What is wrong? Shall we leave?" he asked anxiously. He looked around wildly, wondering how they could make an inconspicuous exit.

"No. I am just being silly."

"Silly?"

"I am nervous," she said angrily, wishing she had never started this discussion.

"You?" he asked. "What do you have to be nervous about?" He inspected her once more, noting the clarity of her skin and the way the dress made her eyes seem even more blue. "You will be the center of admiring eyes."

"Admiring? Richard, there will be people here tonight who have not seen me for eight years. They will be watching me for the slightest sign of weakness."

"You make them sound as though they are the hunters and you are the prey. Surely you do not mean that?"

"Do I not? For some of these people the hunt for gossip is their life, their only life," she said bitterly.

"What will they have to gossip about? You are still as lovely as ever," he said gallantly. He checked to see how many people waiting to be announced were still ahead of them. Edward, who had just seen Arabella join the crush on the stairs, tried to get her attention, but she did not answer him.

Lucy smiled at Richard, her earlier anger and her fear forgotten. That smile carried her through the receiving line and into the ballroom. As she looked at the polished floor and the candlelit chandeliers above it, she remembered the last ball she had attended before she returned home and had her accident. She had danced until dawn.

The musicians began the opening bars for the first dance, and people began to form sets. Lucy stood there longing to be a part of the crowd. "May I have this dance?" Richard asked.

"Dance? I no longer dance," she said quietly, wishing that she dared to do so but afraid of making a misstep on the dance floor.

Her brother, who now had his bride-to-be on his arm, disagreed. "Come join our set." Arabella, her eyes sparkling, added her encouragement.

Soon Lucy was a part of the colorful pattern that twirled about the floor, her cheeks flushed and her eyes wide with enjoyment. When the music had finished and a new set was forming, she allowed her husband to lead her to a seat near a window. Sinking into the chair, she fanned herself. Before the excitement of the dance had completely faded, she found herself surrounded by friends, both hers and Richard's.

When the Earl of Haversham did appear some time later, neither Lucy nor Richard noticed him. Although she had chosen not to dance a second time, Lucy was thoroughly enjoying the party, learning the latest *on dits* and discussing the newest fashions. No one who did not know her well would have realized how nervous she was. Only her frequent glances at her husband gave her away.

Richard too found the ball less difficult than he had expected. Leaving his wife in the capable hands of his friends, he completed his duty dances and then hurried back to her side, choosing to remain nearby instead of going into the gaming room as he would have done with his first wife. When they went into the supper room, they were part of a laughing crowd.

They were still laughing when they got out of the coach at her father's house. The lamps of the carriage and the torches that burned outside made the dark night bright. The watchers who waited across the street in the darkest shadows shrank back into them. Neither Richard nor Lucy noticed. All memories of grievances forgotten, they paused for one moment for a quick kiss and then laughed again, running into the house. Leaning on Richard's arm, Lucy did not even limp.

The laughter was a knife in the heart of the veiled woman who watched them. "It is he," she said incredulously. Her eyes narrowed dangerously. "He must be punished," she said angrily.

Her escort did not try to change her mind. "How?" was all he asked. As they walked toward a busier street where they could find a hackney, she explained. He smiled broadly.

Having successfully passed what they both acknowledged as their first test in society, Lucy and Richard were in alt. Refusing to leave her alone with her maid to undress, Richard watched as Betty brushed out her hair, put her jewels away, and began to unhook Lucy from her dress. "You may go, Betty," he said quietly. She glanced at him and then at her mistress. Lucy, never taking her eyes from her husband, nodded.

As soon as the door closed behind the maid, Richard reached down and pulled Lucy to her feet, pushing her dress off her shoulders. It pooled at her feet. He bent his head and brushed his lips over her shoulders and the tops of her breasts. She caught her breath. Her arms tightened around him. They kissed.

Spinning her around, Richard unlaced her stays and untied her petticoat, leaving Lucy clothed only in her chemise, hose, and garters. She turned back around, enjoying the way his eyes widened at the sight of her. She raised her arms and stretched sinuously. He reached for her. She stepped back. "Not yet," she whispered. She reached for his cravat.

A long time later as they lay in each other's arms, their breath beginning to slow to normal once more, Richard said quietly, "I am sorry for not being honest with you today."

For a moment Lucy was silent. Then she turned so she could face him, one hand tracing the line of his mouth. "I should not have reacted the way I did," she admitted.

"Do you still love him?" he asked. Utter silence followed. Richard cursed himself for not controlling his tongue.

Finally, she asked, "Who?"

"Haversham."

She turned on her back and stared up at the canopy, trying to discover just what she did feel. The silence stretched between them like a wall. Just when Richard was ready to shake her to get her to answer him, Lucy said, "I am not certain I ever did."

"Did what?" Richard demanded, his heart beating faster. He wanted to take in his arms, to crush her to him, but he knew this was not the moment to do so. He held his breath, hoping she would continue.

"Love him," Lucy explained, her voice revealing her own surprise. "Oh, I liked him well enough. He was the most handsome and well born of all my suitors. And we would probably have had a comfortable marriage." Her words stabbed Richard. "I thought I was in love with him, but I wasn't."

"Then why did you stay at home all those years?"

"Pride and fear." The words were so quiet that Richard was not at all sure that he had heard them.

"I do not understand," he complained.

"There is no need that you should," she said, turning so that she could kiss him once again. He was her husband; she had owed him an explanation for the way she had reacted to the man she had once been engaged to, but she did not intend to confess all her fears. As though realizing that she did not intend to say more, Richard kissed her again and pulled her closer.

In spite of all the details she needed to check for the engagement party and the fittings she had scheduled, neither Richard nor Lucy were up early the next day. When they did appear hand in hand, Edward took one look at them and swallowed his comments.

"What do you plan to do today?" Lucy asked, reaching up to smooth a wrinkle from Richard's lapel.

"I promised to look in at the Foreign Office," he explained. He stepped back as her hand stilled.

"Are you going to work for them again?" his wife asked, her face and her voice carefully neutral although her heart was beating so loudly she was afraid he would hear it.

"No. I have done my part," Richard said firmly. Lucy smiled widely and took a deep breath. "Besides I have other things to occupy my time now," he reminded her, closing one eye in a wink. She blushed and turned around so that her brother, who was an interested observer, could not see her hot cheeks.

"Richard!"

"Oh, do not silence him, Lucy," her brother said. "I am learning so much from him." She whirled around and glared at him, but he only laughed.

Then the clock struck the hour. Her eyes widened. "I must go," she declared. "Arabella is waiting."

"I will go with you," her brother said, following her from the room.

"No. We are only going for fittings. You would be in the way. If you must have something to do, check with Father about the wines. I am not certain that we have enough for the party." She put her bonnet on and stepped back. Richard was right behind her. She smiled up at him, and he kissed her quickly.

Then he picked up his own hat. "May I drop you off, Mrs. Blount?" he asked. Lucy thrilled at the sound of her name. She nodded and took his arm. The door closed behind them, leaving Edward staring after them.

He turned to go back down the hall when he realized that the door to his father's office stood open. He walked inside. "Did you hear?" he asked.

"Yes." His father looked up from the books on his desk. He put his pen down and leaned back in his chair. "What do you think?"

"About what?"

"The two of them. Did she make the right decision?" his father asked impatiently.

Edward ran his fingers through his hair, destroying the careful arrangement his valet had worked so hard to create. "I think so. I had my doubts when they first arrived," he admitted.

"As did I. They had had a disagreement. Anyone could see that. But you must keep in mind that no matter how much you care for your wife there will be times when you will argue. Remember that, Edward." He sighed. Then he smiled. "Quarrels, or at least making up after them, can have some interesting consequences."

"Consequences?" his son asked.

"Never mind. I am certain you will find out for yourself." His father smiled again. "Now tell me how Lucy did at the ball last night. I never thought she would agree to go."

"No, you simply created a situation in which she would have no choice," his son reminded him. He looked at the older man closely. In spite of the pain the trip had caused him, his father was in better spirits than he had been in a long time. He took a seat in front of the desk. "She danced," he said baldly.

By the time Lucy returned that afternoon, her good spirits had been truly tested. Standing for hours while the modiste had made innumerable small corrections in the gowns she had ordered had exhausted her completely. All she wanted to do was go to her room and rest. That rest was denied her.

When she had handed her bonnet to the waiting maid, she followed the laughter to the salon where her father liked to sit. There she found him, the children, and her husband. "Good. You are home. Now we can have tea," her father said as she walked into the room.

"Have you waited for me?" she asked, sighing. She gave Caroline a hug and smiled at the two boys. Richard made a place for her beside him on the settee. She sat down, closing her eyes for just a moment.

"Are you tired?" her husband asked, his brow creased with worry.

"A little." She smiled at him, hoping to allay his fears. She sighed again in satisfaction as she felt him relax beside her.

"Grandfather said I could have cake for tea," Caroline said as she came over to whisper in Lucy's ear.

"Did he indeed?" Lucy looked at her father, his head bent over something in a book the two boys were showing him. "Did he say what kind it was? Perhaps you will not like it," she said in a teasing voice.

"Not like cake?" the little girl asked, her eyes opening wide.

"Who does not like cake?" her father demanded, taking her up on his knee.

"Not me," Robert declared, raising his head.

"Or me," David added. He glanced at his father holding his little sister and sitting beside Lucy. A rush of jealousy filled him. He set his lips in a thin line and turned back to the map that Lucy's father's held. "Show me again where you went," he said, turning his back on his father.

Richard looked at his oldest son and sighed. He glanced at Edward, remembering what his brother-in-law had suggested. Perhaps sending the children to Julia's parents in Yorkshire would be the right idea. Then he remembered how ill his first wife's parents had been and shook his head.

That evening Lucy and Richard refused all invitations that had arrived, choosing instead to spend their time with the children. After dinner, served earlier than fashionable in town, they gathered in the salon to play speculation, a card game to which Mr. Meredith had introduced the boys. By bedtime for the children, even David was enjoying himself.

Noting the tired lines in her father's face, Lucy and Richard said their own good nights soon after the children left. Climbing the stairs together, Lucy allowed Richard to help her more than she usually did. Just as they came to her door, she yawned widely. "Shall I bid you good night now?" her husband asked, wondering if the yawn was his signal to find another bed, one by himself.

"Why?" Lucy asked, looking startled. She pulled away from him. "Are you going out?"

Richard recognized that the question carried more meaning than just the words. "Not tonight," he said firmly, opening her door for her and following her inside. Lucy breathed a sigh of relief. In spite of the way he turned to her in passion, she still fought her battles over whether her husband cared for her.

He walked across the room and went into his own bedroom, where his valet waited. As soon as he had finished changing, he returned, crawling into bed. At first he did not notice the peculiar look on her face.

Finally Betty left. Lucy turned to him, a crumpled piece of paper in her hand. "Richard." Her voice was strained.

He opened his eyes and sat up. "What is wrong?" he asked anxiously, sliding out of bed and moving quickly across the room.

"Read this." She held out the paper.

He took it from her, and his eyes narrowed with rage. "Where did you get this?" he demanded.

"Here. On my dresser. It was not there when I dressed for dinner. I would have seen it," she said, her words almost running over themselves.

Richard read the message once again, his mouth set in a narrow line: "Ask your husband why he did not bury his first wife." Each letter was perfectly formed as though it had been traced on the cheap paper. His face grew harder. It was starting again.

"Who would send such a thing?" Lucy asked, getting up from the chair in front of her dressing table.

"Call your maid."

"But she will be in bed."

"Call her," he demanded. She looked into his face, recognizing the determination there. Then she crossed to the bellpull.

When Betty arrived, Richard stood before the fireplace, the paper clutched in his hands. The maid looked at him and then at her mistress. "When did this arrive?" he asked, his voice harsher than the maid had ever heard it.

"It was there when I returned from my dinner," Betty said quietly. She had thought it must be a message that one of the children had sent and had left it alone.

"When was that?"

"After you finished," Betty explained. "Did I do something wrong, sir?"

"No." Richard crossed to stand by the dressing table, his face thoughtful. "Who else has access to this room?"

"Any of the chambermaids and the housekeeper," the maid whispered. "And Rawls, your valet."

"Anyone else?"

"A footman or two who carry the coal when it grows cooler." Betty looked at her mistress, trying to discover just what was wrong. Lucy did not notice but continued to stare out into the night. The words she had read, though innocent in themselves, were burned into her mind. What was the letter writer suggesting? She was not certain she wanted to know.

"Could any one of them have entered this room this evening?" he asked. Betty turned to look at her mistress again.

"Tell him the truth, Betty," Lucy said quietly.

The maid hung her head. Then she took a breath and squared her shoulders. "Not tonight."

"Why was tonight different?" he asked, correctly interpreting her hesitation. "What happened?"

"It is the housekeeper's birthday. Cook made her a

special cake. Everyone wanted to be there to celebrate with her. It was only for a few minutes."

Lucy could tell her servant was close to tears. Quickly, she reassured her. "Very proper. Of course, you had to help her celebrate." The maid relaxed slightly. "Surely, though, you were not all there for very long. Someone must have seen something. Perhaps you could ask around. See if anyone remembers being given this note for me." Richard raised his eyebrows as if in protest, but Lucy ignored him. Betty nodded and hurried from the room, breathing a sigh of relief.

Richard once more studied the note he held, his brow wrinkled. "David was with us all evening," he said quietly, more to himself than to her.

"It could not have been he," Lucy assured him, hoping she was right. "Look at the letters. They are too perfect. David's handwriting looks more childlike." She walked over and took the note out of his hand. Smoothing it out, she laid it on her dresser. "See."

"Are you certain?" he asked, his voice breaking just a little. He did not want to believe that his son was capable of such a cruel act.

She smiled at him. Neither noticed how much her lips trembled. "Yes," she said quietly. Then she closed her eyes and took a deep breath. "Why would someone send me a note like this, Richard?" she asked, willing him to be honest with her.

His shoulders sagged. He sat down and put his head in his hands. "I wish I knew," he whispered. Then his face hardened. "I am going to find out," he promised her.

"How?" she asked, wanting to believe that he could but not completely certain. He could be so unpredictable.

"I have friends who will be able to help," he assured her.

"Friends?" She crossed to stand behind him and put her hands on his shoulders, turning him so that he faced her.

"They will know what to do," he assured her. "They thought they were close to finding out last time."

"Last time?" Lucy stared at him as though he were a stranger. "Last time? You have seen notes like these before?" she asked incredulously. Her voice rose on the last word.

He got up and started to take her in his arms, but she pulled away. His arms dropped. He took a step or two back and went to the window, pushing the curtains aside as she had done earlier so that he could stare into the night. Regretting the impulse that led her to pull away, she walked up behind him and put her arm on his. More than he had wanted anything Richard longed to be able to turn to her, to pour the story out, to feel her compassion. Instead, he was silent.

Reluctantly, Lucy stepped back, an anguished look on her face. "Please explain," she begged. He did not answer. Finally she gave up. Moving as though she were an old woman, Lucy crossed the room and crawled into bed. Richard simply stood there and stared into the night.

Chapter Nine

When Richard woke up early the next morning, he slipped out of the bed in which he had slept alone. Even though he had had little sleep, he was too impatient to stay in bed any longer. Ringing for his valet, he dressed and was on his way before most of the household was stirring. "Tell Betty not to disturb my wife," he told Rawls. "If Mrs. Blount asks, tell her I will not be back until late this afternoon. I will need evening things." Leaving his valet staring after him, he left.

The household he left was not a happy one. As Betty made her inquiries among the servants, the household began to buzz. "Always blaming one of us," one of the footmen complained as he helped Jarvis, the butler, carry the silver into the pantry to be polished.

The butler was quick to silence him. "It is not your place to comment on the actions of your betters," Jarvis said, looking down his nose at the man. The footman knew his place well enough not to answer him.

In the lower regions of the house, others were voicing their opinions. "Never think it was me. Blimey. If me wages weren't all keeping my mam alive, I'd tell him what he could do with this job," the laundress said, curling her lip in disgust. She ignored the disapproving looks the housekeeper gave her.

No matter whom Betty asked, she could find no one who admitted taking the note to Lucy's room. As she herself began thinking about who had been present at the table when the housekeeper received her cake, she realized that none of the household's servants could have done it. "Jarvis even locked the front door after the tea tray was removed so the footman could be present," she told her mistress as she combed Lucy's hair.

"Then how did that note get here?" Lucy wondered.

At the Foreign Office, Richard's friends were asking the same question. "You received nothing like this during the time you were in Devonshire?" his former employer asked.

"Nothing. And that was a surprise. As soon as the announcement of our marriage appeared in the papers, I expected something to arrive. Nothing did."

"Not wise of you to allow that announcement, Richard," his mentor told him, a frown on his face. Dressed in dull gray, he seemed to blend into the gray walls of the room.

"Allow it! I made a horrible scene over it, but it appeared without my knowledge," Richard said, thinking of the strained relationship that had existed between himself and Lucy since its appearance. "But the announcement cannot be the issue. Nothing happened until we returned to London."

"Strange." His mentor frowned. Over the course of the next hour, he led Richard through his actions during the last few days. "They could be anywhere," he finally said thoughtfully.

Richard's face fell. "Is there nothing we can do?" he asked, wondering if his only choice would be isolation. However, he doubted that returning to Devonshire would bring him the peace he craved.

"I did not say that. Let me call in the gentleman who was working on your case before." He paused and looked at the younger man who had always been willing to carry his documents into dangerous places. "He does not come cheap, and since this is not government business . . ." He shrugged his shoulders.

Nodding, Richard said quietly, "My pockets are deep. No matter how expensive it is I must know."

"Good. Here is what we will do." By the time Richard returned home to dress for the evening's events, he had the satisfaction of knowing that someone else was searching for answers to his problem.

Lucy, who had spent much of her day wondering what was happening, had dressed early. As soon as she heard her husband's voice in the room next door, she knocked on the door that separated their rooms and then hurried inside without waiting for an answer. "Richard, Betty did not . . ." Her eyes widened. "Oh," she said, taking in the sight of her husband, who had stripped to his unmentionables and was washing his face. His valet wore a look of horror and rushed to throw a towel over his master.

Drying his face and then tossing the towel aside, Richard crossed the room. "What did she learn?" he asked Lucy, taking her hand and leading her to a pair of chairs set beside the fireplace. His attitude was as formal as though he had already donned his evening dress.

"Nothing. No one in the house seems to know anything." She shook her head when Richard offered her a seat.

"Nothing? That piece of paper did not appear in your room by magic!"

They heard a low sound across the room. Silently, they both turned to look at the valet. "Do you know anything, Rawls?" Richard asked sternly.

"An idea only. If you would allow me to make a few inquiries while you are away this evening?" he said hesitantly. Although he was excellent at his job, he had always tried to hold himself aloof from being too involved in his master's life, a situation that Richard preferred. Even now Rawls was not certain of the wisdom of his actions.

"Make as many as you like," his master told him. "But try not to upset the staff any more than it has been."

"What does that mean?" Lucy asked, already half guessing the answer.

"Jarvis himself met me at the door, complaining about the impertinent questions your maid had asked him," Richard explained.

"He came to you?" she asked angrily.

"Your father refused to listen to him, and your brother has not been at home all afternoon." Richard walked over and picked up the shirt that Rawls had laid out and put it on. Then he sat down and began to pull on his stockings.

"Edward is with Arabella, something about one of her relatives arriving in town." Lucy walked back toward her own room. "Do you think I need to talk to Jarvis?" she asked. "I cannot believe that he did not mention his concerns to me. This is not even your house."

"He said he did not wish to disturb you," her husband explained. "We discussed the matter, and I took care of everything. You do not have to worry about anything."

Made to feel an outsider in her former home, Lucy wanted to protest, but her emotions were too close to the surface for her to feel comfortable about expressing them. With the gossip that had been evident that day, she knew that even one angry word would be reported instantly in the servants' quarters. "I will leave everything to you," she said, her calm manner hiding the storm of emotions that flooded her. Besides being unable to give him children, she was not competent to manage the household.

Richard looked up and smiled. His smile soon disappeared when he realized that she was not looking at him but was walking toward her own room. Before she could open the door that connected their two rooms, he asked, "How are the children?"

"The children?" She slowly turned around to face him, remembering the problem she had faced that afternoon. "Yes, the children. When I explained that you were not available to take them on the ride to the park that you promised them, I told them we would see them before we left for the ball," she said quietly, although her jaw was tight.

"The park." He shook his head and shrugged into his evening coat, letting Rawls smooth it on his shoulders until it fit like a well-made glove. "I hope they were not too much trouble?"

"Trouble?" Lucy lost control of her emotions, and her words came out in a shriek. "Richard, they were hurt and angry. You made them feel as though they were mere inconveniences that you could ignore when you had something else you wanted to do. I was able to fob off Caroline and Robert with promises for tomorrow, but David simply went into his room and shut the door. He refused to come out for nuncheon or for tea."

"He will have forgotten by tomorrow," he said callously, falling unconsciously back into the attitude he had had before the fire. He took the pin his valet had handed him and placed it in his cravat.

"Richard, this is your son you are talking about. The one who needs extra attention." Shocked by his words, she glared at him, the color back in her cheeks. Dismissing Rawls, Richard crossed the room and took her hands in his. She pulled away, entering her own room.

He followed. She refused to turn around and look at him, the flags of anger in her cheeks as bright as the amber silk gown she wore. "Lucy, I am sorry I left you to deal with the children alone. I know I was wrong. But I did not have time to discuss it with you before I left. And David will forget. You will see." He caught her by the shoulders and turned her to face him. She licked her lips nervously. He smiled. Then he bent and kissed her, all his repressed hunger washing over her.

She tried to pull back. Then, wishing she had the strength to deny him, she sighed and stepped closer, wrapping her arms around his neck. All too soon the kiss ended. Shaking her head as though to clear her mind, she dropped her arms and stepped back, determined not to let him twist her emotions any longer. She longed to be able to deny them. "Shall we go see the children?"

The temperature in the schoolroom was as chilly as a winter's sky. Although the two younger children greeted their father reluctantly, David refused to acknowledge his presence at all. Richard did try to reach him. "Shall we go for that ride in the park tomorrow?" he asked.

"Do you think you will have time?" Robert asked, not at all certain he could trust his father's promise. The short time in London had reminded him of the time before the fire.

"Before today have I ever made a promise I did not keep?" his father asked. In spite of what he had said earlier to his wife, Richard knew what it was like to have someone disappoint him. He did not want his children to have to suffer as he had.

"Not since the fire," Robert said slowly, as though the words were being dragged out of him. He kept his eyes fixed on the floor, not on his father.

Caroline, who had stayed close to Lucy's side and was stroking the silky fabric of her gown, looked up, her eyes shadowed. "Da said he would not do it again, Robert," she told her brother. Her face and her voice were more serious than any six-year-old's should be.

"He said that before he left for Russia too," his oldest son said bitterly.

Richard felt as though he had been stabbed by a knife. He looked at Lucy, his eyes dark with pain. He had had no idea that his children harbored such bitterness about his trips. During the time since the fire, he had spent every moment with them, denying his own pleasure so that he would not leave them alone. Then he remembered what he had said to Lucy only minutes before, and guilt ravaged him. "I thought you understood," he said quietly.

"We understand that you do not care for us," David said. "If Mama had not died in the fire, you would have gone somewhere else, and we would not have seen you for months."

Lucy reached out for the sturdy little boy, but he pulled away. "No, David," she said, tears filling her eyes. She put her hands to her mouth.

Caroline pressed close to Lucy's side, her eyes wide. "David is wrong. I know he is wrong," she whispered. "Da loves us." She said it again louder.

Swallowing a big lump in his throat, her father looked at her and smiled. "Thank you, sweetheart." He blinked his eyes a few times to get rid of his own tears. He turned to face his younger son. "Do you think I care as little for you as your brother does, Robert?" he asked. By this time he had forgotten he was dressed in evening clothes and had sunk to one knee so that he could look his children in their eyes.

"He did rescue us, David," the younger boy said quietly, finally looking up at his father. "And he taught us to sail." His smile was tentative, but it told his father that he had not totally destroyed his youngest son's love.

The breath that Richard had been holding escaped in a rush. He sat down on the floor, too weak with relief to think about the sight he made. He held out his arms to his youngest children. Slowly at first and then at last in a rush, they came into his arms. David stared at them and then turned his back.

Lucy sank into the rocker that sat in one corner, no thought of the wrinkles she was putting in her ballgown. As upset as she knew the children had been that afternoon, she had had no idea that their feelings had run so deep. She glanced at David again, wishing she knew how to reach him, wishing she could say something that would make him feel better.

Still sitting on the floor, Richard looked over at Lucy. She smiled at him. The sight of her in her ballgown made him freeze for a moment. His arms tightened around Caroline and Robert. They looked at him curiously. Then he asked, "Can Edward escort you to the ball this evening?"

"Why?" she asked through a throat that was unbearably tight. She held her breath.

"I want to stay with the children."

"We will both stay."

"No, you must go," he said quietly.

His words struck Lucy like a blow. Once more she was shut out. Carefully, she controlled her voice. "I can ask him."

Suddenly aware of the undercurrents between them, he looked up at her. "You are already dressed, and if one of us attends, we will not offend whichever of Arabella's relatives we are promised to tonight," he explained.

Lucy stood up, although every instinct within her urged her to stay, to fight for her right to be part of this family. "I will see if he is still at home," she said quietly. She was gone before he could say anything else. A frown crossed his forehead, wondering at the peculiar tone in her voice.

Caroline began to cry. "I do not want her to go. Make her come back, Da," she said pulling on his sleeve.

"She is not gone forever. She will be back, but tonight I will be here," he said, trying to soothe her. He looked at the door and back at the children in his arms. "You will see her tomorrow."

"Just like a girl. Always crying," Robert said scornfully.

"Do not," Caroline said with a sniff, wiping her eyes and her nose on the sleeve of her dress.

"Do too," her brother said belligerently.

"Stop this, both of you," Richard said, pulling out his handkerchief and wiping Caroline's eyes.

"I do not like London," Robert said, scowling. "I want to go home."

"Me too. When can we go home?" Caroline asked, sniffing once or twice. Even David turned around to stare at him, an expectant look on his face.

Although his first reaction had been to run back to Devonshire, Richard knew that he had set forces in motion that he could not stop, not if he wanted to discover once and for all who was threatening his family. And to find out, he had to stay in London—at least for the moment. He sighed. "We have to stay here for a while."

"Why?"

"Because of the party for Uncle Edward and Arabella," Caroline said importantly. "I got to go in the ballroom today and watch them polish the . . . the . . ." It was obvious that she was searching for a word.

"He is not our uncle," David said, interrupting her. His voice was cold.

"What?" His little sister turned to look at him.

"He is your uncle by marriage," his father said sternly. "Just as Lucy is your mother by marriage."

"Stepmother," David whispered just loud enough to be heard. He glared at his father, wondering if his father would punish him. He knew his tutor would have if he had heard him.

Not for the first time Richard wondered if his oldest son were a changeling. However, much as she had disliked him, he knew Julia had not cuckolded him; the boy looked too much like him for that. Controlling his impatience, Richard took a deep breath. "Yes, she is your stepmother, David. I explained that to you when I told you I was remarrying."

His oldest son muttered something under his breath. Richard held on to his temper, reminding himself that the boy was a child, a child who had had to deal with massive changes in his life. Had he been too soft on them this last year, he wondered. But they had turned to him, capturing his heart in their hands. He had not wanted to turn them away when they reached out to him, finally able to share their daily lives.

A solitary young man whose mother enjoyed the parties and bustle of life in town and whose father was mad for sport, he had longed to be a part of a large family. He had married for that reason, only to find his wife enjoyed being the center of country society far too much to have time for her own family. She had welcomed him to her bed and then railed at him whenever she discovered she was with child, sending him away. After Caroline had been born, she refused to have anything more to do with him. At that time he had begun to make trips for the Foreign Office. As he looked at his children, he regretted those years. He had lost so much of their childhood.

He sighed. Then he got up and sat down in the chair that Lucy had so recently left. "Tell me what you did today," he said, trying to ignore the emotions of the last few minutes. Slowly and then more rapidly, Caroline and Robert re-created their day. Even David added a sentence or two when he realized his father had no intention of leaving.

When he left the schoolroom, Richard wandered about the house, looking for someone to talk to. Discovering that Mr. Meredith had already retired for the evening, he took a book from the library and tried to read. Finally, he gave it up and leaned back in the chair, his eyes closed. He drifted off to sleep.

The sound of a door closing brought him awake. He stretched and looked around. He heard a slight movement in the room next door. "Lucy?" he called. He opened her door.

She sat up in bed. "Yes?"

"Good, you are still up. I wanted to talk to you."

Her heart, which had started racing when she heard his voice, suddenly slowed down. "About what?" she asked, her hands clasped so tightly her knuckles were as white as the sheet that covered them.

He stared at her in amazement. "About the children, of course. You were right earlier this evening. I should not have doubted you."

His words should have been comforting to her. But all she could remember was his sending her off to the ball while he stayed with the children. "I was?" she asked in a voice that sounded more like a croak than a question.

"You should have made me listen."

"How? You know your children better than I."

"Apparently, I do not. You heard them tonight. They hate me."

"Richard, they do not. They love you."

"Even David?" he asked. Then he thought of what he had just said and wondered how many of the men he knew truly cared for their children. Occasionally one would boast of a son being born, but it was rare for anyone to discuss his offspring. He thought of his parents and their friends and realized that his acquaintances were no different than they. Even when he had been at

school, Edward and one or two of the other boys were
the only ones whose parents wrote frequent letters or
visited. His parents had not even been at home when the
school had holiday. He had gone to Wales to be with his
grandfather or, after his grandfather had died, visited
friends like Edward. Had he been that kind of father to
his own children? His face twisted in pain at the thought
that had plagued him all evening.

Lucy watched the emotions rage across his face and
wanted to soothe him. "He would not be so upset with
you if he did not care," she tried to assure him. "And he
has not said any more about wanting to live with Julia's
parents." She reached up and pulled him down beside
her on the bed. Stroking his cheek, she tried to calm him,
to draw his pain to her.

"I wish he had."

"What? Why?" She pulled away from him. The moment she thought she understood him he changed.

"No. I do not mean that," he said. "Or maybe I do. I
do not know anymore."

Lucy stared at him for a moment. Then despite her
own unresolved feelings, she said, "Come to bed,
Richard. Everything will be clearer in the morning." He
stared at her, at first unwilling to release his emotions.
Then he sighed and slid into bed. Lucy blew out the candle and let him pull her close.

The next morning while Lucy finished the final prepa-
rations for the party to be held that evening, Richard
took the children to the park. He did not see the couple
who waited in the carriage on the corner. The woman's
eyes widened. "There is his oldest," she whispered. She
pushed aside the leather curtain and stared at the boy.

"I told you they were all here," the man beside her
said harshly. "Do not let yourself be seen."

"I am not a fool," she said angrily, drawing back and
signaling the driver to follow the other carriage.

"Then do not act like one."

She glared at him but said no more. When Richard's
carriage halted at the edge of the park to let him and the

children out, they drove past them. "Let's get out here," she said.

"It is too dangerous."

"Nonsense." Before he could stop her, she had signaled the driver to let them out. "We must know more. Pay the driver off." Still grumbling, the man did as she directed.

By careful planning, the couple was always a few steps ahead of Richard and his children, far enough away to escape detection but close enough to listen to what was being said. As she cautiously watched David venture ahead of the rest, the woman smiled.

"He's the one?" the man asked.

"Yes." The woman's voice was husky with emotion.

"We must go," the watchers heard Richard say.

"But we have not had any milk," Robert complained. Caroline added a word or two. David simply glared at his father, his anger too deep to forgive as easily as his brother and sister had.

"I must pick up a package." His voice told them not to argue with him. For once Robert listened.

"What is in it?" Caroline asked, turning her face up to his.

"Something special for Lucy."

"For the party tonight?" she wanted to know. "She is going to be beautiful. Not even Arabella will be prettier." She took her father's hand and gave a little skip. David turned around and glared at her, but she ignored him.

Richard merely laughed. "Come. I must take you home." David muttered something under his breath again. His father shot him a hard look.

"There is our carriage, Da," the boy said hurriedly, realizing that his father was watching him too intently. He pointed to it. "Bet I can beat you to it, Robert."

"Try." His brother shot away, and David quickly followed.

"Silly boys," Caroline said, smiling up at him in a way that made him realize why fathers of beautiful young girls often went gray faster than fathers of boys. The couple that now followed them exchanged a knowing glance. The man smiled sardonically; then they watched the family leave before the man signaled for a waiting hackney.

By the time Richard had taken the children home and seen them into the watchful care of their attendants, it was later than he had planned. Refusing nuncheon, he left the house a short time later. When he returned, it was time to dress for the evening.

For most of the day Lucy had been busy checking last minute details. She did find time to visit the schoolroom, promising the three children that they could sit at the head of the stairs and watch the guests arrive. "And I will have cook send up a special supper tray for you," she said with a smile, remembering how exciting it used to be for her when she was allowed to watch and then to share in some of the foods that seemed so exotic back then.

"Will you and Da come up to see us before the guests arrive?" Caroline asked wistfully. Robert and David made faces at her question. She turned and glared at them. "Well, they came last night. And they had a ball to go to then too."

"We shall try," Lucy said with a smile that hid the pain that memory held. "As long as our guests do not arrive too early."

"Papa Meredith can greet them for you," Robert said. "He told me this afternoon he was to attend also. How will he get up the stairs?"

His brother stared at him as though he had proposed that they live in Bedlam. "I heard Jarvis tell the biggest footman to carry him up," David said, daring Robert to contradict him. "His Bath chair too."

"Oh." They both stared at Lucy as if they expected her to add something. She simply smiled at them and told them good-bye.

By the time she reached her room, her limp was more pronounced. Ignoring it, she checked her lists one more time. Then she stretched and closed her eyes for a moment. "I will take my bath now," she said, wondering if she would have enough time to take a nap. While she waited, she went over the details in her mind one more time.

Just when she had given up hope that he would be ready before the guests arrived, Richard walked in, dressed in the black and white that Brummell had made so popular. He smiled when he saw her gown, a sea green sarcenet over a silk slip of the same color. Bordered in gold embroidery about the low neck, sleeves, and hem, it made the perfect frame for her creamy skin. She was once again wearing her pearls. "I think these would look better with that gown," he said as he handed her a gold and diamond bracelet, necklace, earrings, and hair comb. Then he turned her around so that he could unfasten her pearls.

Lucy stared at the pieces that filled her hands. Then she tried to look at him. "Stay still," he ordered, finding the clasp of the pearls more difficult than he remembered. Finally, releasing it, he handed the pearls to Betty, who hovered nearby. "Give me the necklace," he said, letting his fingers drift over the soft skin of her neck.

She gasped. Then she turned her head softly, letting her lips just brush his hand. "Richard, you did not need to do this," she whispered.

He put the necklace in place and turned her around. "I wanted to," he said softly, looking down into her eyes as blue as the sea on a sunny day. Betty shifted nervously. He stepped back. "Let your maid put the comb in your hair," he suggested.

Without protest, Lucy sat down once more before the mirror. Though she normally watched what Betty was doing, this time she did not take her eyes off Richard's reflection. He smiled at her, sending thrills running down her spine. She watched him just as a mongoose watches a cobra. Had they been alone she would have been in his arms, all thought of the engagement party forgotten.

When Betty finished, she stood up once more, taking a last look in the mirror. Then she turned to face him. He took a step toward her. Her lips parted. She licked them nervously. Remembering the guests who would be arriving shortly, he held out his arm, and she sighed but stepped to his side.

As she stood beside her father's chair sometime later, Lucy greeted their guests with a smile, a smile that made her eyes shine. In the short time she had been in London, she had regained her ease in society largely because the gossip she feared had not happened. She glanced at her husband, who had not left her side since the gentlemen had rejoined them after their port. He smiled back at her.

"Will you dance with me tonight?" he asked quietly, his lips close to her ear. She shook her head and turned to welcome the next guest. The music grew louder, and people began to take their places for the first set.

"I cannot dance until all the guests have arrived," she told him, taking advantage of a break in the introductions.

"I will wait," he assured her, a twinkle in his eyes. Almost against her will, she smiled up at him.

Her father turned to say something to her but paused, a pleased look on his face. Although the party had been planned for his son and his fiancée, he had accomplished another goal, seeing his daughter returned to her rightful place in society. No matter how he had disapproved of their marriage at first, Mr. Meredith approved of the change it had brought in his daughter.

By the time the last guest had said his good-byes, all of London was talking—not merely about Edward and Arabella but also about Lucy and her husband. As he had done before, Richard had swept Lucy out onto the floor. And instead of allowing her to retreat after one dance, he had raised eyebrows by claiming her hand for three dances in a row, letting her rest only when she complained of exhaustion. When she had escaped from the ballroom, going upstairs to make certain the children had received their treat, he had followed, unwilling to let her escape from his sight for more than a few seconds. Watching them leave, the gossips had begun to chatter. Although her duties as hostess and his duty dances separated them at times, no one who was present that evening had any doubts of the affection between them.

In a small house in an unfashionable area of town, one woman flared into anger when she heard a report of the evening. "Scandalous it was," her friend explained. He leaned closer. "I heard that the gold and diamond set she wore was a recent gift of her husband. One of the diamonds was as large as my thumbnail."

The listener grew still. Then she smiled. No one who saw it would have doubted the hatred that lay behind it. "Gold and diamonds? Add them to our list." She waited for a moment. "And the letter? What of it?" she demanded.

"Just as we planned." He laughed and pulled off his cravat. "They never even noticed me. I waited until the music had started and slipped inside the house with several people who had just arrived. No one questioned me."

"Have they ever?" she asked, tilting her head back so that he could kiss her throat. "I told you how it would be." Her face grew dark. "But I did not like sitting at home alone. I should have been there too."

"It is too dangerous, my sweet. You are the one who made the rules. Do you want to take a chance and change them now? We are close, so close," he whispered. He put his arms around her and drew her back against him. He put his hand in his pocket and withdrew a small brooch, a cameo set in gold. He handed it to her.

Taking the gift, she smiled. Then she let herself relax. "You are right. I only have to wait for a little while." She looked around the shabby room. "Gad, but I am tired of this place."

"We should have gone to America immediately."

"America? Are you still harping on that old topic? You know I was in no condition to travel." She glared at him as though blaming her poor health on him.

"It was my fault. I waited too long to find you," he admitted, knowing from experience that admitting his guilt was the one way to stop the conversation before it became violent.

"So it was." She slapped his cheek playfully. "But you will never change my plans again, will you, my dear?"

"Never." The man stepped back, his eyes glittering. He waited for the next outburst, but it never came.

The woman smiled at him. Then she turned and walked toward the door. She paused, looking back over her shoulder at him. "Are you coming?" she asked.

Chapter Ten

The second letter was not discovered until the afternoon of the day after the party. The household had risen late, most people choosing to take chocolate or coffee in their rooms. Lucy, realizing that not only they but also the staff would be tired, had arranged that a cold nuncheon be served early in the afternoon.

The sun that had just been coming up when they were going to bed was bright as one after another of the household took their places at the table. "Did you enjoy the party?" Mr. Meredith asked Caroline, whom he had chosen as his nuncheon partner.

"The ladies were beautiful," she said, her eyes growing big. "But not as beautiful as Mama or Arabella." Her brothers looked at each other and made faces. She looked from one to the other, her face set. "Well, it is true."

"I thought so too, my dear," Mr. Meredith said, smiling at her. She gave her brothers a self-satisfied smirk. "Did you enjoy the sights too?" he asked the boys.

David nodded his head and started to say something when Robert interrupted. "Sitting on the stairs was boring, but the food was good. I liked the lobster patties and the little cakes." David looked at his plate, wishing his brother could be quiet.

"Is anyone interested in going for a walk?" his father asked.

David looked up. "I will go," he said quietly. His father smiled at him and nodded.

"And I," Lucy added.

"How tame. Is that the way you spend your afternoons in Devonshire, Lucy?" her brother asked. Since his engagement had been formally announced and he no longer had to worry about anyone sweeping Arabella away from him, he was more relaxed.

"No. We go sailing."

"Sailing?" her father asked, his eyebrows going up. "Is that safe?"

"Da takes all of us, Grandfather Meredith," David told him. "We are all good sailors."

"Even Caroline?" Edward asked with a smile for the little girl.

She frowned at him. "I have been sailing since I was five," she said pompously. Once again the adults exchanged amused glances. The boys snickered. "Tell them, Da."

He nodded, being careful to hide his amusement. "If you are finished, you can prepare for the walk. I will wait for you." Almost before the words were out of his mouth, the children had made their excuses and disappeared. He waited until they were out of the room before he asked his father-in-law, "How soon are you returning to the country, sir?"

There was a note in his voice that made the older gentleman look at him carefully. "I have not decided. I must admit I have enjoyed having friends call. And I like having the papers before the news is a week old. I may just stay even when the Season is over. Why?" He looked at his daughter to see how she would react to his change in plans, but Lucy was staring at her plate.

"A small problem has arisen. If it is agreeable with you, we will stay longer so that I may deal with it." Lucy glanced at Richard and then lowered her eyes once more.

"You are welcome at any time. I regret that any problem exists, but I rejoice in having more time with my daughter. I was already dreading our separation. Christmas is too far away," Mr. Meredith said with a smile that lit up his face.

"Christmas?" Richard asked, trying to remember if he had already promised to visit for the holidays.

"My wedding, Blount," Edward said with a laugh. "If I manage to survive until then. I tried to persuade Arabella's family to move up the date, but her mother would not hear of it."

"She has not finished ordering her bride's clothes, Edward. And the linen takes forever to be embroidered. And you did promise to wait."

"I do not see why we need all those linens with my initials on them. You did not wait for them," her brother said teasingly. When he saw the way both Lucy's and Richard's faces froze, he wished he could take the words back.

"Our situation was different," Lucy said quietly. Then she too made her excuses and left the table.

Edward looked from his brother-in-law to his father. Realizing that to say anything more would be futile, he shrugged his shoulders. "I must be away. I promised Arabella that I would spend the afternoon with her receiving callers."

Richard and his father-in-law sat in silence for a few minutes. Then Mr. Meredith said, "If you wish to discuss your problem with me, I would be happy to advise you."

Slightly uncomfortable and not certain of what Lucy had told her father, Richard said, "I appreciate your concern. However, this is something I must handle by myself." Hearing a noise in the hall, he stood. "Now I must bid you a good afternoon. I believe my party is ready to leave." Mr. Meredith stared after him, a frown on his brow.

By the time they had returned from their walk, the children were red-cheeked and boisterous, all talking at the same time. "Their tutor and governess will not thank you for letting them run about so, Richard" Lucy said sternly as she listened to them telling the footman what they had seen. She tempered her words with a smile. Then she allowed Jarvis to take her reticule and bonnet. "Have a tea tray sent to the drawing room. And ask my father if he wishes to join us," she told the butler. "Will you join us or must you go out again?"

"I will take tea with you," her husband said, enjoying the flush that the sun had painted on her face. "What are our plans for this evening?"

"I refused all invitations." She sighed.

"You can always say your plans have changed," her husband reminded her, interpreting the sigh incorrectly.

"I have no intention of doing that!" she exclaimed. "I deserve a quiet evening."

"We all deserve more quiet than we have now," he said over the voices of the three little ones. Raising his voice slightly, he said, "Children, we are having tea in the drawing room. Wash your hands and faces, and then you may join us." He watched as they made a dash for the stairs. "Like a lady and gentlemen please," he called after them. Obediently, they slowed down and walked up the stairs until they were out of his sight. Then he could hear them begin to run again and frowned.

"What did you expect, sir? They are children," his wife said, tucking her arm into his. The outing with the children had refreshed her, reminding her of some of the reasons why she had decided to wed.

"Shall I bring you your mail, sir?" Jarvis asked as he opened the door of the drawing room. Richard nodded.

As he broke the seal of the letter that lay on top of the pile and saw the words written there, he wished that he could erase the last few minutes. It read: "Ask your wife if she has found the brooch that was missing. Next time the item taken may not be so easy to replace."

He cleared his throat and tried to say her name. Nothing came out. He tried again. "Lucy?"

Something in his tone made her look up. "Yes?"

"Are you missing a brooch?"

"Why how did you know?" she asked. Her face was puzzled.

"When did it disappear?" Although his voice did not get any louder, the way Richard asked the question told her that it was not merely a casual inquiry.

"I am not sure. I could not find it this morning." He frowned. "But, Richard, it is merely a trinket, something Edward gave me during my Season."

Before they could continue their discussion, the door opened, and Mr. Meredith came in. Noticing the heavy atmosphere, he looked from one to the other curiously. Then he smiled at his daughter. "How was the visit to the park? And where are the children?"

"We are here, Grandfather," Caroline said, coming up behind him. She slipped around the chair and sat on his knee. Lucy's eyes widened in surprise, knowing how painful her father's legs could be. She hurried to lift Caroline from his lap.

"Leave her where she is," her father said. "She knows that she must not wiggle, don't you, sweet?" He smiled at Caroline. "The boys can push us and give us a ride." The little girl giggled, and the boys rushed to take advantage of his offer. Although the rugs impeded their progress, David and Robert pushed the bath chair around the room for several minutes.

When the tea tray had arrived and she had poured the tea, Lucy called them to join her. Buoyed up by the activity and the sunshine they had absorbed that afternoon, the children ate a hearty meal. Richard hardly ate anything. When he refused his favorite lemon tarts, Lucy looked worried.

As soon as he could, Richard escorted his children back to their attendants. Calling the boys' tutor to one side, he said, "Watch them carefully. Tell Mrs. Stanhope to do the same. They are not to be out of your sight."

"Is something wrong, Mr. Blount?" Mr. Avery asked, wondering what the children had done.

"Just be watchful." He waited until the man nodded. Then Richard kissed his daughter and rumpled his sons' hair. "I will check in on you when I return," he promised. "But do not wait up for me. I may be late."

Lucy was waiting for him when he came downstairs. "What is the matter?" she asked, coming into his room, where he was allowing Rawls to help him into a fresh jacket.

"Nothing."

Once again she felt the familiar wall coming between them. This time she was determined not be shut out. "Do not try to fob me off, Richard. What is happening?"

"I do not have time to discuss it now," he said firmly. "I will see you when I return. Ask your maid how long that brooch has been missing." Both Lucy and his valet frowned at that. "Rawls, how have your inquiries been going?"

"I hope to have an answer soon," his valet said.

"Let me know immediately." Picking up his hat and gloves, Richard crossed to his wife, who had been trying to make sense of what he was saying. He kissed her cheek. "I will see you later. Have a restful evening."

"Richard, where are you going?" she asked.

"To my club." Before she could ask him anything else, he was gone. She and Rawls stared at one another. Then Lucy walked back into her own room.

Taking advantage of his master's absence, Rawls continued his inquiries. During the ball the previous evening, he had had a chance to further his acquaintance with the upstairs maid, a buxom lass not long in the city. Pleased to have captured the eye of such an important man, she had been more talkative than she normally would have been. As he had suspected from his own recollections, not everyone had been at the housekeeper's birthday dinner. A maid and a footman were absent. The upstairs maid giggled when she told Rawls about the way the two of them had slipped out and then swore him to secrecy. "She'd lose her position if 'twere known," the girl told him.

"Did no one miss them?" he had asked.

"Things were at sixes and sevens all evening. If someone missed 'em, no one said a word." She had laughed then and held up her lips to be kissed.

With his master gone for a time, Rawls now had time to search for the footman. He ran him to ground easily.

A tall, muscular young man who had traveled to London for the first time with Mr. Meredith, the footman was happy to leave the silver polishing to the other men and go to the attic for a case that Rawls said his master needed immediately.

"Set it down there," Rawls said. He pointed to the far corner of the room. The footman did as he was bid and then turned to go. The valet cleared his throat. The footman stopped and waited for further orders. Rawls crossed to him. "I hear you have found a place to take a girl," he said in a husky voice.

The footman's eyes widened. "Not me, Mr. Rawls," he said in a nervous voice. He glanced at the door as if judging how long it would take him to escape.

"That is not what I heard."

"You heard wrong." The footman took a step toward the valet, his face angry. "Those words could get me turned off. You kick up a dust, and I will know who to blame."

Rawls stepped back quickly. "You mistake my meaning," he said hastily, wishing he had never volunteered to help his master find out anything. "I have a friend, a female, and I thought . . ."

The footman laughed in relief. He clapped Rawls on the shoulder. "I knowed what you thought. You came to the right man. There's a spot in the garden just right. Enclosed in shrubbery with a bench. No one there usually."

"But how do you get out without being seen?"

The footman threw back his head and laughed. "Want all my secrets, do you?" he asked. Rawls nodded. The footman stared at him as if trying to read his face. Finally, he said, "Find the door that looks like a window. In the basement."

"What? Where?"

"I'll say no more. I must go." Before Rawls had time to say anything, the man was gone.

While Rawls was talking with the footman, his master had taken the letter to the men he had hired to look into the matter. "What are you doing?" Richard demanded. He threw the letter down on the table in front of him.

"Lower your voice, sir," the little man in the shabby clothes said quietly. He glanced around to see if anyone in the dark and dank tavern had noticed anything. When he was assured that the noise and turmoil in the taproom were so loud that no one had heard Richard's question, he picked up the paper and read it.

"And is the brooch missing?"

"My wife confirmed it. What are you going to do?"

"What?" The man leaned across the table, a mug of ale in his hand.

"I did not hire you to have this continue," Richard said through clenched teeth. "This must stop."

"I agree. But you must give us some time." He returned the letter to Richard. "Do you recognize the hand?"

"It could be anyone's."

"Not quite."

"What?" Richard stared at him in surprise.

"Look at the letters. All perfectly formed. All spelled neatly." The man dressed in shabby clothes leaned forward until only inches separated his face from Richard's. "Whoever writ this has had schooling."

Surprised, Richard picked up the letter again and reread it. "Do you have any other clues?"

"Not now. When my partner returns, perhaps." He glanced around the taproom once again, noting one or two people who looked at them strangely. "You must leave now. And do not return."

Richard glanced around the room and noticed that at least one person had shown an unhealthy interest in their conversation. He nodded. "I want results," he said firmly. "You know where to send a message?" The man nodded. As Richard walked out the door, the man he had hired to investigate the problem stared after him, his face carefully expressionless.

When Richard arrived at the Meredith townhouse, Rawls was waiting for him. "I have learned the way they must have gotten into the house," the valet said, his voice ringing with quiet satisfaction. At his master's urging, he told the story of the footman and the maid, being careful not to give away their identities.

"Have you found this window?" Richard asked, taking off his cravat.

"Not yet. I could not think of a reason to be in the out-of-the-way areas of the basement," the valet admitted regretfully.

"Hmm. It may be a problem for me too." Richard pulled off his shirt, flinging it aside. "Are you sure the footman did not give you false information?"

"I cannot be certain of that until we find the door," Rawls said. His tone of voice and the set of his chin told Richard that his valet was not pleased.

"Of course. Now we must think of a reason to be in the basement." He smiled ruefully. "Mr. Meredith's servants will talk if I just show up down there."

"Perhaps Mrs. Blount could think of something," the valet suggested. He unfolded one of Richard's cravats to see if it needed pressing.

"A capital idea, Rawls. I will seek her out immediately," Richard said, hurrying to the door that separated their rooms.

A check of Lucy's room did not reveal anyone but her maid. "Where is my wife?" he asked, not realizing how his disappointment showed.

"I believe she is in the drawing room with Mr. Meredith, sir," Betty said quietly. She glanced at him and then bent her head over the hem she was mending. Even though her mistress kept her feelings to herself, Betty knew that there had been problems with the marriage. As far as she was concerned, all the problems had been caused by him.

Richard cursed quietly under his breath. He would have to wait. He knew that neither of them wanted to involve her father in their problems. Perhaps after dinner he would have a chance to draw her to one side.

While Richard was waiting to talk to his wife, the

writer of the note was busy. "Did you find the men we need?" she asked, her once beautiful face set in determined lines.

"Four of the biggest and most ruthless men you ever want to see," her co-conspirator said, a wicked smile on his face. "They will be ready whenever we give the signal." As if a thought had just struck him, he paused. "Are you sure this will work?"

"Fool. Of course it will if you do your part when you are supposed to. It was not my plan that failed last time," she said bitterly.

"I told you the window was locked. I had to wait until the alarm was given," he said, wishing as he did occasionally that he had left her where he had found her that night.

As if realizing what he was feeling, she smiled. "I know. I should not mention it." She stepped close to him, running her fingers over his chest and then lower. He shivered. She kissed him while her fingers caressed him. "But the thought of how *he* escaped drives me wild. He should have died."

This time her companion was the one to offer the comfort. "He will pay. I promise you that." Enthralled since the first time she had been intimate with him, he lived to please her. The woman in his arms buried her face in his shoulder and smiled.

Chapter Eleven

Lucy looked up when Richard entered the drawing room, her emotions carefully hidden. It would do no good to show him how angry she was. She had spent most of the time since tea reminding herself that he had never promised to share more than his home, his children, and his bed. Just because she no longer found their once amiable arrangement satisfying, he did not have to share her views.

"Where is Edward?" Richard asked, looking about the room as if he expected his friend to be hiding in a corner somewhere.

"With Arabella. He will be living in her pocket constantly," Mr. Meredith said. "Or at least until her family grows tired of him." He smiled. "Lud, but I remember what I was like when I was courting your mother, Lucy. Never wanted to let her out of my sight."

"Really, Papa. How long were you engaged?"

Both Lucy and Richard were surprised to see a faint blush creep up into the older man's cheeks. "A week."

"A week? Papa, what are you saying?"

"I was so afraid she would change her mind that I convinced her and she convinced her family to allow us to marry by special license. Of course, everyone in the *ton* counted the months before Edward was born."

"Papa!" Lucy was shocked.

"Now don't be missish. I meant nothing by it. He was born a respectable eleven months later." Richard had to hide a laugh at the shocked look on his wife's face.

"That is not what I meant," Lucy said hastily, her own

cheeks colored by a faint blush. "How could you support Arabella's parents in making Edward wait? They would have listened to you. How could you be so cruel?"

"No cruelty about it. When I married your mother, she had not been engaged before, much less in mourning for another man. I could not support a rushed marriage here. There will be talk enough as it is. Much better to do things slowly," he said firmly. "And your brother understands even if you do not."

"I do not think it is fair." Before she could finish her statement, Jarvis opened the door and announced dinner. She took her husband's arm. "Well, do you think it is?" she asked.

"I would not have wanted to wait that long for you," he said quietly, his mouth close to her ear. His breath on her skin made her tingle. She looked into his eyes and smiled. Mr. Meredith turned around to ask a question but turned back, a smile on his face.

Not until they were walking upstairs did Richard have a chance to talk to Lucy about the basement. "The basement? Why do you want to know about that?" she asked, her brow wrinkling.

"It may explain how that message appeared," he said quietly, opening the door to her room and following her inside. She looked up and saw Betty waiting for her. "Send her away," Richard said, his hands on her waist.

Lucy did as he asked, waiting until the door shut behind the maid before she turned to face him. "What have you learned?" she asked, her voice husky and breathless.

He looked at her parted lips. As if he could not resist, Richard bent his head and kissed her. His arms pulled her close so that she could feel him hard against her. He kissed her again, and she wound her arms around him. "You are sweet, so sweet," he murmured, forgetting for a moment why he had followed her into the room. It had been so long since he had held her.

In spite of her desire to sink into his arms, to allow him to sweep her away from all her worries, Lucy pulled back from his embrace after a few moments. "Richard?"

"Hmmm." He bent his head to kiss her again, but she pulled free and took two steps away from him. "What is wrong?"

"You wanted to talk," she reminded him.

"We can do that later," he said, taking her hand and pulling her toward him. He smiled at her beguilingly, sending fresh tingles of desire through her.

However, she refused to give in. "What about the basement?" she asked, putting her hands on his chest and holding him off.

"What basement?"

"That should be my question," she said. He took one of her hands and brought it to his lips. Making one last effort, she pulled away again. "Richard!"

This time, to her regret, he too stepped away. He shook his head as if to clear it. He took a couple of deep breaths. Then he frowned as if trying to remember something. "The basement. Let me tell you what Rawls has discovered," he said, leading her to the settee near the fireplace.

When she had heard the story, she frowned. "A window that is a door? What does that mean?" she asked.

"That is what we hoped you could tell us," Richard said. "Have you ever heard of anything like that?"

"Not that I know of. But Papa did not buy this house until it was time for my Season; he had a smaller one before that. I was only here that one time, and then I had no time to explore. Perhaps Edward or Papa could help you," she suggested, trying to find some way of relieving his worries.

He frowned. "I did not want to involve them in this," he explained. "And Edward is busy with his own life. I would not want to disturb him."

"Nonsense. They would be glad to help."

He got up and stared at the small fire that burned in the fireplace. Even though it was almost summer, the evenings were chilly. Finally, when the silence had grown almost too much to bear, he turned around. "I am

sorry for bringing you into this confusion," he said quietly.

Lucy's heart plunged into her stomach. Was he telling
her he was sorry that he had asked her to help. She lowered her head to hide her tears.

As if he recognized what she was feeling, Richard
crossed to the settee and took his place beside her. "You
must be regretting that you ever agreed to my proposal,"
he said, taking her hand in his. His finger stroked her
palm. When she did not pull away, the low spirits that
held him in their grip relaxed somewhat.

"Regret? Richard, I do not regret that," she assured
him, a faint hope beginning to blossom within her. He
had sounded so forlorn. Her tears were gone. She willed
him to look at her, unguarded for once, and to tell her
how he felt about her.

He looked up, but she could tell nothing. Once again
he wore the mask that had become all too familiar.
"Then I am a very lucky man," he said. A smile lit his
eyes and his face. He bent forward. She caught her
breath, all thought of the problems they faced lost in the
promise in his eyes.

"Richard?" she asked, her voice no louder than a
whisper. His answer was swallowed up in the kiss that
followed. This time neither tried to pull away, allowing
the passion between them to flare and spiral out of control.

As she lay in his arms much later that evening, Lucy
turned to look at him. "Richard?"

"Hmmm," he said contentedly. He reached up to twirl
one of her curls about his finger.

"We must talk."

He sighed and nodded. Pulling away, he shook the pillows and put them against the head of the bed. Then he
sat back. "About the basement," he said, a lazy edge to
his voice.

"Not just that." Over the last few days, Lucy had
come to a decision. She had postponed taking action on
it until Edward's party was over, but she knew she could

not avoid the situation forever. What it would do to her relationship with Richard was her only worry.

She sat beside him, her head on his shoulder. The silence stretched out as she tried to find exactly the right words. "Richard?"

He yawned and opened his eyes. He too was willing to put off this discussion as long as possible. "What?"

"What is it you regret getting me involved in? What is happening? What were those two letters about?" Her questions, once begun, poured out of her like water from a pitcher.

As he had done so often in the last few days, Richard wished that they could go back to the early days of their marriage before the announcement appeared. They had been so happy then. Realizing that was impossible, he sighed. Then he said, "It began about three months before the fire."

"The fire?" Lucy sat up straight in bed. "Are we talking about the same thing? Richard, I do not understand."

"If the truth be told, neither do I."

"Stop being so enigmatic," she demanded. "Just tell me what you know."

"I know the note you received is part of something bigger. Three months before the fire I began to receive notes that threatened me and my family with harm. At first, I thought they were related to the work I was doing for the government." He paused, the lines on his face more pronounced.

"And they were not?" Lucy asked, urging him on.

"Apparently not. The people my employer hired at the time did not think so. I took precautions. They still arrived."

"What did they say?"

"Mostly threats, threats I refused to take very seriously." He closed his eyes, the guilt that he had felt since the fire overwhelming him. "If I had, Julia might be alive today."

"And we would never have married." Lucy had no idea how the tone of her voice gave away the bleakness she was feeling. She had been right. He did regret their marriage.

Quickly Richard put his arms about her and drew her close. "Never say that. I do not know how I would have managed the last few weeks without you," he said. Then he tilted her face up so that he could look into her eyes. "You have brought pleasure into my life once more." As though he expected her to pull away, he kissed her.

The touch of his lips on hers drove most thoughts of regret from her mind. She melted against him, trying to pull him closer to her. Surely he could not kiss her the way he was and still wish her to perdition. Even after the kiss was over and he was simply holding her in his arms, they sat there in a comfortable silence, her head against his shoulder. Then she asked, "Are the letters you have received in London like the ones you received before?"

"How did you know I had received more than one?" he asked. For an instant he wondered if she knew more than she had told him. Then he swiftly rejected the idea.

"Richard, I saw your face this afternoon when you opened that letter. The only time I have seen you look like that was when I gave you the letter that was on my dressing table. And when you saw the announcement in the paper," she added.

He winced. "The announcement." He paused for a moment, hoping she would accept his explanation. "I am sorry about that. I overreacted."

"Overreacted? Richard, you erupted like a volcano. "Why?"

"I was afraid. When I moved the children to Devon-shire, I told almost no one where I was. My man of affairs here in London dispatched any letters to friends for me and sent theirs to me. And while no one knew where I was, the threats stopped."

"Oh." Lucy twisted around so that she could look at him. "What did the men your employer hired say about that?" Her husband looked rather embarrassed. "Richard?"

He cleared his throat. Then he said, "They did not know. I did not tell them."

"You what? Richard, how could you have been so muttonheaded?"

"I know. My mentor has already rung a peal over my head. But all I could think of was protecting my children."

The thought of the danger to the children made her hesitate. Finally she asked, "And the announcement?"

"I was afraid it would give away my location," he said quietly. He wanted to pull her close to him once more but was afraid she would resist.

"And did it?" Lucy asked, her tone of voice more hesitant than usual. If her family had put his children in danger, would he ever forgive her?

"No. The first letter came to you after we arrived in London."

Thoughtfully, she leaned back, relieved. She rested her head on his shoulder once more. He wrapped his arm around her, holding her close so that she could hear the beating of his heart under her head. "Why wait until now?" she asked, her voice so soft that her words seemed more a thought to herself than a question to him.

"I do not know," he admitted reluctantly. Once again he wondered whether he should summon his family, load the coaches, and return to Devonshire immediately.

"Is anyone looking into the problem now?" she asked a short time later. She had been sorting the information they had in her mind.

"I rehired the men who were working on the threats I received earlier," he told her. He rubbed his hand across her shoulders and kissed her neck.

Ignoring the emotions he had sent raging once more, she asked, "Is that where you went this afternoon?"

"Yes."

"Did you take them the letter you received today?"

"Yes."

Suddenly the emotions she had been holding in for so long destroyed the reticence she had learned. Reacting much as she would have done as a young girl, she turned around and hit him in the stomach. "Ouch! What was that for?" he asked indignantly, rubbing the spot where the blow had hit.

"For keeping me in the dark. Now what did the letter you received today say?" She glared at him as though he were the one who had written the letter.

"It mentioned the brooch you have lost and made a threat about my losing some other 'item.'"

"My brooch? What could someone want with that? It is not even very valuable."

"The men I hired suggested that it was a warning. If whoever delivered the letter could take that . . ." He refused to finish the sentence, fearing that giving the thought words would bring it closer to reality.

"Jewelry? Richard, we must put the pieces you gave me last evening in Papa's safe." She pulled away from him and moved to the edge of the bed.

He caught her and pulled her back. "I do not think that is what they meant," he explained.

She moved back to her original position with her head on his shoulder. "Then I do not understand."

Hesitantly, as though he were afraid that putting his thoughts in words would give them power, Richard said, "Lucy, we must take care. If fire should strike this house, your father . . ."

"Papa?" Then her eyes opened wide. She turned sideways so that she could look at him. "Richard, you are not saying . . . ?" Like him, she was afraid to finish her thought.

"That the fire was not an accident." His quiet words dropped between them like hot coals that burned their way into their brains. Although he was filled with horror at what he had just said, Richard's face was carefully blank, but Lucy's wore a look of horror.

"And you think that is what the last note meant?" she asked, her voice husky with emotion.

"I do not know. I only know that last time I let Julia persuade me that there was no danger. I begged her to go somewhere else with me. This time I plan to be better prepared." The icy note in his voice was as sharp as a winter's wind.

"Julia knew about the threats you had received?"

"Yes. Like me, she thought they were somehow connected with my job as courier. We were both wrong, and it cost Julia her life. I do not intend to take a chance with anyone else's life," Richard said angrily.

Lucy's face was thoughtful. She yawned, but her eyes were sharp as though they focused on something far in the distance. Finally she said, "We will be better prepared this time. But we can do no more tonight. But in the morning . . ."

"In the morning we will inspect the basement," he said firmly as he put his arm around her and pulled her down in the bed. Even when Lucy's measured breaths told him she was asleep, Richard stayed awake, on guard.

After breakfast the next morning, Lucy took the first step in their plan to explore the basement. Meeting with the housekeeper, she explained that her father was thinking about making some changes in the house and had asked her to inspect the areas where the renovations would be made. "I do not plan on interrupting anyone's work. If you will inform Cook and the rest of the servants that we will be there, we will try to be as inconspicuous as possible."

"We?" the housekeeper asked.

"My husband and I," Lucy said firmly, wondering how she was to explain Richard's presence, if questioned. Fortunately, the housekeeper nodded and rustled out of the room.

When they descended into the basement a short time later, the housekeeper met them at the foot of the stairs. "I will be happy to answer any questions you have," she said firmly, falling in behind them. Lucy and Richard exchanged glances. They had not expected her presence. As quickly as possible they inspected the rooms where people were working, looking for the window that Rawls had mentioned. At first they found nothing. Just when they were ready to give up, they walked through the food area one more time. That is when they noticed a window in the cool vault that opened into a passage that led to the garden.

"How long has this window been like this?" Lucy asked, pointing at the boards that partially covered the window.

"Since I first came here," the housekeeper said, wondering at their interest.

"Let me check," Richard said in a whisper. "Distract her so that I can look it over." Lucy nodded.

"Are you satisfied with the arrangement down here?" Lucy asked the woman who accompanied them. "What changes would you make?"

"I am sure I will be happy with anything the master wants to do. It was he who insisted that the kitchen be equipped with one of the new closed stoves. It has made quite a difference in the kitchen," the housekeeper said.

"You do not find it dark?"

"We have considerably more light than many other homes have. And the skylights in the kitchen have helped to brighten the entire story. It would not be safe to have more. Anyone could get in." She paused and looked around. Noticing Richard standing by the window, she crossed to his side. "Now, this window is a waste. Whoever heard of having a cool vault with a window. Defeats its purpose it does." Richard merely nodded. "Now that is one thing that should be changed. Brick it up."

"I agree," said Richard, walking to Lucy's side. "We will be certain to tell Mr. Meredith your recommendation." He took his wife's arm. "Thank you for your help. If we need further information, we will return. We apologize for taking so much of your time." Lucy glanced at him but could not tell from his face whether the window was the one they wanted. She said her good-byes and allowed Richard to whisk her up the stairs to the drawing room.

After the door closed behind them, she turned to him. "Well, what do you think? Was Rawls right?"

"Yes. The boards are not nailed in place. Anyone could move them without much effort." His face was thoughtful.

"What do we do now?" she demanded, clasping her hands together so they would not shake.

"We brick it up." He took two steps toward the door and then stopped. "I forgot. What will your father say?"

"About what?"

"About my making changes in his property. We cannot fob him off as we did the housekeeper."

"Oh." Lucy was quiet for a few moments. Then her face brightened. "You can explain what has been happening." She looked at the grimace on his face. "He will understand."

"Understand that I put his daughter in danger. If you had been Caroline and I had been the father, I am not certain I would be very understanding."

"Papa will not stand in our way. You will see," she promised.

To her surprise, her father was just as upset as Richard had thought he might be. "Threats? In my house? Who is it?" Mr. Meredith said in a voice that was only a few degrees lower than a roar.

When Richard explained that they still had no idea, Lucy's father grew quiet. "What can I do to help?" he asked, looking from one to the other.

"We have found a window, a way into the house, that we think whoever left the notes has been using," Lucy said. She perched on the arm of his chair, her arm around his shoulders.

"And?" Mr. Meredith tried to make his voice gruff. He spoiled the effect by slipping his arm around his daughter's waist.

"We would like to have it bricked up," Richard explained. "Your housekeeper thinks it is a good idea. She has had boards put over it to keep the light out of the cool vault. The bricks will only disturb the people who have been using it to sneak in and out."

"Probably knows the maids are slipping out that way to meet someone too," Mr. Meredith said. He glanced from Lucy to Richard and back. Then he cleared his throat. Lucy slipped from the arm of the chair and stood next to her husband. Richard slipped an arm around her waist possessively. "Do it," the older man said quietly. "And let me know if any more of those letters arrive."

Before the day was over, workmen had covered the outside of the window with bricks. Supervising the work from the garden, Richard breathed a sigh of satisfaction and then turned once again to his wife and his children, who had been just as interested as he in the job at hand. Both of the boys would have helped the men if Richard had not kept them out of the way. "We could carry some bricks, Da," Robert had protested when Richard had once again found him dogging the footsteps of the two large workmen.

"Or we could hand them the tools," David suggested. They both wore the pleading looks that Richard found so hard to resist.

"And then be too dirty for a walk in the park," Lucy said. She smiled up at her husband.

"Are we going to the park today?" Robert asked.

"The one with the cows?" Caroline's eyes grew big with excitement. "Da said that next time we could have some milk. Isn't that right, Da?"

"I said that?" Richard asked, his eyes still on the workmen. Then he looked at Caroline and smiled.

"You did. He promised. Tell him, David," Caroline said. She was jumping up and down with excitement.

"You would rather have milk than ices?" her father asked. He watched the workmen put the last brick in place and then turned to his family. "I thought you might enjoy a different outing?"

"Where are we going?" David wanted to know.

Richard looked at Lucy and smiled. "To see the menagerie."

"What kind of animals are there?" Robert asked.

"We shall have to see. I have not been there in years," his father told him. "Now hurry inside and get ready." He watched them go. Then he turned back to his wife. "Will you go with us?"

She smiled up at him. "With pleasure," she said. Unable to resist the temptation although they were in full view of the workmen and anyone else who happened to walk into the garden, he kissed her.

Then she stepped back, her face tinged with pink. "I must change into something more appropriate," she said, glancing down at the amber morning gown she wore. "Tell the children I will not be long." She hurried into the house.

Richard inspected the bricked-up window once more and paid the workmen. Then he too entered the house, satisfied that he had foiled whoever was threatening him.

Chapter Twelve

Across town the nondescript man Richard had hired to find out who was threatening him frowned as he heard the report of his partner. "Then we know nothing more than before?" he asked sharply.

"Strange, it is. Must be someone who knows him well," his partner told him taking a deep draft of ale. He wiped his mouth on the back of his hand.

"Did you talk to the servants?"

"They would have nothing to do with me. Seems someone has already made them suspicious." He leaned across the table so that no one else could hear. "Hired a couple of watchers. No one will go in or out without our knowing it."

"Good idea. Think I will add someone to watch them when they leave the house too."

" 'Twill cost a pretty penny," his partner complained. "Will he pay?"

"Already has." The man who met with Richard held up a bag that jingled. "Told me not to worry about cost." He smiled. "Also promised more when we find 'em."

" 'Twon't be easy. Not like our usual. No real motive. Do you suppose he has told us all?" The second man scratched his head while he waited for a reply.

"Hmmm. Could have been hiding something. Send him a message. Have him meet us but not here. A second visit would cause talk." The two men nodded.

When Richard returned from his outing with the children, the message was waiting for him. Lucy watched him open the sheet. She was trembling. He frowned. "Well?" she asked.

"The men I hired need to meet with me," he told her, frowning.

"May I go with you."

"No. A lady has no place in the part of town where I must go. You rest." The tenderness in his voice softened his refusal. "And do not tell me you do not need to rest," he said sternly. He smiled at her. "You are limping, a sure sign that you are tired. You should have refused to go with us this afternoon."

"Richard, you must not try to wrap me in cotton wool just because I limp. I would hate to be left behind," she said quietly. Her face was serious. Richard stared at her, captivated by the quiet appeal in her voice. "I want to be a part of the children's life, a part of your life. I cannot do that if you insist that I stay at home."

Realizing that they were standing in the hallway with a footman and a maid hovering close by, Richard merely said, "Rest until dinner. We can discuss this further in private." Then Lucy noticed the servants and nodded. "We will talk when I return," he promised. He watched as she walked up the stairs. Then he took his hat and left the house.

As he walked into the tavern where he had been told to come, he looked around. To his surprise, the room was dim but clean. Here and there were tables set in alcoves for privacy. At some of those tables were men dressed as well as he. He surveyed the room, trying to identify faces, but he quickly realized that it would be impossible. While he was standing there, a large man came up to him. "Are you expected?" he asked.

Richard stared at him for a moment. Then he nodded.

"Your name?" Richard told him. "This way." Winding their way through the room, the large man led him to an alcove set in the back wall and covered by a curtain. His escort drew back the curtain and let Richard walk through.

"Glad you was so prompt, Mr. Blount," said the man

whom he had interrogated only yesterday. "Have a seat. This is my partner, Mr. Jones."

"Smith and Jones. Interesting names," Richard said with a sardonic smile. "What is this place?"

"A place where privacy can be had among other things," the man he had been told to call Jones said.

"For a price," his partner Smith said. Richard nodded.

"What have you learned?" Richard asked, looking from one to the other. If he had been in a crowd with either, he knew he would never have recognized them. Even here they seemed to blend into the background.

They looked at one another. Then Smith said, "Nothing. That is why we asked you to come."

"Nothing." Richard stood up. "Then you are telling me that you are giving up the case?" His voice was cold and quiet. He stared at them, his gray eyes hard and filled with a dangerous light.

As if one, the two of them stood up, shoulder to shoulder, ready for trouble. "Sit down, sir," Smith said, his voice calm. "Naught was said about our quitting." Richard looked at the two of them and then took his seat again. "Just need more information."

Richard relaxed. "Ask your questions."

Smith glanced at Jones, who indicated that he should begin. "Tell us where you have been and what you have done since you arrived in town."

"I already told you that," Richard protested.

"Tell us again. Could have missed something," Jones said quietly. Looking from one to the other, Richard complied.

When he mentioned the theater, Smith stopped him. "Anyone show special interest that night?"

Richard did not have to stop and think. "We were the center of all eyes," he admitted.

"Why?" Jones asked suspiciously.

"My wife was the Incomparable of her Season. But she refused to return to town until now. Everyone who had the slightest acquaintance with her tried to get her attention."

"No one special?" Smith asked, his brow wrinkled.

"No." Richard stopped. "There was one person. Her former fiancé."

"Could he bear a grudge against you?" Jones asked.

"Doubt it. It was he who allowed the engagement to be broken. Besides that was eight years ago."

"Grudges have been kept alive longer than that," Smith reminded him. "What is his name?"

Richard told him. Then he frowned. "That would mean that the notes I received before the fire were not connected to these," he said pensively. He frowned. "And I cannot believe that is true."

"Fire? What fire?" Jones demanded. He glared at Richard as though he had never seen him before.

"I told you about that," Richard said defensively.

"In passing," Smith said. "Tell us more."

Richard looked from one to the other. Then he began his story. They listened carefully, interrupting only when he skipped a detail they thought might be important or when they wanted more information. "Then I moved the children to Devonshire," he said, bringing his story to an end.

"And how long were you there?" Smith asked.

"Over a year. I came back to London because my wife wanted to be present at the engagement party for her brother."

"Your wife. Hmmm. How well did you know her before you married?" Jones asked.

Richard's temper flared. "I will not listen to any accusations about my wife. She is innocent."

"No accusations meant, sir," Smith said hastily, trying to soothe him. He glared at his partner.

"Just thought someone in her past might be making the threats," Jones added.

"I told you she was not the problem," Richard said firmly. "She was not part of my life when the first letters arrived."

Smith and Jones glanced at one another. Then Smith said, "You think whoever wrote the letters is after you."

Richard nodded. "Perhaps Jones should visit your former home and make a few inquiries."

"What could he hope to find out there?" Richard asked.

"Perhaps nothing. What happened to your servants?" Jones asked. He leaned forward, staring at the man who had employed him.

"Most still live there. They keep up what is left of the property."

"You did not take them to Devonshire with you?"

"No, most of them had families in the neighborhood." Richard paused, looking at his clenched hands. "And I wanted servants I could be sure of."

"You think some of your people were part of the problem?" Smith asked, his face serious.

"I do not know. At the time I was only interested in protecting my family."

"Hmmm." Smith looked at his partner. "You will talk to them?" Jones nodded. "Be on your way."

Before Richard could stop him, Jones had slipped out of the alcove and was gone. "But what about now? What are you doing to protect my family?"

"All that we can." In the next few minutes, Smith explained about the men he had hired. "But do not let them go out without an escort of their own. I can suggest a footman or two, men who are known for their strength and brains. If you need extra—"

"That will not be necessary," Richard assured him. He rose. "I will expect to hear from you regularly," he said firmly, his hand on the curtain. Smith nodded.

As he made the journey back to his father-in-law's home, Richard tried to convince himself that nothing could touch his family, that he had done all that he could to keep them safe. That assurance did not last past the front door.

As if she had recognized his step, Lucy came flying from the drawing room. "Come quickly," she said, grabbing his hand and pulling him toward the door.

"What is wrong?"

"David." He stopped, but she did not. "Come. He needs you," she said frantically.

He followed her into the drawing room. Mr. Meredith held his oldest son in his arms. The boy was trembling and crying. "What has happened?"

"He returned from playing in the park in the center of the square this way," Lucy explained. "According to Mr. Avery and Mrs. Stanhope nothing out of the ordinary happened."

Richard crossed to the Bath chair. "I will take him now, sir," he said quietly, picking David up in his arms. For a few moments, his son went wild, thrashing about trying to get free. Then he went limp. Richard took a seat on the settee, holding him close. Then he noticed Robert and Caroline, their eyes wide and their faces frightened, staring at them. "Lucy," he said softly. She hurried to his side. "Take the other children upstairs, please." She nodded and gestured to the other two children.

When the door had closed behind them, Mr. Meredith cleared his throat. He watched the way Richard held his son so that the boy did not hurt himself even when he struggled to be free. "Should I send for the doctor?" he asked quietly.

Richard looked up, his face set in hard lines. "Not yet. Let me see if I can calm him." He loosened his arms about David. The boy began to struggle to get free once more. "Hush, David. Be quiet for a time."

"I must go. She wants me," the boy said frantically.

"He has been saying that over and over since they brought him in. What does he mean?" Mr. Meredith asked.

Richard did not answer the older man. All of his attention was for his son. Finally, the boy stopped struggling. But the litany of his words went on. "She wants me. I must go to her."

When the door opened again, David stiffened as if he feared what he would see. Only Lucy entered. He slumped in his father's arms. Richard tightened them about him. Gradually, David's wild sobs began to fade, the words becoming a senseless mumble. The three adults waited until he grew calm; then his breathing slowed as though he were sleeping.

"Exhausted, poor little chap," Mr. Meredith said with a sigh. "Anyone able to tell you what set him off?"

"Mr. Avery and Mrs. Stanhope say nothing out of the ordinary occurred. He stopped to pet a dog that a lady was walking. Apparently he was quite taken with it. He started to follow it out of the park. Mr. Avery caught him. Then, according to Caroline and Robert, David fell into a fit of rage. Mr. Avery had to pick him up and carry him home," Lucy said. "They are quite disturbed, Richard. I promised that you and I would see them before they went to bed."

"A fit of rage? That does not sound at all like David. What could have happened?" Richard asked.

"And who was the lady? Must live about here somewhere to be in the square," Mr. Meredith reminded them. He patted his face with a large handkerchief, his hand trembling slightly. After his attempts to quiet David, he was aching all over and longed for his bed. But he did not intend to be fobbed off with some story that Lucy told him for his own good.

"The lady? Did either of the children mention her?" Richard looked up at his wife.

"They were more interested in her dog," Lucy told him. "We could ask Mr. Avery and Mrs. Stanhope; perhaps they noticed something." Lucy sat down beside her husband, her hand stroking the boy's hair away from his forehead. "He is so young to be so troubled." As she had done before, she wished she could absorb all the pain that the boy felt, leaving him young and happy and carefree.

"I had better get him up to bed," Richard said quietly. He stood up and shifted the boy in his arms.

"Make him drink a sleeping draught when you get him in bed. You do not want him awake before morning." Although Mr. Meredith's voice was quiet, Richard recognized the command. Nodding, he made his way to the door. Lucy was before him and opened it.

By the time they had put David to bed and given him the sleeping potion, both of them were exhausted. They looked at each other and sighed. "What I would give for a nice, quiet, usual day," Richard said, stretching to release the tight muscles in his neck and back. Lucy nodded. She yawned, too tired to cover her mouth. "Are the other two still awake?"

She glanced at the window where light was still streaming through. "They should be. It is still quite early. But I feel as though it should be midnight."

"Let us talk to them. Then we can have a quiet supper in our rooms." He put his arm around her and led her to the door. He reached for the latch and then stopped. "I wish I did not have to do this," he said, his confusion and despair evident in his voice. Lucy nodded her agreement.

The scene in the schoolroom assured them. Caroline and Robert, their faces too solemn and their eyes still frightened, were eating their supper. As soon as they saw their father and stepmother, they froze. Then casting a quick look at their teachers, they started eating again. As she watched Caroline struggle to swallow a bite of bread and butter, Lucy realized that the children would be more comfortable if they were alone with Richard and her. "Why not take this time to yourselves," she suggested to their teachers. "We will stay until the children go to bed." As soon as the door closed behind them, she sent the nurserymaid off to get her own supper. "I will ring when we need you again, Mary," she said.

When they were alone with the children, Richard sat at the table with them, trying to make light conversation while Lucy sat in a chair nearby. Eventually, Caroline and Robert finished their meal. Knowing that he could not postpone the questions any longer, Richard looked at Lucy. She nodded. "I was surprised to hear that you had gone to the square after our walk in the park," he said. "Do you go there often?"

Caroline crawled up in Lucy's lap. Robert stood close to his father. "Mr. Avery was teaching us about leaves. We were to find three different kinds. Here are mine," he reached in his pocket and pulled out a crumpled mass of green.

"I lost mine when David . . ." Caroline said, her face puckering up as though she were about to cry. Lucy tightened her arms around her.

Robert's face lost its brightness. "David ruins everything," he said angrily. "I was going to win a prize for my leaves. Now Mr. Avery does not even want to see them."

"Put them on your dresser overnight. He will feel different in the morning," his father said. "Besides David did not intend to ruin your outing."

"But he did. Why did he act that way? He is always telling me what a baby I am, but he is the one who is a baby!"

Richard hugged his son, wishing that he had some answers. "Maybe you can help me so that I can keep this from happening again," his father suggested.

"How?"

Caroline, who had been silent up to now, sat up on Lucy's lap, bringing an involuntary moan of pain from her as the muscles in her leg protested. But when the little girl would have slipped down from her lap, she held her tight. "I think it was that lady," Caroline said in a little voice.

"What lady?" Lucy asked, her face a mask that hid the hope she felt.

"The one in black. With the dog." Caroline leaned back again, her head against Lucy's breast.

"Did you see her too?" Richard asked Robert. The boy nodded. "Did she try to speak to you?"

"No. I was busy choosing my leaves. But she said something to David."

"What did she say?" his father asked. Richard's heart was beating so fast he could hardly hear the boy's answer.

"I do not know."

"He looked scared," Caroline said. "I stayed close to Mrs. Stanhope 'cause you told me not to talk to strangers." She looked up at her stepmother to see if Lucy approved. Lucy smiled down at her.

"What did she look like?" Lucy asked, smoothing back the curls that clustered around Caroline's face.

"Like the witches in the tales that David reads."

"And how could you tell?" her brother taunted her. "She had a veil over her face."

"Did she?" Richard asked his daughter. Caroline nodded. "What else do you remember?"

"She had a dog," Robert said quickly, cutting off his sister's answer.

"And she was alone." Caroline looked up at Lucy. "She must not have been a nice person." Both Richard and Lucy stared at her.

"Why?" Lucy asked.

"Mrs. Stanhope says a lady does not go out alone." Both Lucy and Richard had to smile because the little girl sounded so much like her governess. Lucy gave Caroline a hug.

Before his father could ask any other questions, Robert leaned against his shoulder, his face serious but also somewhat embarrassed. "Da, can I have a candle tonight?"

"A candle?"

"Me too," Caroline said. "It gets so dark."

"Are you sure that is what you want?" he asked, remembering how the sight of a flame had upset them for weeks after the fire. "You know that Mary will be nearby all night."

"Just for tonight, Da," Robert pleaded. Richard looked at Lucy for advice. Slowly, she nodded.

"Just for tonight," he said, giving his son a hug. "If you remember anything else about this afternoon, you can tell me tomorrow."

"Like how ugly the dog was?" Caroline asked.

"Was it, sweetheart?" Lucy smiled at her. "What did it look like?"

"Like one of those nasty dogs Mama used to have."

"Is that right, Robert?" his father wanted to know. His face did not show the tension he felt.

"Yes. I suppose this means we will not be able to go back to the square," he said angrily. "David spoils everything."

Wisely, his father did not say anything. For a few minutes the four of them sat there quietly. Then Caroline yawned. "Time for bed," Lucy whispered. The little girl tried to protest but yawned again. Reluctantly, she slipped off Lucy's lap. Going to her father, she gave him a kiss on the cheek but ignored her brother. Lucy stood up, her leg shaky from the extra weight it had borne. "I will help you get ready," she said, holding out her hand. Caroline took it and led her into her bedroom.

"Do I have to go to bed now, Da?" Robert asked.

"What do you usually do?"

"David and I play some game while Mary helps Caroline."

"Well, David is not available. Will I do?" his father asked. When Lucy returned from tucking the little girl into bed, the two of them were deeply involved. She kissed Robert's cheek and told her husband that she would be in their room and that she would send Mary up right away. He nodded.

When he rejoined her sometime later, she asked, "Did he tell you anything else?"

"No. I think he was truly more interested in those leaves than anything else. Caroline saw more than he did." He sighed. "I will have to wait until David wakes to learn more."

"Do you think he will tell you?" she asked, brushing her curls back away from her face. She turned to look at him, the rich peach velvet of her dressing gown giving a glow to her face.

He stood behind her, his hands on her shoulders. "I do

not know." The sadness in his voice was more than she could bear.

"Richard, do not let this tear you apart," she said, standing up so that she could face him.

"How can I not?"

"Then you are giving the person who sent those letters to you power over your life," she said angrily.

"What do you mean?" he asked. He took a step or two back from her, not certain at whom her anger was directed.

"Think about what is happening to your life."

"I have done little else since we arrived in London." His temper was starting to build. "I have no intention of ignoring the threats as I did last time."

"Last time you were alone in your fears. Now I am here." She paused. Then a look of terror crossed her face. "You think what happened to David today was part of the threats," she said in a horrified voice.

He glared at her, wishing she had not spoken his fears aloud. He nodded. Her face turned white. "I will tell Smith about it tomorrow."

"Smith?"

"One of the men I have hired to look into the matter. I met with him and his partner today."

"What did they say?" Before he could answer, a noise at the door caused them to start. Lucy smiled. "Probably our supper." She crossed the room and opened the door.

Although neither of them was truly hungry, they made a good meal, each eating in order to encourage the other. When the footman had cleared away the last dish and they were alone once more, Lucy asked again, "What did the men you hired have to say?"

Richard reached up to brush back the curls that had fallen in his face. As little as he wanted to discuss the situation, he acknowledged that she had a right to know. He had put her in danger too. Before he could change his mind, he gave her a rough outline of what the men had said.

"What do they hope to find on your estate?" she wondered, her face wrinkled into a frown.

"Even they do not know." As he sat there staring into the small fire that took the chill off the room, his mind tried to find answers for what was happening. Suddenly, he sat up straight. "The watchers!"

"The who?"

"Smith said he hired someone to watch the house and to watch over us when we left it."

Lucy made the connection immediately. "Do you think he saw what happened this afternoon?"

Richard sank back against the settee, his eyes clouded. "I do not know. I suppose it would depend on when these people started."

Another thought crossed Lucy's mind. "Are they watching everyone?"

"I do not know. Why?"

"How will they know who belongs here and who does not?" she asked.

"Jones said they had already made inquiries. Between your maid and my valet, however, those inquiries were not successful," he said ruefully.

"What do you mean?" Lucy asked indignantly.

"No one wants to answer any more questions. After the way we bricked up that window, Rawls is not in good odor any longer."

"Why him and not Betty?"

"I suppose because he was the one who knew about that window to the garden. Slipping away from the house will be much harder now." He reached over and pulled her close to him. She put her head on his shoulder. For a few minutes there was silence.

Finally, she said, "Richard, I think we must tell Edward what has happened."

"Why? It would only upset him. He deserves to have a carefree existence for a time."

"I agree, but I also know my brother. If we do not tell him, he will be angry. Especially when he finds out that Papa knows."

"How will he find out?"

She turned to look at him, amazement written all over her face. "Richard, you are joking, are you not?"

"What?"

"You must know that the servants are talking—maybe not to the people you hired but among themselves. Edward is certain to find out. You need to talk to him tonight."

"Now?" He realized the wisdom of her words but did not want to leave her.

"As soon as he comes home. He told Papa that Arabella wanted an early night to get ready for the Venetian breakfast tomorrow. He will not be late."

"Unless he goes to his club," Richard reminded her. In spite of his words, he got up and used her brush on his hair, trying to tame it into the style he usually wore. He glanced at the bed. "Do we have to go to this breakfast too?" he asked.

"I must go," she told him, "but you may stay at home." She began to plan an excuse that Arabella would accept.

"You accepted for us both, did you not?" She nodded. "Then we both will go. What time are we supposed to be there?"

"I promised to arrive about eleven, but most people will arrive much later. For some reason Arabella is nervous," Lucy said with a smile. She stood up and took the brush from his hand. With one or two strokes she had tamed the last unruly lock of his hair. She smoothed his collar and then stood back. "There. Now you are presentable again."

"You know I would rather stay here with you," Richard told her, wrapping his arms around her and trapping her within them.

"I will be here," she promised, delighted by the possessive reaction he was displaying. At moments like these she allowed herself to hope that something powerful was tying them together. He bent his head and whispered in her ear. She turned bright red. "Richard!"

"Do not forget," he said quietly. He bent his head and kissed her. The desire that flared between them washed all thoughts of the threats from his mind. His arms tightened around her, pulling her so close to him that she could feel the heat of his body through her dressing gown.

Lucy longed to allow his passion to sweep her away, but she knew she must not. Breaking free of his arms, she stepped back, one hand cradling the side of his face. "Richard," she said softly. He turned his head and kissed her hand. "Richard."

"Hmmm."

"You need to talk to Edward," she reminded him. He kissed her hand again. She wanted to forget about their problems and give in to him. But ignoring her problems had not helped her in the past. They needed her brother's help. And to gain it, Richard had to talk to Edward. She stepped back further. Reluctantly, he nodded. "Do not be long," she said as she walked to the door with him.

While Richard waited in the study for Edward to return, he thought about the changes that his marriage to Lucy had brought. Neither of them had expected to plunge into the *ton* once more. But Richard had to admit that, except for the threats he had received and David's reactions, coming to town had been the right decision. He had not realized how much he had missed the companionship of other men. And Lucy, Lucy had brought happiness back into his life. Before he could analyze the situation further, the door to the study opened.

"You wanted to see me, Richard," Edward said. He crossed to the table where the wine decanter sat. "Shall I pour you some?" he asked. "Drank orgeat all evening. Vile stuff."

"Why?"

"Lud, I do not know. Some fancy of the hostess. Someone told me she's a Methodist."

"And no one complained?"

"Are you mad? Of course, we complained. You should have been in the garden blowing a cloud like I was. Every gentleman there threatened to refuse any further invitations if the situation did not change."

"And did it?"

"Not publicly. I understand that her husband arranged for a footman to provide wine in the library for anyone who wanted some." Edward stretched. "However, I was not about to leave Arabella to the circling wolves."

"Wolves? Come now, Edward. Even the most randy of them know she is spoken for," Richard reminded him.

"Does no good. I still do not like to see them around her, complimenting her hair, her eyes. Makes me angry." Edward yawned and stretched. "But you did not wait for me to talk about my problems."

"No, you are right. What I need to talk about are mine." Richard took a deep breath, wondering where to start.

"Yours? Are you and Lucy having problems?" Edward asked, his face as dark as a thunder cloud.

"No. Not the way you mean. Lucy is the best thing that has happened to me in a very long time," Richard said quickly.

"Explain then." Edward took a seat and pulled a stool over so that he could prop up his feet. His eyes never left Richard's.

By the time that Richard had completed the story, Edward was no longer lounging in his chair. He leaned forward, his hands clenched on his knees. When his brother-in-law had finished, he got up and began circling the room. When the tension between them stretched almost to the breaking point, Richard asked, "Will you help?"

"How can you doubt me? Why did you not tell me before this?"

"Edward, I did not want to disturb you with my problems," Richard said quietly.

"Your problems? Richard, any problems that affect my sister affect me too. Besides, if I have more to think about, watching Arabella flit here and there will not drive me mad with jealousy."

"Jealous? You?"

"Do not mock me, Richard. You cannot know how much I have suffered. Now, tell me what I can do to help."

By the time the two of them walked up the stairs to go to bed the level of brandy had been decreased considerably and both of them were as satisfied as they could be that they had the situation in hand.

In yet another quarter of the city, a man watched a woman pace angrily about the room. "I almost had him," she said through clenched teeth. "If you had been quicker."

"Quicker? With everyone round? We would have been taken before we could get away," he said, grabbing her arm. "Give this up. Let us go to the colonies."

"Go and leave him unpunished?" Her eyes flashed at him. "And what about money?"

"We have enough."

She laughed. "Enough for what? A measly farm? I do not plan to live like a farmer's wife. I must have luxuries." Wisely, he did not remind her that they would have had ample funds if she had not gambled so much of it away.

"Did you leave the other letter?" she asked. Her eyes fastened on his like a wild animal fixes on his prey.

"No." Seeing her face flush with red, making her scars stand out, he explained. "They have bricked up the window."

"Hmmm." She smiled wickedly. "Maybe we will have to find another way. Are the men ready?"

"As soon as you give the signal."

"Good. You watch them. I must not be seen around there again." She picked up the small dog that was pawing at her dress and smiled wickedly.

Chapter Thirteen

When morning came, both Lucy and Richard were determined to find out who was making the threats and what had caused David to react as he did. As she dressed for the Venetian breakfast, Richard talked with David. When her husband walked back into the room a short time later, Lucy knew the news was not good. "What did he say?" she asked.

He looked at her maid and did not say anything. Lucy understood. She sat patiently while Betty put the last pin in place and then dismissed her. As soon as the door had closed, Richard said, "He said nothing."

"Nothing?"

"He will not speak to me or to anyone else. He just lies there as though he had seen something horrible." Richard leaned against the mantel, staring into the empty fireplace. "I do not know what to do." The frustration and sorrow in his voice hurt Lucy.

She crossed the room and put her hand on his. "Perhaps we should send for the doctor," she said quietly. He reached out and took her in his arms, holding her as if she were a lifeline and he was drowning. "I am sure Papa has one he could recommend."

"He is so little. What am I going to do if he is always like this?" Richard asked, his voice breaking. "In spite of the horrible fire that brought it about, this last year I have enjoyed becoming better acquainted with my children. David would follow me around, ask questions." He closed his eyes as though in terrible pain. "Will he ever respond to me again?"

"David has always been the one you worried about. Remember how he treated me when I first arrived. But he began to come around before we came to London," she said in a soothing voice.

"And look where he is now. There must be something I can do." His arms tightened around her, crushing the freshly ironed muslin gown that she wore. She said nothing but held him tightly. Soon he loosened his arms and stood back. "There must be something," he said once again.

Lucy's eyes brightened. "Did you not say that Smith and . . . and . . ." Not remembering the name irritated her. She paused.

"Jones?" he asked.

"Yes. You said they had hired someone to watch the house. Perhaps that person saw what happened to David. The square is only a few steps away."

Richard's face lost its somber expression. "I will get in touch with him immediately." He reached for her and pulled her back into his arms. "You are a wonderful wife and a wise person!" he said as he kissed her. Lucy beamed up at him, thrilled by his reactions. A knock at the door interrupted them.

"Come," Richard called.

Neither expected Jarvis. They looked from one to another in astonishment. "A messenger just delivered this. He said it was urgent," the butler explained, handing Richard a sealed note.

Gingerly, as though he were reaching for a snake, Richard picked it up and broke the seal. Reading the signature, he relaxed. "Thank you, Jarvis. I will ring when I have an answer."

"Who is it from?" Lucy asked. The look on his face told her it was not another threat. "Smith and Jones?"

"No, my man of business." Richard unfolded the letter. As he read it, he frowned.

"What is wrong?" Lucy asked.

"Someone has broken into my house," he said, still frowning.

"In Devonshire?"

"No. The one here in London. I told you I was thinking about getting it ready for us to live in the next time we are in town. I suggested that Mr. Ledsworth hire someone to put it in order." He paused, looking at the letter again.

"And?" she asked impatiently.

"When he took them to the house, they realized almost immediately that something was wrong. He wants to meet me there as soon as possible to see if anything is missing."

"Now?"

"It will have to be later. I must send a message to Smith. Then I will go." As he turned to go, he remembered the breakfast. He smiled ruefully. "Do you think Arabella will forgive me if I do not appear at her party?"

"She will understand," Lucy assured him. This problem on top of the others made her realize how little their social obligations meant. "Shall I tell Papa and Edward?"

"Not yet. I may need their help later." He kissed her, wrinkling her dress even further. "I am leaving you without an escort," he said ruefully.

"Nonsense. Edward will be there. Besides Arabella asked me to arrive before anyone else. No one will notice." Her eyes widened in horror as an idea crossed her mind. "Do you think this is what the threats meant?" she asked.

"Perhaps." As soon as he had read the note, he had wondered. "I will let you know what I find out," he promised, his hand on the latch. "Are we promised anywhere this evening?"

"A ball given by Arabella's cousin. Shall I send our regrets."

"No. Just tell Rawls. I will be back before then." Before she had time to ask what she was supposed to tell his valet, he was gone. She glanced in the mirror, made a face as she realized how crumpled her dress was, and then rang for her maid. She would have to change before she left.

By the time Richard arrived at his townhouse, both Mr. Ledsworth and Smith were waiting, the former keeping suspicious eyes on the latter. "Tell him you hired me," Smith demanded. "He looks at me as if he thinks I'm the thief."

Quickly, Richard made the introductions. Only then did Ledsworth relax. "Interesting. Let me show you around." As they walked into one of the two main rooms on the ground floor, it was evident that someone had been at work. Dustcovers were spread haphazardly around most of the room.

"Did the people you hired do this?" Richard asked.

"It was like this when we arrived," Ledsworth assured him. "Since I had inspected it for you after you left the last time, I knew something was wrong."

"You are right. Let us see what is missing." As they walked through the two rooms on that floor, Richard noted several missing items, including several small figures that his first wife had insisted they purchase. A painting was gone from the wall to the left of the fireplace. And when they walked into the library, there were gaps in the books on the shelves although the dustcovers over the furniture had not been disturbed. "Damn," he muttered as he tried to remember just what books went where.

"Were they valuable?" Smith asked, taking notes.

"If they were the ones I think they were, very," Richard said angrily. He checked the shelves to see if his edition of Shakespeare's First Folio were still there. It was gone. "Damn and blast!" he said, more upset by the missing books than the painting or china figures.

"Can you get me a list of the books missing?" Smith asked, checking the room carefully. Richard nodded. Ledsworth raised his eyebrows as if to ask a question. "May be able to find out who bought them," Smith explained. "Was anything else disturbed?"

"We looked no further," Ledsworth admitted.

"What about the plate room?" Richard asked suddenly. The other two just stared at him. "Where we store the silver," he explained.

"Do you always leave it here?" Smith asked, plainly disapproving.

"Not usually, or at least not all. But Julia saw no use in moving it to the country when we planned to return so soon. We took only a few pieces with us to supplement what was already there. After the fire, I forgot about it."

"Where is this room?"

Richard led them down into the basement, past the kitchen and scullery, and to a small door. It was closed but at his touch sprang open. In the dim light of the candle he carried, they could see broken china and crockery about the floor. "Someone has been here," Ledsworth said unhappily.

"Cleaned you out. Should never leave such valuables lying about," Smith added.

Richard just looked at the confusion. Then he cursed. "I should have hired a caretaker," he said angrily. Wisely, Mr. Ledsworth did not remind him that he had suggested just such a situation.

By the time they had checked the inventory of the house against what remained, the afternoon was far gone. Smith had inspected each room before he would allow them to enter but did not tell them what he was looking for. Finally, Richard sent Ledsworth on his way after telling him to hire servants and clean the place thoroughly. Then he turned to Smith. "Well, what do you think? Is this related to the threats?"

Smith frowned. Then he shook his head. "Too much dust," he said thoughtfully.

"Dust?"

"No signs of a recent disturbance. No signs of footprints being covered over. Had to have happened sometime ago. Probably soon after you left."

"Are you certain?"

"As certain as I can be," Smith assured him.

"Then it was just a robbery," Richard asked, unwilling

to give up the idea that this thievery was connected to the threats.

"I did not say that," Smith was quick to reply. "Whoever did it knew what he was looking for. Knew too not to disturb anything that could be seen through the windows." Smith walked around the room and pointed out what he meant. Although Richard had not noticed it before, the pattern was evident. A valuable painting still hung in the drawing room while another was missing from the opposite wall. "No broken windows or forced door. He had time. Probably made several trips, came in the servants' entrance, carrying a parcel or two. No one would notice if he took something back. Neighbors, if they noticed, would think you were redecorating."

"Then I must count everything as lost?" Richard asked, looking about the drawing room again. As much as he disliked being robbed, the only things he would truly miss were his books. He looked around again, struck by a new idea. Lucy might enjoy replacing the rest, refurbishing the whole place.

"I did not say that. We will ask around, see if anyone has sold any of the items." Smith took one last look around.

As they walked to the door, Richard remembered the other matter. "Have you had a chance to question the men who were watching my house."

"Not yet. Came right here. Will go there now. I will send you word by morning. Want me to send someone to stay here until Ledsworth finds someone for you?"

Richard agreed, giving Smith one of the keys from a ring he had brought with him. Hurrying back home, he made his first stop the schoolroom. "Has he improved?" he asked Mr. Avery anxiously.

"The little lad has not said a word all day," the tutor said, his voice showing his disapproval.

"But he did get up."

"That he did. As soon as you left. He even took tea with Mr. Meredith and his brother and sister."

Richard felt a knot of fear dissolve. "But he has not said anything?"

"Not a word." Once again Richard could hear the disapproval in the tutor's voice. He wanted to scream at the man, to tell him that David was not at fault, but he restrained himself. Slowly, he walked over to the children, who were playing a game. He watched for a while.

"Want to take a hand, Da?" Robert asked. His father shook his head. "David is winning."

As soon as his father took a seat beside him, David folded his cards and put them on the table. He got up to walk away. Richard followed him, ignoring Robert's and Caroline's complaints. "David, tell me what happened in the square yesterday," Richard said quietly, his eyes fixed on his oldest son's.

He watched emotions play across the canvas of his son's face. Finally, David shook his head. "I will see you in the morning," Richard said quietly, leaning down to put a kiss on his son's cheek. David drew back as though he were afraid of being bitten by a snake. His heart aching, Richard told the other two children good-bye and left the room.

Still caught up in the events of the day, he dressed, ate his dinner, and escorted his wife to a ball, whose he could not have said. He did not even notice the way Lucy and he were the center of all eyes, he in his black and white and Lucy in a stunning bishop's blue gown of glacé silk trimmed with ivory ribbons and lace. When her brother whirled her away from him, he stood watching them until the dance ended. From his expression, Lucy was not sure he even knew she had been gone.

When Arabella joined them, his reverie was shattered. "I should be angry with you, Richard," she said with a pout. She glanced at Lucy's dress and wished that she were married and had the final say on her own clothing.

"Why?" he asked after Lucy poked him in the ribs.

"Because you deserted me today. Of course, I understand you had no choice. Was it exciting? Did you catch the robbers?"

Before Richard could open his mouth to rip her up and ruin everyone's evening, Edward glared at him. "What robbery? I thought you were going to tell me everything," he said in a muted roar.

"This is the first time I have seen you. And a ball is no place to discuss this. We can talk later." As if recognizing that his friend was right, Edward nodded, but Lucy noticed that even while he was dancing with Arabella he kept his eyes on them for some time.

Finally Richard had had enough. "May we leave soon?" he asked as he swept Lucy around the floor.

"When this dance is over," she whispered, giving him a warm smile. His arm tightened about her, and the strain he had been feeling lessened.

As they waited for their carriage to be brought around, a gentleman who had just arrived stopped to talk to them. "Good to see you in town again." He greeted both of them. Then he proceeded to his real purpose. "Thought you should know, Blount. Found a matching statue to that nymph you have in your garden. The one with a bow," he said. "Thought it was a copy but have been assured it is genuine."

"Where did you find it?" Richard asked, not letting his excitement show. The statue was one of the items missing.

"A chap I know. Keeps an eye out for things I might like."

"Do I know him?"

"Doubt it. Not telling you either. Do not want your collection to surpass mine," the man said.

"When did you find it?"

"About a year ago. Surprising really. Not much travel to the Continent. Supposed someone with pockets to let selling it."

When their carriage arrived, Lucy and Richard made their excuses. As soon as they were safely inside, Lucy turned to her husband. "Is what he said important?" she asked.

"How did you know?"

"Your face. Oh, do not worry. He did not notice. He was too involved in proving to you how he had outsmarted you. Was the statue stolen from you?" she asked. On their way to the ball, her husband had given her a bare outline of what had happened.

"Yes." Richard picked up her hand and brought it to his lips. "You are very clever, madam."

She lowered her eyelashes and then smiled at him coquettishly. "So are you. You got him to answer all your questions."

"Not all. But maybe Smith will have better luck." He smiled at her. Then for the first time that evening he looked at her. His eyebrows went up. "Is this the dress you were wearing earlier?" he asked, gazing disapprovingly at her neckline.

"Richard, what are you talking about?" Lucy asked, turning to look at him.

"Your dress."

"What about my dress? You complimented me on it earlier."

"I did? Were you wearing a shawl?"

"No. Richard, I do not understand." Lucy's eyes were wide and dark with confusion.

He laughed ruefully. "A husband's right, my dear, to complain about his wife's clothing.

"But you said you liked it."

"I do." He leaned close to her. "But it reveals charms I would rather not have anyone else see," he said, running a finger across the neckline where the tops of her breasts were exposed.

Lucy blushed. "Oh," she said softly, thrilling to his touch as she usually did. She reached out to smooth back his hair. He caught her hand, bringing it to his lips once again.

When the carriage arrived at Mr. Meredith's house, they both were flushed. They hurried upstairs. "Is Betty waiting for you?" he asked. Lucy shook her head. "Good." She blushed again.

Later as they lay in each other's arms, not yet willing

to go to sleep, they talked in hushed tones. Just before he
drifted off to sleep, he remembered what he had planned
to ask. "Care to redo the house?"

"In Devonshire?" She frowned, trying to decide what
she would change.

"Here. Smaller than this. Shouldn't take long." His
voice was slow and sleepy.

Lucy lay there looking at the draperies above her. His
arm pulled her closer to him. Through eyes as sleepy as
his, she watched his breathing slow and his eyes close.
The thought of redecorating his house gave her a sense
of pride and belonging. It would be their home.

As soon as they went down for breakfast the next
morning, Edward pounced upon Richard. "What happened? What were you talking about last night?"

Looking around to be sure no servants were in the
room, Richard told him. When the door opened, he
changed the conversation. It would be impossible to
keep the news from the servants, he knew. But he also
did not know if he could trust them.

"Chocolate. Do you want this or some coffee?" Lucy
asked the two men as though it were the most serious
question in the world. When they requested coffee, she
poured their cups. After the footmen had finished serv-
ing, she dismissed them. "Do you have any ideas, Edward?" she asked when the servants had left.

"Ideas? About what?" She frowned. "Oh, about the
robbery." He paused for a moment. "You could offer a
reward."

Richard thought for a moment. "I will ask Smith if he
thinks it will do any good. Problem is it happened so
long ago."

"When may I see the house?" Lucy asked as she
broke a muffin into smaller pieces.

"Today." Richard smiled at her, enjoying the picture
she made in her jonquil round gown with her hair tied
with matching jonquil ribbons.

"I do not like that idea," her brother said, his face
solemn. He stared at Richard.

"Why not?" Richard asked.

"What if the robbers should come back?" Edward got up and came around the table, his cup in his hand. Lucy poured him another cup of coffee.

"There will be servants about the place. Did you not say that Mr. Ledsworth had orders to have someone cleaning by today?" Lucy asked her husband.

Richard's face lost the frown it wore. "Yes. She will not be alone."

"I still do not like it," Edward said. "Those people will be busy. And they will probably be strangers to one another. They would not notice if another stranger appeared."

Richard nodded his head. "What do you suggest?" he asked. Lucy looked from one to the other and shook her head in disbelief.

"Whenever you go to the townhouse, Lucy is to take her maid and a footman, someone who knows the family."

Lucy opened her mouth to disagree, but Richard answered first. "A good idea. And I will make it very clear that their jobs are to watch after her."

"And have I nothing to say about this?" she asked indignantly.

"No," they said almost simultaneously.

"But Betty has work to do here," she protested.

"We will hire someone else to help her," her husband said firmly. "I will drop a note to Ledsworth today."

"I do not think that is the answer. No knowing who he might send," Edward said with a frown.

Richard nodded. Then his face brightened. "I can ask Smith. He will know someone."

"I do not want a stranger. I will find someone within the household. I am certain Papa's housekeeper will be glad to help," Lucy said firmly. She glared at first one and then the other. Before those determined blue eyes, they gave ground.

"Well, I suppose that might be best," her husband said rather sheepishly.

Her brother nodded his agreement. Then he said, "Arabella will be happy to accompany you. She will enjoy making suggestions about how to bring the house up to the latest style."

"And when will she have time?" his sister asked. "Her days are full. You know that. You are not to insist that she help."

"But . . ."

"Edward, you have no idea how busy she is." He pulled a face. "Oh, I know you think you do, but consider this. If she starts spending time at the townhouse with me, when will she have time for you? And do not tell me in the evenings. I know her mother. Even if you are engaged, she will not allow Arabella to stay in your pocket no matter how much you both wish it. And you do not want to make her the center of any more gossip than already exists."

Feeling as though he had just been run over by a team of well-trained horses, Edward was forced to admit his sister was right. Even though he was not happy about the situation, Richard smiled at his wife, enjoying her spirit.

"When should I be ready to leave?" she asked, pushing her chair back.

She was fastening her garters a short while later when he came into her room. "The men watching saw the lady with the dog," he said, waving the message that Smith had sent him.

Betty muttered something about privacy under her breath while she dropped a petticoat over her mistress's head. Lucy frowned. She turned around to let her maid tie it. "And?"

Richard sat down, enjoying the sight of his wife in shift and petticoat. Betty picked up the stays. "Are you going to wear those?" he asked, frowning as he remembered the marks they left on her skin.

"Yes," Lucy said as patiently as she could. She stood quietly while her maid laced her up. "What else did he say?"

"They have seen the lady before. She walks in the

square every afternoon. But they do not think she lives here."

"Why not?" Lucy turned to look at him.

"They have never seen her arriving or leaving one of the houses here," he said. "They do admit that they did not pay much attention to her. They were watching your father's house."

"Were they close enough to hear what she said to David?" she asked, hoping to have the mystery solved. She sat down so that her maid could arrange her hair, but kept looking at him.

He shook his head. Lucy sighed. "They will be watching for her. And if she returns, someone will follow her."

"And if she does not?"

"Then we will never know." His voice was bleak.

To comfort him as well as herself, Lucy said, "They will find out. You will see." He smiled at the certainty in her voice.

When she and Richard left for the townhouse, neither knew they were followed. Informed by Smith of their plans, one of the men who watched the house had gone ahead to be in place when they arrived. In spite of the warnings he had been given, he did not pay any attention when a man dressed as a gentleman ran up the steps to a nearby house and then disappeared down the steps leading to the lower story.

As they walked through the townhouse, Lucy frowned. Although the servants that Ledsworth had hired had been busy since early that morning, there was much left to do. The ground floor had been put to rights, but the bedrooms were still in chaos. As she walked around the bed in the main bedroom, Lucy stumbled and almost fell. Richard, who was on the other side of the room, hurried to her side, a worried look on his face. Ignoring him, she bent down to pick up an object from the floor.

"You have done enough for today," he said. "I will not have you exhausted." He picked her up and put her on the chaise longue.

"I am not exhausted," she protested. When he put her down, she looked at the object she held. "Richard, look at this."

"What?"

"I found it on the floor. I think it is a miniature of you." She held it out so that he could take it.

"I thought this lost during the fire. I sent it to Julia during our engagement. She must have forgotten it." He turned it over in his hand.

"It looks as though someone stepped on it. Do you think the thief dropped it?"

He looked at it again. "Perhaps." He did not want to admit to her that it looked as though someone had deliberately crushed it beneath a heel. Remembering the discord that had existed between him and his first wife when they came to London the last time, he wondered if Julia had been the one to destroy it. The act would have been like her, he admitted.

"Is it badly damaged?" she asked, trying to remember. "I do not have a miniature of you," she said wistfully.

Richard smiled at her. "Nor I of you. We will sit for them together. And I think I want a portrait of you. It will be the first addition to my new gallery." She smiled up at him, warmed by the expression in his eyes.

"And one of you. And the children," she said breathlessly.

He made a place for himself on the chaise. "And the children," he said as he bent to kiss her. The more time he spent with her, the more he wanted her. The chaos around him and the knowledge that the servants might enter the room at any time kept him from any caress more than a kiss. He sat back and looked around the room once more. "But first we must have some answers. I wish I knew who had done this." His face hardened at the thought of some stranger entering his home at will.

Lucy, who had no previous attachment to the place, looked around carefully. "Are these colors you particularly like?" she asked, inspecting the red and gold fabric that covered the walls and furniture. The curtains in particular had not worn well, showing streaks where they faded.

"No. I prefer something brighter." He looked at her again and smiled. "Like your eyes."

She lowered her lashes and then swept them up again. Her breath caught in her throat at the passion she saw on his face. Then she heard a noise in the hallway. She swung her legs off the edge of the chaise and stood up, swaying slightly as she regained her balance. He held her steady, his eyes on hers.

The door to the hall opened. A footman carrying coals for the fireplace stopped, wondering if he would be reprimanded. "Didn't know you was here," he said, trying to keep his face from revealing both his fear and his interest in them.

"Dispose of everything in this room," she said, looking to Richard for approval. He nodded. The footman, realizing his good fortune, smiled.

Their enemy was also smiling when she heard that the townhouse had been opened. "The very place," she said, her eyes lighting with glee. As they made their plans, a wicked smiled played about her mouth. When she had explained what she wanted, she sat back. "Now we wait."

As Lucy visited the house over the next few days, she was pleased with the progress they were making. Only the study paneled in rich woods had been left alone. When most of the general cleaning had been finished and before the painting had begun, she invited the children to go with her.

She watched in amazement as they stared at the place as though they had never seen it. David, who had begun to speak once again, stared at one painting that hung in the drawing room. "My mother hated that picture," he said quietly. Since the episode in the square, he had shown no excitement about anything.

"She did?" Lucy asked, sitting down beside him on

the sofa she planned to re-cover in pale blue satin stripes.

"She told Da she wanted it out of the house. I guess he sent it here." Lucy looked at the picture again, wondering what Julia had found to dislike in the pastoral scene. David stroked the satin he was sitting on. He looked around the room. "I do not like this room. It is too dark." He turned to look at her. "Are our rooms like this?"

"You do not know?"

"This is the first time I have ever been here. Mama always insisted that we stay in the country because she did not intend to be gone for long."

"And was she?" Although she disliked what she was doing, Lucy felt an overwhelming urge to learn more about her predecessor.

He sighed, his face set in lines more usual in an old man than a young boy. "No. She did not like to be away from the manor," he said.

"Or from you," Lucy added, trying to bring more cheerful memories to his mind. She ached when she saw him in so much pain. If she had not insisted that they come to London, he still might be a somewhat happier young child.

"Oh, we did not see her often unless Da was home. She was too busy," David said casually. "We see you more." His hand was beside hers on the sofa. Lucy covered his with hers, and he did not pull away.

"Well, as soon as this place is in order, I promise you will see more of your father and me than you do now." She smiled at him. When a faint smile crossed his face, she felt as though she had won a great victory.

Remembering his words about his mother not having time for them, when the painters had finished, Lucy began taking them to the townhouse with her as she inspected the progress each day. Although the house was much smaller than her father's, the garden was large and provided them space to run and play after they had grown tired of watching the house change. Following both her husband's and her brother's orders, a footman always stayed outside with them. Busy and happy, she was able to put the thoughts of the threats behind her, simply enjoying the life she had made for herself.

Chapter Fourteen

While Lucy and the children were busy at the town-house, Richard and Edward investigated every possible source that Smith turned up. Mr. Meredith, refusing to be left out, made careful inquiries of his friends. Nothing turned up the answers they needed.

Several days passed without either new threats or a resolution to the problem. When Jones returned to town, Richard had hopes that he might have discovered answers. All he had discovered were further questions. At their next meeting, Smith asked Richard, "Did you know a Mr. Ashton?"

"Yes, why?"

"He sold his property and left shortly after the fire," Jones said grimly.

"He was always talking of going to America," Richard told him. "He had no family to hold him back. And his property came to him from a distant uncle. No real ties to the place." Jones frowned, not willing to give up a clue as insignificant as this one might be. "What else did you learn?" The two men exchanged glances. "Tell me."

"According to your servants, your wife had a lover."

Richard laughed. "I could have told you that." The men stared at him, their shock written on their faces. "She told me, gloated about it. He was why she was so unwilling to come to town."

"And you did not care?" Smith asked, shocked to his middle-class soul.

"Of course, I did. But there was nothing I could do."

Smith and Jones glanced at each other and then back at him. "Oh no, I did not set the fire to get rid of my wife. She was willing to leave. All I had to do was provide her an income that she approved of, and she would not have bothered me or the children again. I was seriously considering her offer. It would have been more pleasant than living with her," Richard said bitterly.

Finding nothing else to say, Smith and Jones left, promising to send him word if their search turned up any answers.

With no more threats evident and no other confrontations, Lucy thought they had nothing to worry about. Then disaster struck. As usual, Lucy had taken the children to the townhouse with her. After they had walked through the house to see what had changed, they went into the garden. When it was time to leave, Lucy called them in. She waited a few moments and called them again. Caroline and Robert ran to her side.

"We cannot find David," Robert said. Lucy's blood ran cold with fear.

"Where is the footman?" She could hardly get the words out.

"Looking for him. We were playing Hide and Go Seek," Caroline said. "I found Robert twice, but David is a good hider."

"Maybe he thinks the game is still going on," Lucy suggested, beginning to breathe once again.

Then the footman returned, his face white. "Well, have you found him?" she asked.

The man shook his head, too breathless to answer. Lucy closed her eyes and whispered a brief prayer.

"Is David lost?" Robert asked, his voice quavering just a little. Caroline grabbed Lucy's hand as if she were afraid her stepmother would disappear too.

"I do not know." She put her arms around both of them and ushered them into the house. When she saw Betty waiting, Lucy motioned to her. "Take the children home. Then tell my husband and brother that I need them immediately." Frightened by the harshness of her mistress's voice, the maid nodded. "You go with Betty," Lucy told the children. "She will take care of you."

"But I do not want to leave without David," Robert protested, digging his heels into the carpet.

Lucy had no time to ease his fears. "You will go with Betty," she said sternly. "David will follow you soon."

Once again she uttered a prayer that she was right. She kissed his cheek and hugged Caroline, sending them on their way. Ignoring their pleas, she turned back to the servants who were clustered on the stairs to the kitchen. "I will need you, you, and you," she said, picking out the strongest, most sensible of the lot. "Search the gardens, the alleys, and the streets. He must be here somewhere."

By the time her husband and brother arrived, she knew David was not anywhere where they could find him. Taking one look at her husband, she burst into tears. Brushing them away angrily, she gained control and said, "I have lost David." Then she waited for him to upbraid her.

"Nonsense. He played a prank on you. He is having tea with your father as we speak," he said quietly, taking her in his arms. The comfort in his voice did not reach his eyes. Edward, who had been instructed to keep an eye on the servants, noticed one start. "We have come to take you to him. I plan to scold him severely for having frightened you." Her brother nodded and stepped outside.

Relieved yet not secure, Lucy allowed Richard to usher her into the waiting carriage. As soon as the door closed behind him, Richard's mask fell. "How did he get home?" Lucy asked. Neither man answered her.

"Did you see that maid's face when you said David was at home?" Edward asked his friend. "She gave everything away."

"Did you tell Smith?" Edward nodded.

"Smith? Was he there? Why? What is wrong?" Lucy asked, fixing first one and then the other with her gaze. They shifted restlessly.

Her husband cleared his throat. "David is not at

home," he said as if every word were being dragged from him.

"What?" The panic she had been holding at bay for so long threatened to overwhelm Lucy. Her face lost its colors. "Why did you lie?" Her eyes widened in terror. "They have him," she whispered.

"They? Who? Did you see who took him away?" Richard asked, his hands gripping her arms so tightly she knew she would be bruised.

"The ones who have been making the threats. It was David they wanted, not my jewels. David." The last word was merely a gasp.

"Did anyone see anything?" her brother asked her. "Where was that footman?"

"That is a question I intend to have an answer to as soon as this coach stops," Richard said. Lucy was glad he had not used such a harsh voice on her.

"What will they do to him?" The two men exchanged glances. Neither planned to explain the countless possibilities. "He is only a little boy," Lucy said, her sobs punctuating her words.

"Pull yourself together, Lucy," her brother said, looking out the window. "We do not want to spread word of his disappearance about town. If the conspirators have doubts, so much the better." He nodded as she stifled her tears and took the handkerchief her husband held out to her. "Smile."

Although she fought against her tears, Lucy obeyed her brother, allowing Richard to whisk her from the carriage into the house. When the door closed behind them, she crumbled. "David," she sobbed. Richard held her for a moment and then handed her to her brother.

"Take her to your father," he said. "I plan to talk to that footman." He turned to the butler who waited nearby. "Send him to us. We will be in the study. He should be in the kitchen by now." Jarvis bowed, deeply shocked by the horror that had struck his family.

When the butler ushered the young footman into the study, both Richard and Edward were waiting, their faces set in hard lines. They looked at the man; he began to tremble. Before they could say a word, he began to babble. "I had nothing to do with it. I—we were having a go of it in the shed in the garden."

"We—who?" Edward asked.

"Daisy, a maid from the house next door. But I checked to make sure nobody was around. Just like always." The man was shaking so badly he could hardly stand up.

"Always?" Richard's voice was dangerously low. "Has this happened before?"

"Not Master David but the girl and me. We have been meeting on the sly whenever she could get away," the man admitted. He knew his position was lost. But he was afraid they would send him to Newgate.

"At the same time each day?" Edward asked, raising one eyebrow.

"If she could get away." The man hung his head. "I didn't think anything would happen to the children. They was just playing." The careful tones he had cultivated since coming to London disappeared, leaving a thick country accent.

"And how did you meet this maid?" Richard asked.

"She popped over to say hello to one of her friends, and I was there." He mopped his face with his handkerchief. Dark circles began to appear beneath his arms as he realized just how serious this might be. "I would never let something happen to Master David on purpose," he said, staring Richard in the eyes. "I wouldn't, I couldn't."

Richard turned away, trying to control his urge to beat the man into a bloody pulp. "You should have been doing your job," he said through clenched teeth. "Why did you think we sent you?" He pounded the desk instead. The footman gulped and looked at Edward. He took a step or two back.

"Tell us the name of the maid who introduced you to the girl you have been meeting. Then go to your room until I send for you." The footman nodded. "Do not talk about this with anyone; do you understand?" Edward asked. The footman nodded once more. He whispered the information and left.

"He scurried out of here like a scared puppy," Richard said, gaining control of himself again.

"You must admit you deliberately set out to frighten him. You frightened me," his friend said. "What am I to do with the names?"

"Smith said he would contact us within the hour. We will tell him."

"Are you sure that we should wait?"

"What choice do we have? Can you see me questioning the maids without giving it all away?"

"No, but Lucy could do it."

"Lucy!" Richard looked stricken. He dashed down the hall to the drawing room. "Lucy!"

Like a moth to a flame, she ran into his arms. "I am sorry. So sorry," she sobbed. His arms tightened around her as though he were afraid of losing her too.

"It is not your fault," he whispered, recognizing the guilt she felt. His own threatened to overwhelm him. For a few minutes he held her while she cried. As her sobs ceased, he led her to the settee and sat down beside her.

"What have you learned?" Mr. Meredith asked, his face pale but his voice steady.

"Not much. A maid may have helped whoever it was. Smith will be questioning her in a few minutes," he said. His voice was not exactly steady.

Lucy took a deep breath, trying to steady herself. "Why was he here? Has he learned anything else?"

"Fortunately, he was here when Betty sought me out. He had come to tell me they had done everything they could; they thought there was no immediate danger." The bitterness in Richard's voice was strong.

"What?" Both Lucy and her father were astounded.

"We must do something. Now!" she said angrily. "We must go back and talk to the maid. I do not trust those men. If they find as little this time as they found last, we may never find David." Although she had begun angrily, by her last word Lucy was crying again. "He is only a little boy." Richard took her in his arms again, wishing that he too could cry.

Jarvis entered, his face pale and haunted. "A Mr. Smith to see you, Mr. Blount. I have put him in the study with Master Edward."

"I will go with you," Lucy said, gaining control of herself once again.

"And I too," Mr. Meredith said firmly.

"Ask them to join us here," Richard said. His hands were trembling. Smith had to have some news.

Neither Edward nor Smith looked happy as they walked into the drawing room. "Well?" Richard demanded. Smith bowed to Lucy. He straightened his coat and pulled down his sleeves. "Speak."

"Mr. Edward Meredith was right. The maid knew more than she was telling. Introduced myself as your steward. Hope you do not mind my assumption of the role, Mr. Blount." Richard shook his head. "Threw a good scare into the lot. Then talked to the maid alone. She gave me the name of a man and the tavern where he likes to go. According to her, he was the one who snatched the boy. Had a coach waiting at the crossroads."

"Is David all right?"

"Where have they taken him?"

"What can we do now?"

"Do you think she is telling the truth?" Questions began flying around him. Finally he put his hands over his ears, the noise grew so loud. One by one his questioners were silent. "I sent Jones to find the man the maid thinks was involved," Smith said into the silence.

"I'll go with him," Richard said, the light of battle in his eyes.

"I too," Edward echoed.

"No, sirs, you will not. The sight of you would frighten the man off. Just show up there, and everyone would know you had guessed the game. They would disappear before you could find them."

"They?" Mr. Meredith asked. "How many are we speaking of?"

"Cannot tell for sure. Had to have been someone in the coach. And if the maid is right, the man who took David is not the one who thought of the plan. She still thinks the boy got away. The threat of being transported did the trick."

"What can we do now? We cannot just sit here," Richard said, glaring at the man who was supposed to save them from this trouble.

"I am afraid that is just what you must do. They may get in touch with you," Smith said. He stared at his employer and avoided Lucy's eyes.

"Why?" she asked. He refused to look at her or answer her question. "Why?" she asked again, this time more defiantly and louder.

"Hush!" her father told her. He rolled to her side and took her hand. She looked wildly from one to the other of the men.

"What will they do with him?" she cried.

"Tell her, Richard," her brother said quietly.

Drawing her back to the settee, her husband sat her down and took a seat beside her. He linked his fingers with hers. "Smith thinks they are holding him for ransom."

"Ransom? For money?" she asked. Her eyes were wide. "For money?" she repeated. He nodded. "Then they will let him go?" None of the men would meet her eyes. "They will let him go, won't they?" she demanded.

Her father was the one who finally answered. "We hope so," he said quietly. His voice said something different.

"Hope? Only hope? We must find him!" She was frantic. "What can we do?"

"Wait." The one word brought her up short. She stared at Smith, urging him to give her more directions. He was silent for a moment. Then he turned to Richard. "I would like to speak to the footman."

"He is in his room," Edward said. "Shall I send for him?"

"I think I'll talk to him there. More privacy. Can you have someone show me the way?"

The silence that fell when Smith had left the room was not an easy one. Everyone wanted to talk, but no one knew what to say. Lucy kept a hold on Richard's hand as though he were the only sanity in her existence. When the door opened again some time later, they all jumped.

"Well?" Richard demanded as Smith entered the room. Mr. Meredith moved his chair so he could see the man's face. Lucy's hand tightened on her husband's.

"He knows nothing," Smith said quietly. "He was a pawn in someone's hands." The hope they all had felt disappeared like fog on a warm summer's day. "I need to talk to my partner," he told Richard. "If you need me, you know where to send a message." Reluctantly, they watched him go, every step he took telling them over and over again that there was nothing they could do. Lucy closed her eyes and lay back, one tear trickling down her cheek.

When the silence stretched into pain, Edward got up. "I'll send word to Arabella not to expect me to escort her tonight." He sighed.

"Do not change your plans," Richard said, his voice incredibly weary.

"Of course, he will," Mr. Meredith said firmly. "If that little man finds out anything, we will need him to help." Edward nodded. A faint smile crossed Lucy's lips as she watched her brother walk from the room.

A thought suddenly crossing his mind, Richard followed him. "Do not tell her anything about David's disappearance, Edward."

"Why? She will soon be his aunt."

"Since we do not know who is involved, someone from my townhouse might find out David is really missing and try to warn their conspirators that we are suspicious."

Edward nodded. "When she finds out that I have hidden this from her, you are the one who must answer her." The wry humor in his friend's voice made Richard smile faintly.

"Henpecked already, my friend?" Edward merely shrugged and walked into the library.

Before he could reenter the drawing room, Jarvis stopped him. "Should I ask Mrs. Blount if I should serve tea now?" Richard started. Although it seemed like several hours since they had discovered David's disappearance, it was only the middle of the afternoon. Richard nodded.

The appearance of Jarvis and his question brought Lucy out of the self-imposed slough of despair. She sat up straight. "Robert and Caroline," she exclaimed. "I must go to them."

Although he normally would have agreed with her, Richard knew his children. "Have someone bring you news. Do not worry them unnecessarily."

"Unnecessarily? Someone has David. They could be next," she argued.

"Not if they are in the schoolroom. Ask Betty to check in on them occasionally. You and I will go up later."

"And if they start asking where David is?"

"Have Betty tell them he is being punished for hiding from you." Mr. Meredith, who had been listening, swallowed the comment he was going to make and nodded his head. With her husband and father allied against her, she gave in.

When the tea tray arrived, she poured each of them a cup and had the footman pass around a tray of sandwiches. Richard shook his head, his stomach too uncertain for any food. Edward took several of his favorites and then stared at them. Mr. Meredith drank his tea and asked for a second cup, which Lucy poured, glad to have something to do.

The hours of the afternoon dragged by. Each time they heard footsteps approaching, they sat up straighter. When they led to nothing, they slumped. Although

Richard tried on more than one occasion to persuade his wife to go upstairs and rest, Lucy refused to leave.

Finally one set of footsteps approached the door and entered. They all leaned forward. "This just arrived for you, Mr. Blount," Jarvis said, handing him a message.

Breathlessly, the others watched him open it. His eyes narrowed. He looked up. "Smith was right."

"What does it say?" Lucy asked, grabbing his arm once more. She trembled.

"It is a ransom demand."

"How much?" Mr. Meredith wanted to know. "I keep some money in my safe."

"I doubt if you have this much on hand," his son-in-law said, still looking at the note. "They want ten thousand pounds by tomorrow evening."

"What?" The old man was shocked.

Edward gripped the back of his father's chair so hard that his knuckles turned white. "Can you raise it?" he asked. "If not, I will help."

"And I," Mr. Meredith added.

"I have more than that in the Funds. It will be a matter of selling out," Richard assured him. "If I can do it in time."

"What about David? What does it say about David?" Lucy asked frantically, not caring about the money involved.

Richard looked at the note again. "If I leave the money where I am told to do so, he will be released."

"Then we must do as they say," she said firmly. But she could not miss the looks that the three men exchanged. "What? What is wrong?" Although they tried to soothe her, she refused to be silenced. "Why do you look like that?" she asked her father.

He took her hands into his own, sorrow wrinkling his face more than it was already marked. "Lucy, you must be brave. We have to trust that they will do what they say they will."

She looked into his eyes. "But you do not believe they will keep their word," she said dully. The three men shook their heads. Pulling her hands away from her father, she sank down into a chair, tears beginning to trickle down her face. "He is just a little boy," she whispered.

Before long, both Mr. Meredith and Richard had letters ready to be delivered. "Tell Mr. Ledsworth that this is urgent. I must see him immediately," Richard said as he handed the footman the message. Her father used almost the same words when he sent for his man of business.

By the time the moon rose, their plans were made. "I will see to this as soon as I can in the morning," Mr. Ledsworth promised, shuddering both at the horror his client must be facing and at the loss he would be taking. He and Mr. Meredith's man had a list of buyers they had split between them.

"If you cannot do this, let me know before noon," Richard said. "I will need time to arrange an appointment with a moneylender."

"I do not think it will come to that, Mr. Blount," Mr. Ledsworth said. His horror was evident.

"I will do whatever it takes to get my son back," Richard said, hoping the villains would take just the money. Edward nodded.

When the others had left, the three men made their way to bed. Lucy had gone up an hour before, her limp more pronounced because of her exhaustion. As she lay in bed, visions of David ran through her mind. And her own guilt plagued her. Why had she not gone into the garden earlier? Why had she been so careless?

A door opened. Richard walked to the bed and took his place beside her. Realizing that she was awake, he said, "I did not want to be alone." Then as if he had absorbed all the pain he could stand, he reached out for her. "Hold me. Please hold me," he begged. She wrapped her arms around him and felt something wet on her cheeks. Whether it was his tears or hers she never knew. For a short time all they did was hold each other close. Then as if he needed to be reminded that he was alive, he began to make love to her frantically, desperately—as if he had no promise of the morrow.

When they finally closed their eyes, their sleep was restless. When the first light broke through the windows, they both rose and stood staring out into the morning. "Where is he?" Lucy wondered, her hand pressed to her lips to keep from sobbing.

When a knock sounded on the door sometime later, they were both dressed. "Come in," Lucy called, her hands clenched in fear.

"A message for Mr. Blount," the sleepy footman said, his uniform hastily donned and badly buttoned. His eyes widened as he realized that they were ready for the day.

Lucy closed her eyes, praying, while Richard opened the letter. His eyes narrowed. "Well?" she said anxiously as she waited for him to speak.

"Smith asks that I not leave the house until he arrives." Richard looked at the note again to see if he had missed anything. Lucy sighed. "Perhaps he has some news."

"And if he does not?"

"We pay the ransom." And hope they keep their word, he thought to himself.

"I wish we could do something," Lucy said, twisting her handkerchief. The frustration she felt was evident in her brother and father as well when they met at breakfast a while later. No one ate much. The men downed countless cups of coffee, and Lucy shredded a muffin and drank chocolate.

When Smith arrived, they were in the drawing room once more. Slightly surprised to find them all together so early in the morning, he stopped on the threshold.

"Well, tell us what you have found," Mr. Meredith demanded, his voice gruff and his eyes deep set from lack of sleep.

Smith looked at Richard, who nodded. "We think we have found where they have taken him," he said quietly.

"Where?" The word could have come from any of them.

"A barn not far out of town."

"On the road to Tunbridge Wells?" Richard asked, remembering the orders in the note he had received the night before.

Smith frowned. "On the road to Maidstone."

"An attempt to throw us off the scent?" Edward wondered out loud. "A man on a good horse could travel quickly across country without much trouble."

"Or his partners could arrange to meet him somewhere else later," Smith added. "Jones is keeping watch over the place in case they decide to move your son." Lucy gasped. "Do not think they will try that, not in daylight."

"And I am supposed to pay the ransom and receive directions to where I can find my son shortly after sunset," Richard said, his mouth set in a straight line. "Can we take them?" he asked.

Smith looked uncertain. "Still not sure how many people are inside."

"You make contact with your partner. I must stay here until I find out if Ledsworth can sell those Funds."

"Do you plan to pay the ransom?" Smith asked.

"Not if I can help it. But I must be ready in any case." The threat in Richard's voice sent chills up Lucy's back.

"You realize that we do not know what they will do?" Smith asked, trying to make certain that the man who hired him knew all the risks.

"I know." Edward and Mr. Meredith nodded too. Lucy, her eyes big, pressed her hands to her mouth to keep from crying out. "Do you still have those men we can hire?"

"Too many men may be a mistake. The road beside the place is well traveled. I planned to hire a farmer's wagon loaded with produce," Smith said with a smile that did not reach his eyes. Richard and Edward exchanged glances. Then Richard nodded.

"Ask the servants for some of their clothes," Edward suggested. "I will see to the guns." Pleased with the activity he had stirred up, Smith left, promising to return within the hour.

As soon as he had gone, Lucy turned to her husband. "I am going with you," she said firmly. "And do not try to convince me otherwise." An hour later as they were leaving he was still trying to make her to stay behind. Dressed in their servants' clothing, they slipped out the servants' entrance and hurried to the closed carriage that was waiting for them. Mr. Meredith and Mr. Ledsworth, who had been left with the responsibility of delivering the ransom if they did not return in time, watched them go. "God speed," Mr. Meredith whispered.

Chapter Fifteen

The first part of their journey was a silent one. Lucy wanted to reach for her husband's hand, but he was too forbidding. She clasped her hands in her lap and prayed wordlessly.

As soon as they were close to the inn that Smith had selected, they climbed down, sent the coach home, and walked the rest of the way. To Lucy's surprise no one paid any attention to them. "Keep quiet. I'll do the talking," Smith said. He looked at the two men. "Slump more. You've been working for hours." Richard let his shoulders fall and put a stupid look on his face. Edward followed suit.

Before long they were in the wagon. Lucy sat on the seat beside her husband while Smith and Edward rode in the dirt and rubbish left by the cabbages and other vegetables it had once carried. Edward had suggested that they pretend to be drunks, but Smith had disagreed, reminding him that farmers who were anxious to better themselves could not afford to spend their money on drink they did not produce. Instead, they curled up, pretending to be asleep.

The road was bumpy, and before long Lucy was as sore as Richard had told her she would be. But no complaints passed her lips. She shut them tighter until they formed a white line. Richard glanced at her once in a while but said nothing. She had known what this trip would be like.

They had recently passed the George Tavern in Greenwich and then a bunch of men walking into town when

Smith told Richard to stop. Fearing they had been discovered, Richard pulled off the road under a big tree,
hoping it would provide some cover.

"Thought you'd never come," said a man, pulling
himself over the end of the wagon. "Then I had to chase
you." He was panting so hard he could hardly speak.

Ignoring the introductions, Smith began questioning
him. "Are they still there?" The man nodded. "How
many?" The man simply lay there, trying to get his
breath. "Jones, how many?" He held up three fingers.
The others stared at him.

Taking a deep breath, Jones let it out slowly. When he
was breathing more normally, he said, "Two men and a
woman. Were more, but they left."

Richard leaned forward, a feral smile on his face.
"How far?" he asked.

"About two miles down this road." Jones took the
water bottle that Smith held out to him and drank deeply.
"Why'd you bring a woman along?" he asked, raking
Lucy from head to toe.

"She insisted," Smith said quietly, giving his friend a
poke in the ribs. "She's the boy's stepmother."

"Have you seen him? Is he all right?" Lucy asked. Her
heart was beating so loudly that she could hardly hear
her own voice. Richard leaned over in order to hear what
he said more clearly.

"Peeked in early this morning before they were up.
Had him wrapped in a cloak beside the fire. Didn't look
like he was too uncomfortable," Jones told her.

"This morning? Have you seen him today?"

He shook his head. "Give me more of that water. It's
hot and dry watching."

"Tell us about the barn," Edward said. Jones drew
back in surprise at his polished speech. Then jumping to
the ground, he drew an outline in the dust.

"Only the one door?" Richard asked. The man nodded. "No chance to rush them then."

"Not through there." Smith frowned.

"But what if they think we are someone else?" Lucy

asked. She stared down the distant road as if she could see that weathered structure where David was held.

"What do you mean?" Smith asked.

Richard turned around and kissed her. She blushed. "What if something happened to the wagon as we went past the place?" he asked, keeping an eye on his wife. She nodded. "You said the road goes by there. We could claim we were looking for something to help us repair our wagon."

"Only if you was silent," Jones said. "One word out of your mouths they would twig the game right away."

Smith nodded. "And your missus had best be my daughter," he suggested. "If Mrs. Blount could act like she was sick or something."

"Your limp. You could pretend you injured your leg when the wagon lost its wheel," Edward said.

"Finally, it is good for something," she said, trying to smile but yet afraid. She looked at Richard, who was frowning. "Will David give us away?"

"We will have to take that chance. But he has never seen us dressed as we are now. If you keep your bonnet pulled over your face and we yank our hats down and keep our eyes on the ground, we may fool him," Richard said. "And I think we need to be dirtier."

"I already feel as though I am wearing more dust than clothing," Lucy complained. But she allowed him to hand her down, holding on to him until she had regained her balance. Then she reached down for a handful of dust and sprinkled it on her face and dress. Her husband and brother did the same. "Am I properly disguised, Mr. Smith?" With something to do, her fear was, if not disappearing, at least being pushed out of the forefront of her memory.

When they met Smith's approval, they climbed back into the wagon. This time Richard joined Edward and Jones in the back while Smith drove the oxen.

As they jolted along the road, they made their final plans. The barn was on the other side of a small hill, hidden away in the valley. Just before they reached the crest of the hill, they would loosen a wheel. With the ruts in the road, it was certain to come off before they got to the bottom. Neither Edward nor Richard made any objections, although both wondered what they would do if these people had placed a lookout at the top of the hill.

Fortunately, they were lucky. Shearing off the pin that held the wheel in place, they sent the oxen forward at a slow walk. No one was anxious to be thrown from the wagon when the wheel came off. A large rut two-thirds down the hill performed the deed. With a jolt worse than anything she had suffered since her accident, Lucy was pitched into the wagon while Mr. Smith tried to hold on to the team. When they stopped, both Edward and Richard huddled around her while Smith and Jones unhitched the team.

"Are you all right?" her brother whispered, lifting her from the wagon. She nodded and moaned. Richard's face turned white.

"Tell him I will be fine," she whispered into her brother's ear. He glared at Richard and motioned him to come on. "Now put me down," Lucy demanded when they were well in sight of the barn. He did as she said. She took a step or two, her limp very pronounced, and collapsed. The men grabbed for her, but she fell at their feet. Edward picked her up again. "Good job, little sister," he whispered as he tried unsuccessfully to wipe some of the dust from her face.

She gave him a faint smile and then closed her eyes. Smith, acting like a frantic father, gave contradictory directions and dashed about like a puppy who has just discovered his tail. "Get her in here," he ordered in a country accent. "Then we will send someone for help."

Before they could open the door, a large man stepped out. "Is this your barn?" Smith asked. "Can we ask you to send someone for a wagon? My daughter is hurt." The man looked behind him as if asking for instructions. He hesitated for a moment, looked at the broken wagon up the hill, and then nodded. As though too worried to notice the man's attempt to stop them, Smith led the way into the barn.

With Smith hovering beside them, Edward carried Lucy toward a pile of moldering hay at the other end of the barn. One of the men started to object, but the lady beside him shook her head. Edward put her down carefully and then stood up and stretched. "Are you all right, my dear?" Smith asked, still in country tones. As he had walked beside Edward, he had noted the position of the other two people, but he could not see the boy.

Lucy felt a movement in the hay behind her. She opened her eyes cautiously and turned to one side. David was staring back at her. His hands and feet were bound, and he was wearing a gag. He recognized her and began to struggle against his bonds. As if she were testing herself to see if she was hurt, Lucy shook her head from side to side. The movement stopped.

"We will have you right in a moment," Smith said, patting Lucy's cheek. "Jones, you fetch the water bottle from the wagon. And you, you young ne'er-do-well," he pointed at Richard, "see to the oxen. If you had checked the wagon carefully before we left London, this would never have happened." He watched Richard follow Jones out of the barn. As if noticing the two other people in the barn for the first time, he made a bow. "Appreciate your letting us rest here until I can get my daughter attention, my lady. Did not expect to see someone like you in such a rundown place."

The lady smiled. "I am here to decide what to do with the place. My estate manager"—she motioned toward the man at her side, ignoring the sour look on his face—"has suggested that I tear it down." She pulled the veil on the small riding hat she wore across her face so that it hid all but her eyes. Outside the door where he waited for Smith's signal, Richard worried about his son. When he heard her voice, he froze.

"F-Father," Richard heard Lucy call, disguising her voice with a stammer. He could hear but not see as Smith hurried to her side.

"You will be fine, my dear," Smith said comfortingly.

"My youngest," he explained after apologizing for leaving the lady's side, "would come to town with me. Now see what has happened." He looked to the door, unobtrusively signaling his partner that the child had been found.

"I am certain she will be fine. Now I will bid you good day." The lady picked up the skirt of her velvet riding skirt and turned to leave. She had taken only a few steps when Richard, his heart in his throat, stepped into the doorway. "Richard," she whispered, her hand pulling on her stock as though she were choking.

"You never expected me to find you, did you, Julia?" Although Richard's face was white, his voice was steady. Rage burned in his eyes. "Where is he? Where is my son?"

"He is with me," Lucy called. She could feel rather than hear the boy's sobs. Digging through the moldering mess, she reached for David and pulled him into her arms.

"He is mine too," Julia reminded the man she no longer thought of as her husband. She stepped forward, smiling as though she welcomed the opportunity to see him again. The man at her side went pale. He slipped his hand into his pocket. "Are you not happy to see me?" she asked coquettishly. "What a happy threesome we will make—you, that girl you married, and me. I do think people will talk, but surely we can overcome that. I prefer the country anyway. If only you were a duke, we might pull this off." She took a few more steps toward Richard. The man who had been standing beside her slipped into the shadows. Lucy, who had not heard Richard clearly before, gasped. Edward, stunned at the thought of what Julia's appearance would mean to his sister, stopped where he was, his eyes on Lucy's face. It grew paler, but she never lost her composure.

"Why? Why this charade?" Richard asked, ignoring everyone else in the place.

"Why not? You cannot say you were not glad to be rid of me. And so inexpensively too," Julia taunted him. She stopped only a few feet from him, her veil still about her face.

When Julia began to taunt Richard, Lucy wrapped her arms about David, pressing him close to her and covering his other ear with her hand. She was more concerned about him that about herself. "Richard, remember your son," she called as she listened to their angry words. With her other hand, she pulled frantically at the knots that held his gag in place.

Richard paused, some of the anger draining from his face. Julia turned, her eyes flashing. "Mrs. Blount, I presume," she said with a bitter laugh. "I can imagine what society will say when it finds out that Richard has two wives living. You will be the talk of the *ton*. And when the gossips get through with you, you will be an outcast even though some people will feel sorry for you. Think of it; you have been sharing a bed with a man who is not your husband." She glanced at her husband. "You have been sleeping with her, haven't you, Richard?" Her wild laugh echoed in the barn.

Trying not to show how horrified she was by the scene Julia painted, Lucy stood up and pulled David up beside her. "Edward, will you take him outside and release him, please?" she asked, never doubting that her brother would do as she asked even though she knew he would prefer to stay. Her eyes were fixed on her husband's first wife. David tried to cling to her. She merely bent her head and kissed him. "Go with Edward, my dear. I will join you shortly."

"Do not listen to her, David. Come to your mother," Julia beckoned, forgetting the ropes still tied about his ankles, ropes she had instructed one of her conspirators to place there. He wet his lips as if he were going to say something but only shook his head. Edward lifted him and began to walk toward the barn door, keeping as far away from Julia and her partner as he could manage.

When she realized that her son would not or could not obey her, Julia frowned. "Do not take my son from this building," she ordered. Edward kept on walking. "Stop!" she screamed. David buried his face in the rough coat that Edward wore.

Smith, who had been listening, drew back into the re-
cesses of the old structure, half hidden by one of the
stalls. He tried to watch the door as well as the man in
the shadows. Richard moved out of the center of the
door and further into the barn. Smith smiled. He now
could see that the man who had tried to keep them out
lay on the ground outside. Jones slipped inside the barn,
moving so silently that only Edward and Smith, who had
been watching the door, saw him come in.

"I will not give him back so easily," Julia cried.
"Simon!"

"Yes, my dear?" said the man who stepped from the
shadows with a gun aimed at Richard.

"Make them give him back."

Jones tried to get a clear shot, but Edward and David
were between him and Julia's lover. He moved silently
further into the barn. Smith cursed silently when he realized that he too was blocked.

"Take the boy back to where he was," Simon said.
"Or I may have to shoot him." Edward paused, his face
white. He looked down at the boy he held and back at
his sister. He had a pistol in his pocket but could not
reach it. David whimpered. "And after that, I think I
would rather see all of you," Simon told them, motioning Lucy and Edward to join Richard. Both he and Julia
seemed to have forgotten Smith. He took several steps
backward until he could see all three of the others.

Julia laughed. "Did you think I would allow all our
planning to go for naught?" she asked, tossing her head.
She smiled at her fellow conspirator and moved to his
side. Her heart beating loudly, Lucy clasped her hands
tightly to keep them from trembling. She watched Edward put David down carefully. Not by one gesture or
change of expression did she reveal that the boy was free
of his bonds. Caught up in the confrontation with her
husband, Julia ignored them. "Do you not want to know
what my plan was, Husband dear?" she asked, longing
for a chance to prove how clever she was.

Richard shrugged his shoulders. Her eyes blazed. She

took a step or two toward him but then stopped. "Naughty man. I will not fall for that. No, it will be best if I keep my distance. We still have so much to discuss? Simon, tell Richard what we have planned."

Her companion frowned. "Tell him," she demanded. When he remained silent, she glared at him and then laughed. "Are you afraid of them?" she asked. "As long as we have David, we shall be fine." More astute than his lover, who was flushed with anger, Simon kept his eyes on Richard, Lucy, and Edward, recognizing their threat, and did not answer her.

Although Lucy had her eyes fixed on Julia, she was listening to the rustling sound that told her that David was moving through the hay. Willing him to escape, she held her breath. Richard, who was facing that end of the barn, saw a movement out of the corner of his eye but did not let his hope show on his face. Edward thrust his hands into his pockets as if in disgust, his fingers curling over his gun.

"Get closer together," Simon demanded. Reluctantly, the three obeyed. He looked at the little group as if realizing for the first time that someone was missing. "Where is your father?" he asked.

"Her father?" Julia laughed, but the sound held no joy. "Where are you, little man?" she called, inspecting every side of the place.

Smith had moved cautiously from stall to stall, taking advantage of Julia's ranting to hide the noise that he made. Jones, seeing what his partner was doing, had taken up a position on the other side. When Julia began her search, he hid behind a half wall, his heart beating loudly. David, still hidden in the hay, raised his head cautiously. Realizing that neither Julia nor Simon had noticed him, he looked at his father and Lucy. His father, trapped by Simon's gaze, did not show that he had seen David. Using her skirt to cover her gesture, Lucy pointed at the door. David crept slowly toward freedom.

Realizing the boy needed a distraction to cover his escape, Smith drew their attention to himself. He stepped out into the center of the barn, his hands showing. David darted out of the barn, the sunlight clearly revealing the bruises that marked one side of his face. Lucy felt Richard stiffen. She put a hand on his arm.

"They made me pretend to be her father," he complained. "I did not want to lose my position. What is a man to do with a master like him?" He pointed at Richard and deliberately stopped some distance from the others, as if he were afraid.

"Stay out of my way, little man," Julia said angrily. "And keep quiet." As if finding Smith had keyed a memory, she turned around. "David? Where are you, darling?" She glanced around as though she had forgotten where the boy had been placed. Richard took a step forward, drawing her attention back to him. Forgetting her son for the moment, Julia inspected the rest of them. "What shall we do with them?" she asked. "Perhaps a fire. This old barn will burn nicely, and Simon starts wonderful fires. Don't you, my love." He smiled and nodded.

"Why are you doing this?" Richard asked.

"As if you did not know." She laughed again, hysteria close to the surface.

"And how did you escape the last one?" Lucy asked, her eyes fixed on Julia's.

"The last one. That was a . . . disaster. But then I was relying on Simon. Had everything gone as I had planned, then it would not have been necessary for me to steal my own son in order to finance my life." She frowned at the memory. "Simon left things too late that time." Her scarf had begun to slip, and she rearranged it hastily.

"I told you. I had to wait until the alarm was given," Simon said. Smith, hoping he was not paying attention, started to put his hand into his pocket, but Simon threatened him with a gun.

"All I was able to take with me then were my jewels. I had to wait for a more luxurious life." She smiled at her husband. "Did you bring the money?" she asked sharply.

"As if he would think of such a thing," Lucy said scornfully.

"If his children are threatened, he will do anything I

ask." Julia stroked Lucy's shoulder. Lucy shuddered, glad that the other two were safe from her clutches. She hoped that David would be safe too. Richard looked on, helpless. He measured the distance between himself and Julia, but he knew he could not reach his wife before she could harm her again.

As the groups shifted positions, Jones stayed out of sight. Finally seeing a clear path to Simon, he fired. Simon staggered. As he fell, Simon's finger closed on the trigger of his gun. It fired. Julia, who had run to Simon's side, wavered, swaying in her place. Then her knees crumpled, and she fell. "Julia," Simon whispered and hit the ground.

Pulling his gun from his pocket, Smith approached the downed pair. Edward shook his head as if he could erase the memory of the last few minutes from his mind.

"She wants you," Smith told Richard. Reluctantly, he let Lucy go and kneeled beside the woman he had thought dead long ago.

Julia felt him beside her. She opened her eyes. Richard leaned forward, ready to listen to her pleas for forgiveness. "It should all have been mine," she said. "Mine." She coughed and a bloody froth appeared at the corner of her mouth. "Had you not spoiled it I would have had everything."

"Everything? You asked for only ten thousand pounds," he said, shocked.

"Before. The fire." Her voice grew weaker. "All of you should have died." She coughed and doubled up with pain. "Simon?" she whispered. Smith looked at the other body and shook his head. For a moment Julia opened her eyes wide, and then they went blank.

As soon as Richard had gone to Julia's side, Lucy had run outside to search for David. Filled with horror over the scene that had just occurred, she wanted to erase the last day from his mind. She found him hiding behind a tree. He stood there looking at her, his eyes no longer innocent or happy. "She did not love me," he said quietly.

"She wanted you with her," Lucy reminded him, pulling him into her arms and holding him close.

"Because Da would pay her money to get me back. She was alive and did not tell me. All she wanted me for was to get money." He buried his face in Lucy's shoulder, his tears beginning.

Richard walked out of the barn, looking for them. His heart raced to see his oldest son in his wife's arms. David looked up and turned and ran to him. "Why did she do it, Da?"

The question lingered in all their minds. Leaving Smith and Jones to turn the bodies of Julia and Simon Ashton over to the magistrates, the others climbed back in the wagon and headed for London. David curled up on Lucy's lap and slept most of the way. The others rode in silence.

As soon as they arrived, Lucy and Richard took David back to the schoolroom, leaving Edward to explain matters to Mr. Meredith. Full of bread and milk, he crawled into bed. "I will stay with you until you go to sleep," his father promised. "And I will leave a candle burning in case you wake up. Mary is close at hand if you need her." Lucy said good night and left the two of them talking quietly.

"How were Caroline and Robert today, Mary?" she asked.

"A trifle anxious, but they settled down nicely, ma'am," the girl said.

Lucy nodded to her. "Tell them I will see them in the morning," she said, longing to have their little arms wrapped around her one more time. She walked down the stairs to her own room, her limp more pronounced than usual.

She let Betty undress her and bring her a bath. The warm water relaxed her muscles and her tears. When her maid asked what the matter was, she would only shake her head. Refusing any refreshments, she climbed into bed, wishing nothing more than to be able to erase the day from everyone's memory. But Julia's taunts lingered. She glanced at her wedding band and pulled it off. Her fingers curled over it as though protesting. Then she laid it carefully on the table. Not tonight, probably tomorrow, she told herself. That was when they would talk about their problems.

Hours later she was sleeping fitfully when the door to her room opened. Making little noise, Richard crossed the room and got into bed with her. Half asleep, she sighed and moved closer to him as she usually did. Then her eyes flew open. "What are you doing here?" she asked, pulling the sheet up to her chin and moving away from him.

"Did you expect me to sleep alone after today?" he asked, reaching over to light the candle. He was turning back to her when the candle flame caught a glint of gold. He stiffened; then he picked up her ring. His fist closed around it. "What is this doing over here?" he asked, keeping his voice steady only with effort. If she left him . . . He could not finish the thought. It sent shivers up his spine.

"I could not go on wearing it," she explained, her voice breaking.

"Why not?"

"Richard, our marriage was not legal. You heard her today gloating over the fact that you had two living wives. My brother heard her."

"Now I have only one."

"Richard!"

He put his arm around her. She stiffened. He pulled away. "Lucy, listen to me," he begged. She fluffed her pillows and leaned back, careful not to be touching him. He sighed and did the same. "For me, Julia died long ago. That poor scarred woman who died today was not the mother of my children. I did not know her."

"Scarred?" she asked.

"From the fire, I suppose. We will never know. She slapped David when he asked about it. It must have been hard for her to go from being beautiful to being disfigured. But even before the fire, something had affected her mind, and I never realized that something was wrong. Whether it was her relationship with Simon Ashton or something else, I suppose it does not matter now."

"But her being alive matters. It means we are not legally married."

"No one knows."

"No one except your son, my brother, my father too by now, and those two men. You cannot expect them to keep silent forever."

"I do not." Impatient, he turned on his side and put an arm around her. She stiffened. He leaned over and kissed her, wrapping his arms around her. "We will obtain another license. I will have to think of some reason, but after today that should not be difficult. Then we can slip off and be married legally."

She froze, her heart beginning to pound. "You want to marry me again?" she asked. The light in her eyes sparkled as she looked up at him.

"Of course, I do." He rolled over so that she was on top of him, her face only inches from his own. "What did you think I would do, abandon you?" She closed her eyes, but she could not hide her blush. "You did. You thought I would leave you." His face showed his astonishment.

She blinked rapidly to keep her tears of joy from overflowing. "You never told me how you felt."

"But you know. You had to know that you are the light of my life, my joy, my happiness," he said fervently. "I love you. My marriage to Julia was nothing. She meant nothing. But if I lost you, I could not continue."

She kissed him, stopping the flow of words that was music to her heart and to her ears. The words of love she whispered as she covered his face with her kisses made his heart race. His passion flared, and he pulled her closer to him.